THE WRITING CIRCLE

ROZENA MAART

We acknowledge the support of
the Canada Council for the Arts for our publishing program.

 Canada Council   Conseil des Arts
for the Arts   du Canada

ONTARIO ARTS COUNCIL
CONSEIL DES ARTS DE L'ONTARIO

We also acknowledge support from
the Government of Ontario through the Ontario Arts Council.

Cover design by David Drummond

Library and Archives Canada Cataloguing in Publication

Maart, Rozena, 1962-
    The writing circle : novel / Rozena Maart.

ISBN 978-1-894770-37-8

    I. Title.

PS8576.A29W75 2007   C813'.6   C2007-902733-4

Printed in Canada by Coach House Printing

TSAR Publications
P. O. Box 6996, Station A
Toronto, Ontario M5W 1X7
Canada

www.tsarbooks.com

To Anne Mayne

for her courage and determination in starting Rape Crisis in
Cape Town, South Africa, with three women, in 1976, when
no one else dared to.

Part One

In Cape Town, there is a group of five women who gather together every Friday night to share their experience of writing memory, writing the body. They call this gathering, *The Writing Circle*.

Isabel

It was the cold mouth of the gun against my temple as I sat behind the wheel of my car that alerted me to the fact that this was indeed a hijack. I sat there breathless, shaking and shivering. My eyeballs darted left to right. My hands wrapped in black gloves, I gripped the steering wheel as tightly as I could. I tried to hold my head still while my mind raced past the situation in order to seek a way out. The mouth of the gun moved as I moved, and moved to the corner of my eye as I jerked momentarily and failed to meet the gaze of its owner. The swift tap of it against the bone behind my eyebrow was a clear indication that its owner did not want to be looked at. I looked into the mirror and gasped as I fell back into my seat, turning the ignition off, as my tormentor instructed by moving and pointing the gun. Not quite sure that it was my face I saw in the mirror, I moved my head back slightly, and hastily drew in the very puff of breath I had just exhaled. I could smell the staleness against my hollow palate as I inhaled. My breath was trapped by the gun, which inhaled it each time I opened my mouth. The mirror was blurry and I felt hot and cold each time I tried to keep my heaving mouth still. I looked piercingly everywhere for signs of movement.

The lights at the front of my house were all on. Beauty, Carmen, Jazz, and Amina were in the living room waiting for me. My hand was close enough to the hooter but my temple throbbed behind the mouth of the gun that menaced me. My fingers were stiff, clawed, curled side by side wrapped in the daintiness of black silk. Beauty had the other set of keys where the second remote was attached; she usually peered over the gate from the kitchen window to check for my car at the entrance, then opened the gate and shut it and met me at my car. I had telephoned her earlier in the afternoon, after I spoke to Jazz, and asked her to inform the group that I would be running late and they should start without me. I chewed my lips so hard, praying that she would open my back door, that I tasted blood; it swam in my mouth with no possibility of going anywhere.

"Get out of the car," he ordered, his voice soft and his tone harsher than his eyes, which were sheltered by a ridiculous-looking blue baseball cap. His movements were that of a well-trained cat. He kept the gun at my temple with both his hands. I looked down at his expensive-looking luminous white trainers, lined with navy blue all around the side. He moved swiftly, the padded trainers allowing the calculated silent hop and bounce, his blue windbreaker, which lay brisk against his broad shoulders, shielding him somewhat from the Cape Southeaster.

"Turn the lights off and gimme the keys, lady," he ordered as he looked over his left shoulder, touching the tip of his nose with the gun as though inhaling its power. His voice thundered in my ears; there was no evidence of Cape Town in his voice, in the order he issued. I swallowed the blood immersed in saliva in fast gulps and choked. The gagging sound forced his attention upon me and he pushed my head down and swiftly managed a chop behind my neck. I gasped out loud as the gun moved from my head to his face, my lungs still battling for air. I absorbed all of the air in the car in that instant, shivering and panting. My breaths were short and intermittent. My mouth was open and dry. I could feel the coarseness of my own breath against my quivering tongue—too dry to beg for mercy. That small space I left for the smoke to release itself from my cigarette as I puffed pleasantly while listening to the sound of *Freshly Ground* was exactly where he inserted his fisted, loaded, hand. He pointed then jerked the gun in the direction of the radio and CD player and I knew what he meant. My hands shook as I touched the knob and turned the music off. I was sniffling, crying and shaking. I looked towards the back door hoping Beauty might make an appearance but there was no sign of her.

"Shut up or I'll blow your bloody head off, lady," he uttered, in a cool crisp voice. I pictured the women from my writing circle at the front end of my house, in my living room, seated on the black sofa chairs, which were usually loosely scattered in a circle, or sitting on the floor, no doubt, reading their writing for this week's session. I saw Amina's car on Cambridge Street, stacked to the brim with all sorts of fancy material, and Carmen's parked right behind hers. Beauty's car was parked at the station and so was Jazz's oversized four-by-four. They were all secured by rather expensive alarm systems; one has to be so careful these days. Jazz's brother, Manjit, usually dropped her off and waited for her to telephone him before he collected her; they must have changed their arrangement for this evening. Someone should be coming to see where I was, even though I was quite late, I thought, biting my lip and hoping, as I counted from one to one hundred, for my back door to be opened. I was too afraid to wipe my lips, although the small trickling taste of my own blood did alert me to the unfortunate realization that this was not a dream. My whole body shook and I cried out achingly as he grabbed at my hair with his left hand and pulled chunks of it through the window.

"Now, take the keys. If you touch the car I will blow your head off, lady," he said, as he let go of my hair. He looked at the chunks of hair in his hand then thrust them into his pocket, smiling, after wiping his hands on his trousers—as though he wanted them to be clean for the purpose he intended for them.

I touched the keys in the ignition, and at the moment when I made contact with them I exhaled and burst out crying so loud I thought my lungs would drop onto the seat.

He put his arm through the small space of the window and took the keys from me, just like that, as if my frightened face gave him that final permission.

I tried to remember Tom's face, which I had seen moments ago in his consulting room at the hospital, his loving hands stroking my hair, as the man with the blue windbreaker pointed the gun at my flaring nostrils.

"Your cell?" he demanded. I handed it to him.

He turned my cellphone off then shoved it into the pocket of his jacket; I could hear it dropping among coins and other items there.

"At least it's over . . . he got what he was after . . . just be calm . . . just be calm," I kept saying to myself, ready to leave my car in his hands. He shifted the peak of his cap to the back of his head.

"Don't get out, lady, stay where you are!" he demanded, in an icy voice.

"Just take the car . . . please . . . just take the car!" I called out, my mouth too bloody to offer anything else and my eyes focused on my back door.

"Shut up!" he shouted, fury and agitation written all over his face. My eyeballs darted about, expecting a stir of some sort from one of my many nosy neighbours.

"Move!" he instructed.

The mixture of tears and nasal fluids combined on my lips as I bit and swallowed simultaneously, gasping and crying into my sweaty gloved palms, as I covered my face with them. He climbed into the seat beside me, shoving my bag of shopping from Woolworths to the floor, and shut the driver's door quietly. He locked all of the doors in my car with the remote control attached to the keys I had handed him. He stared at me coolly, then electronically double locked my backdoor, just like that, without hesitation, as though my keys and remote belonged to him. He certainly knew enough about remote-controlled electronic gates. He pointed the gun at me, indicating that I should move to the back seat. The *Argus* and the morning's *Cape Times* were on the back seat and he shoved them with his left foot. He must have caught a glimpse of both front pages, each of which featured the beloved deputy president Zuma who had been charged with rape, and he smirked.

"Gah!" he exclaimed, in a vulgar sort of way as the stench of his breath circled the inside of my car, then looked back towards my house where the lights were all off except for the far front corner where the writing circle met.

"He knows," I said to myself, afraid he might hear my thoughts. Speaking to myself was like having someone with me as a witness, an alibi, someone to guide me, as I contemplated what to do next. I tried to stay focused, fearing my death at the hands of this stranger with a gun. He knew that there were four women in my house waiting for me . . . he must have been watching me. I never drove home at night unaccompanied. I hadn't called the security watch, as I usually did, to alert them of my time of arrival, nor had I allowed Tom to drive behind me. Tom usually followed me and waited until I was indoors or he came inside with me to check if everything was all right, except for Fridays when he was on call and Jazz and Manjit usually collected me from my office. Jazz worked in Neurosurgery, which was two blocks from mine at the hospital. Tom had asked me to stay with him to talk about the future of our relationship and I agreed, even though my Friday nights were reserved for the writing circle. I needed to talk to Tom. My mammogram was frightening. I had no idea how to proceed with treatment, should I need it. I could not tell Tom about it despite the speech I had rehearsed. My gynecologist had found several small lumps in both my breasts. I looked at them differently after those tests. I did not want Tom to drive behind me because I didn't want Beauty to know that I was dating him ... not yet anyway. Beauty had only met Tom once at a social gathering and was very quiet; this usually means that she does not like someone. A part of me wondered whether she knew about Tom and Frank; I doubt very much whether Frank would have told her before he died.

With the gun still in his hand, the man with the blue windbreaker put the seats of the car down then put the gun inside my mouth. He simply opened my mouth and shoved the gun inside it, as though he was looking for a place to stash a nuisance item. The gun barrel faced outward. I gagged and the gun dropped to the floor. I was choking on my own saliva, and he pulled my hair, yanking my head towards him so that I would face him. My head bounced up and down. I think I might even have wet myself slightly, because my muscles gave way under me and all I could see was fury and agitation on his face, as though I was a clumsy schoolgirl who could not carry out a simple request. I could feel parts of my legs; although I knew they were there and I could see them, they felt rubbery in some places and numb in others.

"If you do that once more, lady, your life will be over," he said, pointing at me with his calloused left hand.

I shook, and my head bounced in agreement. He opened my mouth again, as wide as he could, and stretched every muscle within its range. He placed the gun inside of my mouth again, this time using his fingers to stretch the sides of it, and looked into my eyes. I could not look into his. I could taste the fish paste from the sandwich I had had in Tom's office as his fingers slipped around my teeth. I tasted the nicotine from his fingertips as he dug, like an eager child on a sandy beach, and opened my mouth wider and wider. The gun fitted into his hand like a glove; inside of my mouth it felt like a large heavy rock, weighing me down and forcing me to sink into his hands. My whole body was coerced into compliance. My shoulders fell and my body curved into a ball to hold the gun inside my mouth. My mouth was this thing, this useless thing, which he just played with and opened and shut, as though it was an ornament. My breath competed with the gun for air as I held onto it with my lips. I watched with muted obedience as he told me where to sit. I looked down at the bridge of my nose as the barrel of the gun hung outside of mouth, incapable of sustaining its full grip.

He used both his hands to undress me after shoving my arms above my head. Four women were inside my house waiting for me, sharing their writing on the body, which was the focus of our group. Mr and Mrs Sedgewick, the neighbours across the street, were watching the eleven o'clock news on television and I could see the reflection of the screen on their front window. I waited for Mr Sedgewick to look in the direction of my yard but he was turned away from me. There was some report on the war in Iraq and I caught a glimpse of American soldiers running in and out of crumbling homes, with guns pointed in every direction. I had no idea it was that late. The man with the blue windbreaker moved my head and removed his baseball cap, in a gentlemanly fashion, then stroked his lower face, bringing his fingers to the point of his chin. Why are neighbours never nosy when you want them to be? Mr Isaacs, the neighbour across from me, two doors down, formerly an English teacher, slammed the lid onto his rubbish bin and looked about the street, and at the small garden he kept, as he usually did every evening while he watched the news halfheartedly and roamed about the house, looking for unsavoury items to collect while uttering atrocities at whomsoever offended him on the televised news broadcast.

"Bloody Zuma!" I heard him cry out, as he banged the lid back onto the rubbish bin in his yard and as my head was being thrust further back into the leather seat of my car. I looked towards Mr Isaacs as my head bounced up and down, hoping for his eyes to venture over to my direction, as the man with the blue windbreaker held me down and lowered me into the back seat of my car. Mr Isaacs was too busy to steal a glance in the direction of my yard to see whether I had brought another load of lesbians to my house, as he regularly remarked when he was angry at me for not inviting him to our writer's circle even though I explained to him it was a women's writing group. He had started checking up on me just over a year ago when Calvin left and appeared perfectly entitled when I questioned him about it. Biscuit, the cat, which belonged to that busybody Mrs Applebaum, watched in quiet contemplation while her owner blew out the candles in the living room and bolted the security door before she retired for bed. I hoped and prayed for her alarm to go off, as it often did at eleven o'clock, because she would either forget to reset it or forget the combination, in which case she would rattle the gate on my front door and demand my assistance. I could almost see her walking around the house groping at furniture in order to get to her bedroom. "Damn that Mrs Applebaum," I thought, what's the point of having so many lamps and lit candles in her house if she can barely see? She'd asked me for names of eye doctors every week and tried to force a prescription out of me, even though I had told her I was only a social worker and not an optometrist, despite my white coat. She cornered Jazz once, but Jazz's abruptness put her off completely. I begged for her bedroom light to remain on, as the glare was still casting a light onto my car. My head was forced further back and I shut my eyes. The tears that rolled from them made small puddles on the leather seat—they, along with Biscuit the cat, perched high on the opposite wall, were my only witnesses. The only time I had previously stared at my tears forming puddles on a car seat was when my uncle Reggie had once asked me to take the bag of fishing tackle from his lap as he was driving us back from Kalk Bay harbour, then grabbed my hand and put it inside his pants. He drove with my hand between his legs, then forcibly held my hand down with his hand, the left one that had the tattoos on it, and jerked my hand up and down on his penis. I sat beside him in the front of the van too afraid to say anything, and saw my tears roll down my cheeks and form puddles right in front of me, between my legs, on the leather car seat. Minutes later he pushed my right hand out, as he shrieked—the same right hand which minutes earlier held a delicious chocolate ice cream cone, which he had bought, having refused the payment I offered, excitedly, from the pocket money my mother had made available to me since my tenth birthday. When we arrived at his house at the top part of Steenberg, where his wife and my parents were waiting for us to join them for afternoon tea, he stopped the car a few metres away from the house, then muttered under his breath that I had to clean up, wash my hands with the water in the rubber water bottle he kept under the driver's seat.

"You can't go into the house smelling of fish, little girl," he said, without once looking at me. I took the water bottle and washed my hands at the side of the pavement, watching as the clouded water ran along the gutter that was cluttered with stones and cigarette butts. My hands smelled of him for years, I think. Two years ago, almost thirty years to the day, he came into Emergency Unit after suffering a stroke. He asked me to forgive him—and I did. He had suffered enough, I thought. My father broke his leg when I explained why I never wanted to be around his brother and why I did not want him to come to my twenty-first birthday. I thought twenty-one was old enough to tell my father that my uncle, his brother, had molested me, that day on our return from the fishing trip, and several times after, when my mother and father insisted that I go and help out at Uncle Reggie and Auntie Katie's house.

My father never went near him after he broke his leg with a cricket bat. Uncle Reggie lived alone after Auntie Katie died, which was shortly after my twenty-first birthday, and none of our other family members went near him either. My mother made sure she told the neighbours, for which she was severely criticized. My mother wasn't the kind of woman who paid attention to what others thought of her, and when the women from Kalk Bay harbour went around spreading rumours about me, from Kalk Bay to Steenberg, she sorted them out right away. My mother did not even attend Auntie Katie's funeral.

"Wives always know when their husbands are up to no good," my mother said, as she cleaned the dishes the night before my twenty-first birthday and scrubbed the tea towels with sunlight soap. "That woman kept quiet! Gmf! She must have known what Reggie was up to, and she never had the guts to stand up to him!" she exclaimed as she ground the spices with the pestle and mortar and pounded the spices into the meat, in preparation for the breyani. "I wanted tomorrow to be a special day for you, Issie," she said, as she sobbed. I stood by her side and put my arms around her. My mother was not a crier. I knew she was thinking of Dolores.

My sister Dolores killed herself at the age of twenty, after spending two years in and out of court. She took her high school teacher to court for raping her and my parents stood by her, as each and every day she faced the stares, the sniggers, and the remarks of those who praised Mr Jacobus for being such a wonderful teacher. I was only fifteen at the time. I think of my sister every day, and what she would have done in situations I faced with people who were unkind. Dolores had guts. She challenged everyone and everything; she was not afraid of anything. Her suicide came as a surprise to all of us. Dolores once told me after one of the court sessions: "Not being believed is the worst fate a woman can suffer . . . and everyone knows it. They won't believe *me* because they're afraid no one will believe *them*." I cried myself to sleep for two years after she died, not sure if I missed her for being Dolores or just missed her because she had stood up for me and stood up for everything she believed in. She never liked Uncle Reggie.

I hadn't thought of Uncle Reggie since his death and the puddles on the car seat grew larger as the man with the blue windbreaker thrust himself on top of me. He was busy with the lower side of me. He made no attempt even to look at me, not my face anyway. My head and face did not exist for him any longer. When Mrs Applebaum's lights went out, some thumping moments later, I shifted my gaze inside to the ceiling of my car. I remember looking down from it and all I could see was my car jerking; someone was being violently jerked around in my car. As I looked down I saw a man on top of a woman. The woman had a gun in her mouth; her arms were shoved above her head. Her body was causing the car to jerk because he was jerking her, pushing her from the inside. I saw her scrunched-up face, the stream of continuous tears running off the top of her nose, and the balls of her eyes turned away from her body. She had agony written all over her face, as her arms and hands jerked with the rest of her body to the detestable pounding the man mounting her put them through. In that brief moment when I saw her face, all of it, in muted tearful silence, I recognized her. I recognized her because she looked right at me. In a drawn-out almost dreamlike moment I recognized myself as though I were staring at a mirror, except the reflection in the mirror was not the same as the one on the other side of it. I was looking on, while this man had entered me, and there I was, lying still . . . still, with a gun in my gaping mouth, saliva streaming out of it, meandering down my face, sliding on my oily makeup, into my throat, as my body was being ravaged by an intruder. I saw myself looking down on to the top of his balding head because he had buried his face in my bosom—a bosom he separated carelessly and desperately to suit his purpose. Within seconds he touched my hair, held it in his left hand, then brought it to his mouth and nose, inhaling it, to absorb the scent of my extravagant conditioner, as though we were lovers—bloody cheek—then buried his head in my bosom, my possibly cancerous bosom, which he swooped together, like two castles in the sand, and pulled my reluctant body closer to him. As his grunts grew louder he rammed himself further inside me for the final round of his victory. He nestled himself in my flesh, his mouth gaping open triumphantly, salivating onto my breasts, his lips dripping with delight. I saw different images flashing in front of me each time I heard him slobbering. He was winning a boxing match with a fragile, underweight, opponent who was no match for him at all. He was the dog at the dogfight foaming at the mouth, and I his smaller, fragile, opponent whose flesh he devoured, after he stole my bark. I was still wearing my black silk gloves, and I must have looked quite a spectacle to him. He moved my arms above my head, again, as though he had calculated every move in order to obtain the picture-perfect moment of his deviously delicious accomplishment. I could hear the Simonstown train at the station and I knew that within minutes it would take off with a deafening roar—just the kind of applause he needed. The saliva in my mouth circled and softened the gun. I could feel it slipping further back and needed to prevent it from going down my esophagus. I realized that my hands were free and he did not care what I did with them; they were of no use to him at the moment, they were simply attached to the parts of my body that interested him. I could hear him salivating then panting, anticipating his overdue emission, and his shoes squeaking against the bottom of the leather car seat, his short legs heightened with voracious tension allowing his knobby knees to knock me further back. The gun moved further back into the roof of my mouth. In a slow and casual movement, I lowered my shaking hand to my mouth because my teeth were aching from the grip I was forced to endure. I inserted my fingers around the various holes the handle offered me and I gripped it with the intention of removing it. Suddenly I heard a loud bang and felt a stream of warm clotted liquid gushing into my face—warm, thick, salty, red liquid, erupted from his head and spewed all over my face. I felt his head and his whole body go limp inside of me . . . as though his batteries had suddenly been removed.

Jazz

I was the first one to jump up. We all looked at one another for a few seconds, perhaps to distinguish between the sound of the train and the bang we had just heard. It took a few exchanged glances before everyone else jumped up, screaming, leaping from chair to sofa to carpeted floor. My heart throbbed in my face. I paused cautiously, in the moment, as I turned Vivaldi off, to collect myself, while the others scurried about and screamed hysterically. We listened to Vivaldi's *Four Seasons* at our writing circle gathering. Beauty's partner, Ludwig, is a violinist and it was after attending one of his concerts that we all agreed that Vivaldi's violins suited our purpose on Friday evenings. I moved away from the stereo and covered my face with my hands and groaned. My mind was racing. Several images flashed in my mind. I had to think about possible responses to what I feared had happened. Beauty, Amina, and Carmen were either jumping on one spot or flopping about from sofa to carpeted floor screaming and crying at the same time, all of them quite hysterical. Beauty grabbed the two sets of keys from the floor, which she kept beside her: one her own, the other Isabel's.

"Isabel! Isabel!" she called out, loudly and with such a jerk in her voice that it made us all tremble. Amina held on to Beauty and cried into her blue silk scarf, which had now slipped from her head to her neck. She leapt towards her brown leather Gucci handbag on the adjacent black leather sofa and retrieved from it several small packets of Kleenex tissues. She threw it on the sofa as she helped herself to the tissues, wiping tears and nasal fluids, trembling and crying. In a swift moment, when her body jerked into realization, Amina grabbed her cellphone from her handbag and pressed the speed-dial set for the number of her parents, with whom she lived, with her son and daughters. I grabbed it from her, looked at the screen and pressed the stop button before the call could be transmitted. She stood there shaking. "Ebrahim! Ebrahim!" she called out, as she trembled, which came as a bit of a surprise to me since we all knew that she was romantically involved with her children's grandfather even though she never mentioned him or the romance. Carmen, the drama queen, gripped my arm so hard I had to throw her off me. Beauty, who was dressed in black, as usual, grabbed Amina by the arm and they ran towards the back door, while Carmen covered her ears and jumped up and down. Carmen always wore many colours and they flew in and out of my vision, like front-runners at the Coon Carnival, forcing my eyes to bounce up and down in order to absorb the full spectacle she put on. She leapt to the floor to collect her cellphone after she saw me grab Amina's—typical of her, really—and I took it from her. She placed her arm around my shoulder, and said, "Oh God, what is going to happen to me? To us," she added, as she saw my face drop to its usual level of disappointment at most of the self-absorbed things she uttered.

My heart was pounding and my thoughts were racing. I knew I had to pull myself together to face whatever was awaiting me outside Isabel's back door. Perhaps Carmen's impertinence forced me to. I took a deep breath, and when I had gathered myself, all I could think of was whether Harminder was outside at the back door. My hands formed fists each time I thought of him making those threats about coming to Isabel's house on Friday nights, when he knew I would be among my friends, whom he, in his deluded mind, blamed for the breakup of our marriage . . . as though a group of women getting together sharing their writing was hazardous to marriage.

"What is going on?" Carmen shouted again, as her overweight body bounced up and down.

My face transformed itself from fear to thoughtful contemplation; I had to take charge of the situation. Carmen was looking at me very closely with those beady eyes of hers.

"Jazz, you know what's happened don't you, Jazz? Oh God, please tell me . . . ," she cried out, holding onto my face with both her hands.

"I don't know! I don't know!" I yelled, all at once, as I knocked her hands off my face. She's often impersonal in a personal sort of way.

Carmen started screaming again.

"Stop that! Stop that!" I shouted.

I was thinking of Harminder but did not dare to reveal my thoughts to Carmen. My thoughts raced back and forth between Harminder and Sipho. I could not possibly telephone Sipho because he refused to listen to my complaints about Harminder since I did not see the need for a restraining order. The thought of obtaining one and going through formal procedures involving the police gave me the creeps.

"Arghhhh! Arghhhh! Arghhhh!"

Three loud agonizing cries were released, followed by softer exhalations, then two loud thumps against the back door. I knew that something horrific had happened and that Beauty and Amina had fainted. Beauty is generally quite brave and Amina is so meticulous about everything and very controlled most of the time that I knew they had been knocked back by something quite beyond their anticipation. Playing doctor to my friends was not a favourite pastime. If Harminder had shot himself, then I would have to telephone the ambulance and his parents, I thought to myself, as I bit my lip and coiled my hair at the nape of my neck and stuck my pencil in it. I still had his note in my office. Sorry beggar. Some men are just fools. The paperwork that comes with divorce gives me headaches, and as a consequence I delayed it. I shifted my attention elsewhere. I bolted towards the outside wooden kitchen door, while Carmen followed on, dragging her feet and holding on to the sleeve of my cardigan. I rolled my sleeves up to my elbows to ensure that she had nothing of mine to hold on to before running towards the back door.

Beauty and Amina were crouched on the floor, against the door, crying and holding on to one another. Amina was asthmatic and could hardly breathe. I stood back for a few seconds, my mouth gaping, shocked at the state of Amina, whose hair was all over her face. I've always known Amina to be the kind of person who would rather endure an insufferable inconvenience than be seen in an unsatisfactory state of attire. I dashed over to Isabel's kitchen cupboard and found a brown paper bag for Amina to breathe into and handed it to Carmen. "Carmen, use your lighter under their noses while I go outside to check things out." She nodded and did as I asked, for once. Beauty panted at me, waving her arms about as a cautionary measure, I think, but I assured her that I would be fine. I squeezed her hand and walked towards the backyard, which doubled as Isabel's garage.

The black electronic garage gate was closed and I could not see the street nor could I see anyone standing about within it. I glanced back at Beauty and Amina and could see them beginning to stand up. They had opened both the back doors, including the electronic one, but had left the garage door locked. The sight of something in the backyard had caused their collapse—of that I was sure. The backyard was quiet; not a sound could be heard. I stuck my head out quietly, and tiptoed about, making use of the light the street lamp offered to see where I was going. Only Isabel's white Honda was in the backyard and I did not see anyone in it. None of us had heard her arrive; she must have left with Tom, I thought, and just parked the car since he often drove behind her and she did say that she would be with him and would be quite late. I knew she would not want to enter the house with him on account of Beauty. There was no sign of Harminder. I looked over my shoulder at every corner of the backyard. Harminder and Amina have been friends since high school. If he was in the backyard, he would never harm Amina, nor harm anyone, only himself. If Amina had seen him she would have said so. My walk was slow and my steps were cautious and guarded. I walked towards Isabel's white car, rather slowly, looking about in the dark, not sure of anything else in the garage. There was movement in the back window. It and the side windows looked murky, as though some fluid had been spilt on them. My heart pounded faster and my body shook as though a fist was forcing itself out from inside my chest. I scrunched my nose and eyes against the window and peered through it, cupping my hands at the side of my face in order to see through the light and dark striations in the window caused by the street lamp. I saw a blood stained face staring back at me. My mouth flew open and I gasped, falling back against the white wall behind me, uncertain what to do next. I looked about and saw no sign of Harminder and looked into the car again. I did not recognize the person's face, but the remains of a white shirt did seem to resemble Isabel's. I looked into the car again, and at that moment when I recognized her, I could hear my breath competing with my eyes. Isabel was sitting almost upright and had a gun in her hand. She was wearing her black silk gloves and lifted herself rather awkwardly in order to turn the light on in her car.

There was blood everywhere. My eyes shut on it, just like that, as though a stage curtain had been closed on the scene. In a flash of light, I opened my eyes again, and saw spattered bits of flesh amid the blood, pulsating, as though they were still alive. I tried to say her name but I couldn't.

"Isa . . Isa . . Is."

I could not breathe. I could not speak. It was very different to being at the hospital; I was looking at a dear friend and my lack of coherent speech made me fearful, almost hopeless. She gestured with her left hand for me to come closer.

"Isa . . . Is . . Isabel."

I blinked hard. All I could see was the colour red. I felt my blood racing. I thought I was going to faint. Each time I opened my eyes I saw red. Once at a dream clinic the researcher had asked me to describe all the images I saw in front of me, and I could not. Just like then, everything looked familiar now, as though I had seen it before, yet I could not speak, nor could I see clearly. I blinked as hard as I could, so that the red would go away. Each time I had that red flash, the image of Dr Govinder would come to mind. His wife, Auntiejee, had insisted that I call him by his formal, professional name. I had had red spells before, sometimes at family gatherings—from which I was usually ushered by Auntiejee, who hated me intensely—but never at work, and certainly not with my patients, but each time I had them, Dr Govinder's face popped in and out of them. Auntiejee had her spies whom she sent to follow me about and it was she who reported to my uncle that I attended art classes and continued playing the flute on Saturday mornings in London's West End, when I was meant to be assisting with food at the temple they attended. I gritted my teeth and looked towards Isabel. Isabel gestured again, and I understood that she wanted me to get into the car. I stood there for a while, not sure whether I should touch the car at all, let alone enter it. My heart thundered in my toes, and I looked at the door handle, then at my henna-patterned bare feet.

"Open the door!" she shouted, as she sat upright.

Isabel knew that I did not wear shoes in the house, and she must have known what I was thinking.

"Open the bloody door!" she shouted. "Leave your shoes. Beauty has the remote attached to her set of keys. Fetch it, pleassssse!" she shouted out, all at once.

I walked towards Beauty and Amina, who were staring up at me with frightened eyes.

"Isabel is okay, she's okay," I said, then knelt down to take the set of keys and the attached remote from Beauty's hand. Both Beauty and Amina held on to me. My body was still for a moment; I had to tear myself away and return to the car.

I pressed the first green knob and could hear the buttons in Isabel's car pop open. I opened the door slowly.

Two feet in trainers, limp and lifeless, dropped from the car onto the cemented yard. I contained my outburst. For one, they were not Harminder's feet and I felt relieved and confused all at the same time.

I held my hand to my heart, as I often did when confronted with personal difficulties, even though I have been a medical doctor for ten years. I had no idea what to expect.

There was a man lying on Isabel, his bleeding head at her waist. His trousers were half way down, and his naked buttocks stared at me, without shame. I could feel my heart sinking, and I saw red again. I saw blood red with not a sign of anything else in sight, except Dr Govinder's face. Oh, how I despised that face. My whole body shook, for I feared I would have one of my episodes again. I blinked hard, begging for the red to go away. I could hear Isabel calling my name, and I blinked again, until I could see her. Isabel's chest was covered in blood; she must have lifted herself from under him, and pushed him further down on the seat, since the direction of the long stain on her half buttoned white shirt showed evidence of the blood moving downwards, the wound being in his head, which now hung limp and dented in a pool of blood on the car seat. There was a blue baseball cap on the floor of the car. Isabel pulled her black linen skirt down, and wiggled herself out from under his lifeless weight. My eyes darted up and down, back and forth, all across the car, with great concern, for all I could see was evidence of activity, and blood trails of an unknown man being dragged as my friend Isabel tried to rid herself of him. I noticed a black undergarment sticking out from his jeans pocket and I was uncertain whether to remove it. I knew that Isabel did not wear suspenders. I slipped my hand into his pocket and grabbed the black silky item and shoved it into the right pocket of my chunky cream-coloured cardigan. I still had to stare at his bare buttocks, which offended me. I knew she did not know him; none of us are friends with the new African immigrants and his appearance looked as though he was one of them. Although I did not care to look at his face, the rest of him fitted that profile—the unfashionably high-cut baggy denim jeans, with Adidas white trainers, were certainly a giveaway. He was dead, without a doubt. I tried not to look at him. I was not at work and had to stay focused on assisting my friend and had to remind myself that the dead man with the gun wound was not my patient but an assailant who had attacked my friend, and most likely raped her with the intention of killing her. I used my foot to push his denim trousers up—as far up to his waist as my foot allowed. I did not want Isabel to see his bare buttocks.

At the moment when my eyes met Isabel's, she trembled and shook, breathing as fast and feverishly as a frightened child. She knew that I knew. Perhaps she read my thoughts, as she often jokingly said, when we looked at each other on Friday nights during our writing circle meetings. She cried, intermittently.

"The bastard . . . hijacked me!"

"Ssssh, I'm here. It's okay, sweetie," I whispered.

"He . . . hijacked me . . . I . . . had . . . no idea . . . he . . . was standing there," she uttered, with stammered speech, as she pointed to the driver's seat with the gun still hanging from her black silky gloved hand.

I got the picture. I kept my eyes focused on her.

"You're safe now. Put the gun down, sweetie," I whispered.

"I can't," she replied, as she looked at her hand holding the gun and shook it, attempting to be rid of the object.

"Put your hand down, Isabel," I said again, trying to make sure that she stopped moving the gun about.

"I think my . . . fingers . . . are swollen. Look!"

"Isabel, please. Put your hand . . . over there . . . on the seat and try to relax your hand. Keep it facing away from you and try to ease your hand . . . then wiggle your fingers . . . out of the rings of the handle." I spoke as slowly as I could without arousing further anxiety.

"I can't," she said again.

"Try, Isabel. Please try," I urged, in a soft and gentle voice.

"Look! My hand is swollen," she cried out, tears streaming down her face.

"It's okay, sweetie," I said, "just keep your fingers as still as possible and relax your hand. I have some tissues here, let me try and wipe your face."

She nodded. Her eyes were fixed on mine. My head was spinning with all sorts of thoughts, and I knew that I had to telephone the police.

I looked over at Amina and Beauty, who were now standing up; Carmen stood beside them and handed them each a glass of water. Carmen must have administered her homeopathic drops because I saw them both throw their heads back and swallow down gulps of water. Carmen seemed the calmest of the three as she clutched her multicoloured sling bag under her arm.

"Everything's okay," I said as softly as I could.

I focused my attention back on Isabel.

"Shall I call the others?" I asked, as I looked at her sobbing, blood smeared all over her face, which my tissue paper had only redistributed. At least I could see her eyes.

"Beauty! Amina! Carmen!" Isabel was screaming, uncontrollably.

"Carmen! . . . Carmen! . . . Amina! . . . Beauty! . . . Robert! . . . Jazz! Jazz! I want Robert! Bring me Robert!

"Muuuuum! Muuuuum!"

She called out everyone's name three or four times, including her brother Robert's, finally calling out for her mother, which made my heart sink. The lump in my throat burst. The sound of her voice made me tearful beyond control. I did not want Isabel to see me lose control so I turned towards the wall and wiped my face with the sleeves of my cardigan. Isabel threw back her mane of long black hair and called out again.

Within seconds, all three of the other women were standing behind me. Amina and Beauty were still sobbing and holding on to each other. Carmen dropped her glasses and cried out, falling forward against the car.

"Oh my God! Ja, Allah," came from the usually very controlled Amina.

Carmen stood dead still, her fingers to her mouth. I glanced over at her momentarily, but tried to keep my eyes fixed on Isabel. Amina and Beauty found a spot to hurl against—a few metres away from the car.

"Isabel, we have to call the police. Sweetie, I think it may be the best. He's dead, and they're going to want to know why."

There was no other way of telling her.

"No, not the police. I don't want to see the police. I don't want anyone to see me like this . . . just get me out of here, please, and call Robert. I want Robert."

Isabel held the tears back as she spoke. Her lips were quivering.

I could not possibly see her being inspected and questioned by the police. There were bits of spattered flesh all over the car, not just the back seat. I counted twenty-seven of them, mostly from the brain area, which I noted as I scanned the car's interior, without making it too obvious to Isabel. I did momentarily think about taking notes, since I had a pen and a notepad in the pocket of my cardigan, but abandoned the idea. Instead, I took a few discreet photographs with my cellphone, keeping my back towards Isabel on each occasion. I slipped my mobile back into my pocket.

Beauty came to stand beside me; she had used her cape to cover her neck and arms since it was a little chilly and she too was barefoot.

"We have to get Isabel out of here," she said. "I'll help you, Jazz. We'll all help. Let's just do it now."

"I want Robert! I want Robert!" Isabel called out again.

"Shall I telephone Robert now, Isabel?" I asked.

"No. Get me out of here. He took my bloody cell . . . my cellphone is in his jacket pocket."

"Isabel, look at me. I am going to go to my car, sweetie, to get some supplies. Everyone is here. I'll only be a minute."

The look on Isabel's face grew weary.

"Sweetie, look at me. I will be back here now-now, okay." The blank silent stare offered only understanding and I waited until I saw her blink then shift her eyes in my direction. She bit her lips together and sobbed. She touched my hand and I squeezed hers.

I grabbed the keys from Beauty and let myself out by pressing the remote so that I could squeeze past the gate, then pressed it again, so that no one else could enter, or look into the garage.

There was not a soul outside. The wind had picked up quite a bit and I could hear it whistling as I took the corner on Milner Road. There were yellow leaves scattered all over the pavement, from the trees lined on the lower side of the road. The wind swirled them around, lifted and gathered them in gusts, then spat them out at the closest person who sought to walk within the circumference of its circular and vibrant, frothy, spin. Some of the leaves stuck to my hair and feet, which upon looking down I noticed had traces of blood on them. I used the bottom of one foot to clean the top of the other, while looking over my shoulders. I ran to my car parked at the train station, which was less than two hundred metres away, and used my remote to open the door then undid the yellow security bar from the steering wheel. I was panting as I looked about. I had no shoes on my feet, and although it was late and very dark, I prayed that no one would see me. I opened the boot and grabbed my first aid box as fast as I could, looking about the street as the wind whistled in and out of my car. I opened the box to ensure that I had enough latex gloves for all of us, then rummaged through another bigger supply box, which I used on my mobile clinic days in Khayelitsha and grabbed several small packets containing swab kits. I poured surgical spirits on both my feet, straight from the bottle, then used one foot on the other, like a cloth, to clean the specks of blood splattered on them. The wind smacked against my cheeks and funnelled into my ears. I had to go through the same procedures to lock the car as I did to unlock it, and I found myself shaking suddenly, overcome by the mountain right above my head whose carved and sculptured grey presence sizzled with condemnation. Table Mountain often had the appearance of ash from a gigantic cigarette and I could feel it beckoning, even though I kept my head down. Each time I lifted my head I could feel it pulsating, throbbing with disdain. I held my head high towards my right side, pointing at the bridge above the Mental Health Clinic, because I could not bring myself to look at the mountain any longer. I kept both first aid boxes between my knees and realized that the few cars that I spotted over the bridge could easily come towards me. I rummaged through the boot of my car for newspapers, and found the remains of *The Voice*, which had the face of Dina Rodriguez on its cover, the woman accused of orchestrating the killing of baby Jordan. How dreadful, I thought, as I wrapped my first aid boxes in the newspaper, knowing full well that the parking attendant, whom I paid to clean my car, including the windows, must have left the popular Cape Flats choice of a newspaper in my boot. Tearing the newspaper across Dina Rodriguez's face brought a little childish satisfaction and scrunching it to suit my purpose brought another. I tore several pieces from the same page with the knowledge that I would be wiping blood with it; what other purpose could there be for a woman who had planned the murder of a young child. I proceeded to lock everything as securely as I could while holding onto the wrapped boxes between my wobbly legs.

I ran back to Isabel's house as fast as I could.

The insomniac Mr Isaacs was at his gate and frowned as he looked at me.

"Is everything all right? Are you girls having a party again?"

Mr Isaacs was staring at my bare feet, and looked me up and down. My hair was blowing and I had to push it away from my face with one hand in order to speak to him, while keeping the oversized first aid box under my long cardigan and the smaller one in my other hand.

"Everything's fine, Mr Isaacs," I said, without knowing what to say next. I even managed a slight giggle for the awkward occasion.

"Molly says she swears she heard a loud bang after that train took off a few minutes ago. Oh, probably those Africans who walk the streets at this time of the night, that's what I said to Molly," he remarked.

Mr Isaacs was as black as my winter boots. I found the kind of ignorance he exhibited quite unforgivable—he was, after all, a teacher and should know better. I had to remind myself not to get into an argument with him, as I have in the past with men of his level of ignorance. I did not want him prying or following me to Isabel's house, as he often did, explaining when confronted that it was his old-fashioned gentlemanly nature that urged him to act in a manner befitting a guardian of some sort to women who did not have men to look after them. He did have quite a gorgeous niece who was about my age and apparently divorced, and whom I fancied. I have been meaning to ask him about her but abandoned the idea as I fumbled for my keys and Isabel's remote.

"It's getting cold, Mr Isaacs, you should go inside," I remarked casually.

"Yes, my dear. You're the doctor, aren't you? The one who lives in Rylands," he said, as he gave me the once over with his eyes again, this time squinting just a little longer.

It was clear that I was Indian, and I suppose he thought all Indian people lived in Rylands. Of course, he was not aware that I was born in Uganda, like many Indians who were Indian by ethnicity but not by culture or identity, and when he referred to Africans he certainly did not include himself or me.

"Good night, Mr Isaacs," I said quickly and opened the electronic gate with my back facing it, so that I could keep my eye on him as he looked about the street.

Amina, Carmen, and Beauty joined me as I opened my small first aid box and handed them each a pair of gloves, which I had stuffed in my pockets. I left the scrunched-up unsightly face of Dina Rodriguez on the cemented floor. I handed Beauty her set of Isabel's keys, since she was responsible for it. I found my pencil near Carmen's feet and stuck it back into my bun, which I had formed hastily at the nape of my neck. We looked at one another, all four of us—a fashion designer, a psychodrama therapist . . . or whatever Carmen calls herself, a sculptor, and myself, the medical doctor—as we observed our friend, the social worker, trapped beneath the body of a dead man. None of us were strangers to latex gloves and we each slid a pair of them on within seconds. I handed each of them a mouth guard before putting on my own.

"Let's lift. Two of you in the front, please. Carmen and Amina, that'll be the two of you! Two at the legs . . . Beauty that'll be you and I. Try and get him on his side. We'll put him down in the alley, which is out of sight and I have several black rubbish bags here to throw over him and perhaps cover him for now."

I pointed to my first aid box and three pairs of eyes followed along. Isabel's eyes were shut; she was shaking.

All three of them nodded. Beauty was beside me.

The glances I gave Carmen ensured that she remained silent and took care of the situation and refrained from offering unsolicited advice—the kind she was accustomed to dispensing at whim.

We gazed at one another, then at Isabel.

"Shouldn't we . . . ," Carmen started.

"Arrgh!" I sighed, sounding annoyed and rather fed up. Carmen lowered her head.

Perhaps the others thought I was tired or bothered, but no one said a word as we looked at the load we had to carry, and upon further examination we closed our eyes almost collectively.

Carmen and Amina grabbed the top part of him, and both pulled a face as though they were going to be ill. Beauty muttered something under her breath, and I was uncertain as to whether she was swearing or praying, since she often spoke in Xhosa and my limited knowledge of the language along with the softness of her voice did not allow me to understand what she was saying. He was quite a heavy fellow, but his weight was the least of my concerns.

"Huh!" I gasped, alarming the others somewhat.

As we tried to lift him, so that we could remove him from Isabel and place him on his side somewhere out of sight, although I had pulled his trousers to cover his behind, his offending organ was visible hanging from his unzipped denim trousers. It was clearly still in use at the time of his passing. We were all aware that he had most likely attempted to and perhaps did rape Isabel but none of us were prepared to think about the possibility that we would see his penis or would have to pull up his trousers in order to cover it. I stuck my bare feet under his head to guard it from further damage, scattering bits of flesh. Within seconds he was dropped on the cement floor, his penis in full view, dripping with fluids.

"Oh God!"

"Oh my God!"

"Oh for God's sake!"

And of course there was this one from Amina, "Supergaan Allah!"

I bent down and looked at the organ closely, checking whether there were any lacerations on the skin; I saw none. I could not tell whether the secretions contained semen and I refrained from further inspecting the organ, since Amina, Beauty, and Carmen showed signs of disgust and discomfort. They were keen to continue despite the different shades of mortification and bewilderment the event had produced.

A lumpy bloody trail emerged as we moved him and I gritted my chattering teeth to stop myself from failing the medical exam I had set myself when I first saw him. I had already failed miserably.

Biscuit, the cat, came running towards me, and I had to shoo her away. She was probably after the bloody pieces of flesh.

"Leave her!" Isabel called out.

I directed the women to move the body to the far corner of the backyard, close enough to the alley, which was still part of the house. Manjit, my brother who is an architect, always comments on the uses the alley could be put to, but a dead man's body lying within it was not a use he might ever have imagined.

I looked over my shoulder and saw Carmen massaging Isabel's hand—the one that still had the gun in it. Carmen had special talents, very useful ones, even if I did not care for her much.

As we lowered the dead man close to the alley, I proceeded to undertake a further examination of him, but my hands were slapped away by Beauty.

"Just leave it. Let the man rest in peace," she said, in that holier-than-thou tone one sometimes hears emanating from her.

The nerve of it all, I thought. He just raped our friend and tried to kill her. I stared at Beauty coldly.

"Could I have a minute with him?" she asked, instructionally, as though my presence offended her.

"What on earth for?" I replied, completely dumbfounded by her request.

"We need to let him go . . . he needs to go in peace," she said as she held both her hands above her head, palms facing upward.

"I don't give a damn how he goes. He got what he deserved . . . actually a lot less than he deserved," I replied, with all the contempt for her and the ritual she was about to perform. Beauty held her hands in the air, as though calling on a spirit, and I knew that I could not possibly watch the performance. It was moments like these that had convinced me that she and I, although we were friends, were quite different. I am not the kind of person who allows differences to stand in the way of my friendships, but her self-righteousness annoyed me intensely. Isabel and Beauty have been friends for years, and I often feel that they feed off one another's good deeds. I met Isabel at the hospital when I first arrived in Cape Town, ten years ago, and our friendship grew over the years. Isabel was an important part of Beauty's support system from the time they met at university, and they became even closer when Beauty lost her brother to AIDS last year. Beauty lost her husband many years ago. He apparently died of police brutality while in detention. Her son Kwame lived with her, yet spent a great deal of time with her mother and her grandmother. Kwame was really a lovely boy. I could understand some of Beauty's sentiments around death and dying, but this man she wanted to send off in peace did not deserve that kind of consideration.

I looked behind me and saw Isabel running from the car into the house with Biscuit following her. Carmen stood holding the gun in her hand. Thank God, I thought, at least that part is out of the way. I motioned with my eyes for Carmen to drop the gun in the larger first aid box, and she complied without fuss.

Carmen, Amina, and I ran after Isabel. I stopped and returned to Isabel's car momentarily to see whether I could collect any of her personal items. I stuck her panties, which I had collected earlier, into a plastic bag. I saw the straps of her bra loosely draped around the receptacle of the seatbelt, while the cups were tucked into the creases of the leather seats. I grabbed it and placed it into another bag. I placed both the sealed bags at the bottom of my small first aid box, which I put in the bigger one, which had a lock on it. I grabbed my cellphone and rang Robert, whom I was not particularly fond of, but whom I tolerated. He sounded inebriated, as I expected, and was somewhere in the Kirstenbosch area at a braai with several rowdy friends, whose voices sounded muffled in the background. I could almost smell the combination of spicy meat, nicotine, and alcohol on his breath. It was a Friday evening, and close to the end of May, but I did not engage him on the details of his social life, nor did I answer his questions about when he and I would go on a date; I simply informed him that Isabel had asked for him to come to her house urgently. As soon as I ended my telephone call I gathered the unsightly baseball cap. I remembered that I had seen something sticking out of our dead man's pocket. I ventured over to the area of the backyard where Beauty sat crouched beside him. She had her eyes closed. She looked as though she was at a funeral. Her beautiful black dress and her black cape, an outfit she wore regularly at this chilly time of the year, gave the moment a very different mood. I'm not sure if she knew that I sat beside her. He was lying on the black rubbish bags I had put down before placing him on top of them. Beauty had uncovered his face; she had him facing the wall. I placed the baseball cap beside him, then stuck my latex hand in the pockets of his jacket and recovered Isabel's cellphone and put it inside one of the plastic bags I had in the pocket of my cardigan. I then stuck my hand in the right pocket of his denim jeans and recovered bits of hair, identity cards of men and women, coins amounting to about forty-two rand, a used bus ticket with today's date on it, a silver chain, which did not belong to Isabel, one gold stud earring and a stick of gum . . . but no wallet. I wondered whether any of these belonged to him. I walked back towards my first aid box and stuck all of the items from his trousers in a separate plastic bag then went indoors. I could hear Isabel screaming. I ran into the house, closing the back door behind me without locking it, since Beauty was still outside crouching beside the dead man.

Isabel ran up and down the passageway between her bedroom and the bathroom, screaming out loud and touching herself, as we followed on.

"He touched me everywhere!" she shouted.

"He was inside of me . . . the bastard!" she called out, pulling at her hair.

"Isabel, what do you want us to do, sweetie?" I asked, from a distance.

Carmen and Amina went closer, and she cried out loud, causing them to step back.

"Please . . . please . . . don't come near me. Please don't leave me. Don't leave me. Please stay . . . just stay!"

We looked at one another. I was the only one who managed not to cry.

The collar of Isabel's white Foschini shirt was soiled with tears and runny mascara; her black linen skirt was torn. She must have only partly buttoned her shirt, since the splattered blood was also on the inside. She was fumbling, looking for her bra, but I chose to remain silent about having collected it from the car seat, acutely aware that my disclosure might be a painful revelation. It appeared as though the rapist had taken some care in concealing various items of clothing in Isabel's car. Isabel grabbed the soiled shirt and threw it in the small rubbish bin in the bathroom. I stared at it for a while, quite determined that I would collect it when she was not looking, as part of the evidence that could come in handy at a later stage.

I put the smaller first aid box beside her, hesitant as to whether I should suggest a proper cleanse and bandage. I opened the box and took out the surgical spirits and cotton balls, then placed them on top of the lid; it was as suggestive as I could be.

Isabel ran back into her bedroom, screaming and shaking; we all followed.

Before I knew it, bits of food were spewed onto the maroon-patterned Indian mat at the foot of her bed, a smaller and darker version of the one in the living room. She stood across from the mirror and watched herself hurling uncontrollably and cried out loud, at the top of her voice. She could not stop herself. Amina and Carmen stepped towards the door momentarily.

"Don't leave . . . please don't leave!" she called out at them.

She undressed herself but could not complete the task and ran towards the shower. We all followed.

"Oh God!"

"Oh God!"

"Oh God!"

"Oh God help me . . . help me please."

"Oh God!"

We stood at the door of her bathroom.

Isabel was screaming and crying at the same time.

"Why didn't I close the gate faster? . . . Why didn't I see him standing there? . . . He slipped right into the yard without me noticing. . . That bloody electronic gate . . . Why did I smoke? If only I was paying more attention. . . I shouldn't have had the music on so loud."

"Sweetie, don't. Don't!" I called out, amidst the running of the shower.

She scrubbed herself everywhere with a nail brush and held her mouth under the running water, fingering every tooth, every part of her gums. She coughed and gargled, then let the water trickle down her throat and hurled it out again, throwing her head forward. She poured shower cream all over her body, then shampoo, then conditioner, and scratched herself, using her fingernails as extensions of the small nailbrush, until her skin was raised and long welts appeared on it. Isabel had no pubic hair, which surprised me a little. She looked like a frightened little girl.

Beauty walked through the bathroom door and headed for Isabel. Isabel fell into Beauty's arms like a baby.

"You have to stop hurting yourself. It's not your fault. You have to stop hurting yourself," Beauty said, repeatedly.

Carmen, who wears glasses occasionally, removed them and wiped the steam off the glass with the cuff of her jersey. Amina ran the bath and Beauty lowered Isabel into it. Beauty grabbed the washcloth from the rack and dipped it into the water, which she had scented with bath oils. She released the water over Isabel in a slow and careful motion, then repeated the process. It seemed to work, since Isabel stopped crying and her arms fell limply at the sides of the bath. Beauty and I made eye contact, and she gestured to me that the keys and remote were in her pocket. I slipped my hand into her pocket then slipped out of the bathroom quietly. Amina, who had been sitting in the corner on the tiled floor, winked at me. She squeezed the scrunched-up, soiled, white tissues in her left hand. She nodded at me; she had pulled herself together and seemed keen to assist me. We had to check up on our dead man. We tiptoed out of the bathroom without Isabel noticing. Amina held on to me and whispered in my ear, "Jazz, I have to call my mum just to let them know that I am still here. I always check up on Abdullah and the girls when I get back, even if they're asleep and they have to go to madressa tomorrow morning."

"Okay, quickly," I said as I looked at my watch. "And you're not mentioning anything else, right?" I added, seeing her face transform from one of concern to fear. Amina nodded. The street was quiet and Isabel's garage and backyard looked quite a sight. Beauty had covered the dead man in the remaining black bags I had left beside him; she had cut the plastic bags with scissors and tucked the plastic all around him, to ensure that his entire body was covered. She must have zipped his trousers since he was now lying on his back. I could see by the outline that his arms were folded. He looked almost ready for the morgue, even for the kind of burial given to unknown, unclaimed individuals whom the city had to bury in the condition they were received. The black plastic allowed him to blend into the night. The stacked rubbish bags, all of which were almost bursting, which Isabel had neglected to put out earlier in the week, were close to him, and the black rubbish bin stood between them. Beauty had blood all over her latex gloves, which she had carefully placed in a plastic bag beside the kitchen bin. I grabbed it and put it with the rest of the bloodstained items in my first aid box. Thank goodness for Amina and her cleaning habits. I looked behind me and there she stood dressed in rubber gloves, with her scarf on her head, a bucket of water, several cleaning agents in a rather large plastic container, and a small black torch. She was also wearing Isabel's unsightly rubber slippers. She stared at me, and I nodded. She looked for bloody spots and threw Vim on them, then scrubbed them with a brush, perhaps actually a yard broom, which she moved swiftly and quietly up and down, until each spot was gone. She had disinfectant with her too, and as she poured it over the spots she stared at me. My eyes were focused on the redness of the blood as it mixed with the whiteness of the cleaning agents, and the pink frothy mixture they created when she wiped, as a child might on a piece of drawing paper, before the water in the bucket erased their colour and eliminated their presence, down the drain, just like that. The pink circles left their mark in my mind, and each time I blinked I saw them spread, as though they were attempting to infiltrate a canvas. When I looked back at the cement floor, I saw them again, but this time inside the palm of my hand. I rubbed my hand against my body. I wished I knew what Amina was thinking because her face looked hard and cold, and she hardly blinked as she performed her tasks. I had never seen her in cleaning clothes; I could not imagine her in them, although she always commented on cleaning and how she liked surfaces to be clean when we sat down and had our tea.

I looked about and could not hear anything on the street. It was after midnight. I quickly rummaged through Isabel's car but it was difficult to collect anything significant, more than what I had already collected or taken photos of with my cellphone. The car simply had to be washed. I knew she kept a hose close by in the garden. The green hose lay curled beside the rubbish bin. There was something troubling me, something ticking annoyingly, like a cricket. I looked around and realized that the outside tap was dripping. I tightened the tap. Without further ado, I grabbed the hose and inserted it into the mouth of the tap, allowing the water to run evenly. I was still barefoot, and kept the spout low, so there would be no gurgle—not even a sprinkle. The water flowed steadily and quietly. I kept my head up as I cleaned an area in the car. The scrubbing brushes in Amina's basket proved rather useful. Each time I looked down, the redness coloured my vision. I was prone to these episodes when faced with certain circumstances; they had nothing to do with blood, because I was around blood all day. I think it was the sight of blood that provoked my thoughts and allowed my mind to conjure up images of past events whilst suppressing them at the same time. I could never get past red; it always held me captive, like a fish in a net that can only find its way once lowered back into the sea. I did not know my sea. Two years before I took my internship in London, I had worked with a dream specialist at a sleep clinic, and while I learned a great deal about the methods used to analyze dreams and interpret data, I came nowhere near to understanding the nature of my own problems, much as I would have liked to. I worked with Dr Lassiter for two years and decided that I could never fully immerse myself in that sort of work, since as an insomniac with a limited ability to recall dreams, especially ones which provoked my fears, I would be of little use to others. I shook my head, thinking through some of the images that had flashed in and out of my mind when I saw Isabel in the car, but abandoned them when I felt the cold sensation of the water against my feet. I walked casually about the yard, ensuring that each area of cement that I scoured was now clean. Each time I walked with my bare feet over to a new area, I followed the water with its bloody contents down the drain. "It's for the best," I said, quietly, as I looked at Amina. She was scrupulously inspecting the cement for traces of blood. I coiled up the hose and hung it in its rightful place. Amina looked over some of the spots I had attended to and sprayed them with her bottle of disinfectant. She wore a Fendi scarf on her head, not in the way that a Muslim woman wears when cooking or cleaning but in the way of one who's going to a ceremony or a wedding. Amina was fancy like that. I did not question her dress sense, ever, and she and I never spoke about religion. Punjabi women like me, of the Sikh faith, know better than to engage our friends on religious matters. I knew Amina's father had a butcher shop, perhaps even owned a few supermarkets, and that her mother was a dressmaker. I also knew that she had a relationship going with an older man, who bought her very expensive presents and whom she saw secretly. It was Isabel who revealed to me that the man was Ebrahim, the grandfather of her children. Her daughters, Faiza and Faroza, named after their maternal and paternal grandmother, were lovely girls. Her son, Abdullah, was simply adorable. I observed Amina's cleanliness each time we shared food. I gathered that she must have worked in her father's butcher shop as a teenager or was just accustomed to high standards of cleanliness. Even though I have only known Amina intimately for a little more than two years, she has become a dear friend. I patted her on the back to indicate that I was done.

I entered the house quietly, wiped my feet, and dried them on

Isabel's welcome mat. I returned to the small, unused guest bathroom, which only had a toilet and basin in it, panting quietly into the sleeve of my cardigan. I needed a moment alone. I sat back and sighed, then took a moment to attend to my unwelcome womanly visitor. There is nothing more unwelcome than the redness of bloodstained underwear, three days earlier than expected, to remind one of the regulation of the body by time, or sometimes by circumstance. I poured myself a cool drink in a tall glass, the granadilla Oros cordial, which I mixed with water. I love the stuff. I returned to the living room and Amina followed shortly after, reeking of disinfectant with only a slight hint of the Chanel No. 19 perfume she wore. She managed to look composed under the worst of circumstances. Her scarf was now loose around her neck, and her hair was behind her ears, revealing her beautiful pearl earrings. Amina held on to me for a brief moment.

Beauty ran her fingers through the water, and each time she raised her hand, she poured water over Isabel, uttering a few words in Xhosa, some of which Isabel understood because she kept on saying, "thank you."

My cellphone rang, and I was quite taken aback. I slowly took the phone from my pocket, looked around at everyone as I was about to turn it off.

Isabel nodded at me to answer the phone.

"Isabel, it's Manjit. He's outside. What shall I tell him?"

"Tell him to come in," Isabel remarked, without hesitation in her voice.

There was a long moment of silence. We all looked at one another, realizing that someone other than the five of us would now know of Isabel's ordeal.

My brother Manjit usually lets me know when he is outside Isabel's house, when he collects me on Friday nights. When I am out on my own, he prefers to follow me home in his car, unless he knows that I am with friends who will drive home behind me.

"Is Robert on his way?" Isabel asked, her head down, as she draped several white towels around her body.

"Yes," I replied with a nod.

"Go and sit with them in the lounge, I'll get dressed. Please don't say anything until I get there."

We all looked at one another.

"Thanks, Beauty," Isabel said. "I'm okay now."

Beauty raised herself from the bathroom floor and whispered in my ear.

"Just going to call my Mum," she said, as though she needed to report to me. I was not in charge, although I was often made to feel as if I were, by everyone in the writing circle, each time we went out together or had to deal with a situation that did not require verbal accounts of the sharing we partook in when discussing one another's writing. I nodded. She turned her back towards me and walked into the kitchen. Everyone else left the bathroom. I observed Carmen's delicate composure—she's frightfully English even though she dismisses any sort of comment that depicts her as such.

Isabel did not once ask about her assailant; she looked at me and I nodded. The look on her face ensured me that she got my meaning—which was of course to indicate that he was safely out of sight for now. Isabel usually read my gestures well.

"Jazz, there's a bowl of food for Biscuit under the sink. Please give it to her. I'll be out of here in a few minutes."

Isabel seemed ready to receive my brother and hers, and I carried out her request while the others continued to occupy themselves with tidying up where they could. Biscuit stared at me then sniffed at the bowl, which did not seem to arouse her interest. She looked about, then back at her bowl, almost as though she was disappointed by its content. She scrunched her nose up at the little porcelain plate that Isabel fed her in, appalled that she was not partaking in the fresh potential dinner she saw scattered in the backyard.

Carmen

I was panting, breathing heavily, and took a brown paper bag from Isabel's kitchen cupboard and breathed in and out inside it in the bathroom with the door tightly bolted when I heard that Manjit would be arriving. Isabel was distraught and clearly quite traumatized, despite her professional familiarity with the emotions women endured when raped or otherwise sexually assaulted—women she counselled on short-term and long-term bases. My face was red with indignation. I suffered terribly at Jazz's unkind treatment of me; she seemed completely oblivious to my suffering. I was flustered, biting my lips to prevent any outcry, as I walked into the kitchen and took a seat at the table. The humiliation Jazz inflicted on me, in the way she spoke to me, along with the manner in which she ignored me, made my blood boil. She announced that Manjit was outside the house but never once glanced in my direction. She simply refuses to acknowledge me. Jazz knows that Manjit and I are lovers, because he told me he had finally told her, yet she operates on the pretext of ignorance. I splashed cold water on my face in an attempt not to appear bothered. Isabel's attack came as a shock to all of us, but for Jazz to then invite Manjit into the house, and simply ignore me, was more than I could bear.

Manjit nodded at everyone and smiled awkwardly at me as he came through the door quite unaware of the evening's happenings. He was still wearing his cricket gear and brushed his hair back when he heard Beauty's voice, then Amina's, coming from the living room, only glancing in my direction intermittently; perhaps he was simply uncomfortable, he certainly looked it. Although it was May and not really cricket season, which ended the last week of April, I knew Manjit had had an unexpected game, but I did not think for one minute that I would see him under circumstances where I had to keep a distance one can only describe as ceremonial—an etiquette enforced by a sister who saw it as her prerogative to uphold Sikh formalities on behalf of her entire ethnic group, by withholding her brother's personhood from English women like me with whom he had dishonourable sexual relations, and orchestrating how he behaved towards me, even if merely for the sake of appearance. If Manjit and I were only socially acquainted, she would have made an effort to introduce me to her brother, in order for me to observe how cultured and well educated he was—what a good product he was of superior breeding—just the kind of performance a Thatcher girl like her would indulge in. Manjit looked wide-eyed and out of sorts, like the rest of us, although our discomfort had worn off as we took on the various tasks throughout the night. I don't think I have scrubbed my own house as much I did Isabel's. We were handed latex gloves, one fresh pair after another, by Jazz, who kept them in her first aid box and grabbed several bits of cloth from Isabel's bathroom cabinet and wiped every surface—not only where there were traces of blood but everywhere where it was necessary for the bleached tiles of cement to blend in with the unbleached portions.

Manjit knew something had happened; it was clear from the dishevelled state of the house, and his nervous, wary, stare indicated that he was respectfully awaiting some sort of declaration. He looked as though he were in a trance. He wandered about the house, casually, looking about as though he were waiting for Jazz to inform him as to the reason for its present state while the narrowed look on his face also suggested that he was scrutinizing its design. He is, after all, an architect, and I am sure he was observing the layout of the house as part of the shyness he was so good at hiding, while noting how awkward we all seemed in a house where we met every week. I observed him sniffing, then shifted my gaze elsewhere. Everything looked and smelled sterile. He usually waits for Jazz in his car on Friday nights. I brushed past him, unintentionally, partly because he walked about with his back determining the direction of his steps. I apologized hastily, keeping my head down, as he turned to face me, and walked towards the kitchen. Jazz brushed past between us; there were no introductions forthcoming on her part. I sat at the kitchen table, as Jazz accompanied Manjit to the living room. I glanced back at them, momentarily, and felt a warm rush of blood to my temples. I did not realize that I would feel so awkward seeing him with Jazz, and certainly seeing him inside Isabel's house made matters worse. I was tearful and jittery, and felt ridiculous—like a feeble-minded teenager in love. I am not accustomed to being told what to do and found myself at loggerheads with Jazz on a regular basis. She has an unbearable manner and her impertinence is beyond compare. She is incapable of understanding the emotions of those around her, let alone her own. Perhaps it is what medical doctors of her specialization are trained to do—ignore emotions. Perhaps it is what her parents instilled in her. By all accounts, she is their pride and joy, and it was with her education in mind, after they were kicked out of Uganda by Idi Amin and immigrated to South Africa, that her parents insisted she stay with a relative in England where she was sent to a proper English girls' boarding school. Her uncle was apparently quite wealthy and well connected. Little Miss Jazz grew up with boys who went to Eton and with girls who were the friends of my younger sister, all educated towards further superiority. It has been rumoured that Jazz is older than she says she is, and that due to some sort of trauma, the details of which I do not know, she entered school in England with pupils much younger than she. Her uncle ensured that various documents were altered and that she, like the rest of the privileged elite in England, would graciously be educated towards their further superiority. The Thatcher years made them bolder and brighter, arrogantly so, and made women like me, her senior by only a few years and cut off from the wealth we were born into, more and more bitter.

After the first volley of screams and after Jazz had rudely reprimanded me for asking her if she knew anything, I had to compose myself. I had to go to my quiet place, my work mode; it is what I do and how I function. I use psychodrama in my therapy and am quite accustomed to hearing people scream and shout, but among friends, and when one's life is threatened, my emotions always seem to get the better of me. I played out everyone's screams in my head, then my own, and found myself confronted by my own tumultuous nervousness. I could feel the guts in my belly trying to escape. Unlike my sister and mother, I have my father's poor disposition as far as emotions are concerned, as is evidenced by all of the lower classes. I exhibited mine quite against my own better judgment. I was regularly instructed by my mother during my adolescence on how unbecoming it was to exhibit one's emotions in public. I was easily provoked in any sort of crisis where death was imminent. I feared it more than anything. As I heard Amina and Beauty scream, I was taken back to the day when two school girls had found me lying in the parking lot of a theatre. They were screaming when they saw me, holding on to each other and ready to faint. I had been knocked out by my attacker and had no recollection of the actual incident, other than the fact that I knew he had grabbed me and pulled a cloth to my mouth, then forced me into the back of his van. When he was done, he threw me into the parking lot, like a used, soiled rag and all I remembered was the inside of my body aching, and the pain I felt between my legs. I was dazed and confused when I opened my eyes and saw the faces of two young Coloured girls, screaming. The bump on my head was aching, and I touched it and felt the warm blood sink into the palm of my hand. The girls assisted me with tissues they kept in their trendy beaded sling bags and walked on each side of me. The older one, Cynthia, talked endlessly in the car and tried to get me to talk to her. At each pause I cried, and she kept talking while the younger one, Esmeralda, placed her hand over my shoulder from the back seat. If it were not for the fact that Cynthia had parked in the lot outside my office, instead of the one in the cinema, which she said was full when they arrived, I would never have experienced such kindness. They called me "lady" for the first ten minutes, and I corrected them, insisting that they call me by my name. Coloured girls are raised that way, which I think is sweet, although I did feel rather old in their company and felt my years as I glanced at their youth, and by the manner in which they spoke to me and treated me—like a poor old lady, perhaps a poor old White lady, who was really not that poor but a little lonely, because I could not give them the name of one friend whose house I could go to at midnight. Cynthia told me that she had a sister, who had four young children, and as a result the house was quite noisy and would not be a good place to take me. She held her fingers to her mouth as she spoke to me and thought through her decision. She then suggested that she would take me to her brother's house, which was closest. "I am a *laat lammertjie*," she said casually. "My brother and sister are more than ten years older than I am. I live with my mother but there are too many people in the house. My aunt and her children also live with us. My dad's brother often stays over too."

She looked at me for some time. I was quiet and thinking over the matter. Finally I nodded, and agreed to go to her brother's house. She mentioned that she would have preferred to take me to meet her mother but there would be garments all over the living room as her mother was a dressmaker and had clients who would be visiting for fittings. When we arrived at her brother's house, Cynthia came to the passenger side of the car and assisted me, then accompanied me inside, while Esmeralda stayed in the car. I was concerned but she insisted that she did not want Cynthia's brother to see her and she knew the area quite well and would be fine. Cynthia nursed my wounds and assisted me as much as she could. Her brother was really sweet, as sweet as any man can be who is exposed to a woman who has been raped. He said his wife was away at a family funeral in Johannesburg and if she were home she would insist that I stay until I felt well enough to be on my own. Englishness could never muster such sincerity, not among people who share and declare their emotions so openly and who, forced to live in such close proximity to one another, brought excellence to their own benevolence without realizing it. I felt deliriously unhappy, overcome by my own suffering. Cynthia fussed over me, and her brother even brought me a blanket. She rang her mother, then put her brother on the phone; she asked me if I wanted to report the incident to the police, and she would go with me, if I needed someone. When I declined, she looked a little relieved, as otherwise she would have had to admit that she had been alone with Esmeralda, and not with other women friends, as she had intimated. Both their parents were completely unaware of the fact that they were gay. When I nodded, she bent over and said, when her brother wasn't looking, "I will go with you, really, and I feel so sorry for you for what has happened, but I don't want to get Esmeralda in trouble. As long as we keep her out of it."

I looked up at her, as her brother collected some items from the bathroom to clean my bruises.

"You're very mature for your age," I said. "And thank you so much for being so caring and so kind."

"Oh, I attended a workshop held by one of the women from *Engender*," she replied as she tucked her hair behind her ears, "and she talked to us about what to do if we were raped or sexually assaulted or if someone else was. You really don't have to thank me. I would do this for anyone."

I nodded.

"I need to call my Mum again," she said, apologetically. "She knows that I am staying here tonight and that I took the car and went to the cinema with a few of my school friends. She wanted to speak to you earlier, but I told her that we had just arrived. She is quite concerned for you. I am sure she wants to speak to you, if you don't mind."

"No, I don't mind," I replied. "Thank you once again. This is very kind of you," I added.

Cynthia's brother brought me several boxes of bandages, cleansing ointments, and surgical spirits; the little box he placed beside me had cotton balls, the ones women used for makeup, and I could tell that he was quite comfortable being around women. He even stroked my head, which I thought was rather endearing.

"I'll stay here with you if you like, until the morning, but I have to take Esmeralda home," Cynthia remarked, as her brother made another trip to the bathroom.

I had just met this young woman and immediately felt drawn to her.

Cynthia rang her mother and handed me the telephone, then she took Esmeralda home. Cynthia's mother was very sweet and offered to help, considering that it was now after midnight. She was kind enough to give me her number if I needed to talk to someone later. She even asked whether I had reported the incident or wanted to. "We can't let these men get away with this," she said. "This country will never move forward if we women don't stand up for ourselves." I burst into tears, so overwhelmed by the kindness and consideration that had been offered, and this from people I did not know.

I could not understand why Cynthia thought her mother incapable of understanding the nature of her relationship with Esmeralda. Surely she would extend the same wisdom she had shown me to her daughter, who had reached the age of consent and had just lied to her about being alone. She didn't know that I was already forty-five, and that it was the second time a man had raped me. She kept telling me that it was not my fault, which I appreciated, adding that men of all ages, creeds, and colours raped women.

" . . . all ages, creeds, and colours. Now don't blame yourself, my dear. It's not your fault. Don't blame yourself."

As I sat there that day, drinking the Cadbury's hot chocolate Cynthia's brother had offered me, I thought about those words, how simple they were, the sort of feel-good advice neighbours gave one another, without realizing how true they rang for me. I, more than anyone, should know that men of all ages, creeds, and colours rape women of . . . "all ages creeds and colours." My father first raped me when I was twelve. My mother found out on the day of my sixteenth birthday.

"Carmen," she said, prolonging the sound of my name, "you know I love you, darling," in that upper-class English tone she was fed in child-hood.

I stared at her with contempt. "She knows," I muttered softly to myself. "She bloody well knows. She's always known."

How could I be fifteen, weigh almost nothing and still not have my menstrual period? I cursed the damn thing away for good. That morning, the day of my sixteenth birthday, I reluctantly lifted myself from my bed and realized, as I stared at the spotted sheets, that the much-dreaded event had arrived. I sat in my bed crying for hours, screaming at the maid as she tried to enter my room. The spots were lower down on the sheets, not under the pillowcases as the maid was accustomed to seeing. The discreet, small, self-inflicted lacerations, skillfully done on my shoulder were usually not visible to anyone, except of course to my father, who ignored them and robbed me of the joy of lying about them. My mother always insisted that my sister and I be properly dressed, without revealing an arm, knee, or clavicle, and that if indeed they were revealed it would be through sheer lace or silk stockings of abundantly unflattering proportions. Later that afternoon when my mother came towards me and placed my grandmama's pearls round my neck—she even fitted the clasp and made sure it sat just right for him to admire, I thought—I stood still, wearing my sullen face and wretched posture, hoping that my mother, in her attempt at publicly handling me, even if it was only to display and pass heirlooms onto her children, would touch my arm to adjust my posture and uncover my secret. But God had decided not to grant me that wish. My father sat there on the golden sofa, his legs spread, his beady eyes following every gesture my mother performed to dress me up for my big day. Indeed, what a big day it was! I turned away without saying a word, as he sat there, as she called after me, adamant that I apologize and exhibit the manners befitting her class and position in society. She may even have mentioned that I was ungrateful and unmannerly. I went downstairs to Betty, our housekeeper. She understood. She knew. One can tell servants things. They always understand.

"Oh, what a lovely pearl necklace you have, Miss Carmen . . . oh pet, it looks lovely on yah," she said, in that common Eastender accent she had. She called me "pet" when we were alone: a term of endearment the working classes used to address their children, whom they usually wanted and whose birth they did not regard as a duty to society or to the Queen of England. Betty's mother was from the north of England and Betty often used phrases Londoners were not accustomed to; being around her since birth allowed for an easy relationship with her.

"Thank you, Betty," I said. "It looks so damn lovely that he'll try and get my knickers down again."

"Oh, love, now now . . . your father hasn't been near you for some time. You said so yerself, Miss. He's stopped."

"He hasn't stopped, you silly woman," I said, quite annoyed at her. "I've been putting these huge sanitary pads in my knickers so that he would stay away. I came on this morning for real, and soon I will have those fleshy protrusions with speckled dots on them, pointing at him faster and further than my nose."

I didn't realize my mother was standing only a few feet away.

She had heard every word I said. How was I to know that she

would come downstairs to the servants' quarters?

"It's no place for a lady," she would say every time I ventured downstairs. I knew that I was meant to ring a bell for Betty, one of those that were evenly distributed around our house, but I could not bring myself to use them on her. I didn't mind using them for the maids. My mother stuck her nose out at me as she reprimanded me.

"When I was a little girl, grandmama forbade me to go anywhere near the servants except my personal maid, and then *she* came to my chambers."

Upon overhearing my conversation with Betty, my mother simply collected me, twisted her lips and eyes in a manner befitting the situation from which she wished to be released, nodded at me and asked me to take up my position at my harp. Betty lowered her head like a good servant and busied herself with some irrelevant detail, without once looking at my mother.

The party went ahead as planned, of course. All my cousins and relatives on my mother's side were invited, many of whom are related to the royal family, however distant. My mother smiled the kind of smile all mothers of her class and generation wore—controlled and contrived and apparently very contagious, since everyone she associated with wore one too. I took up my position at the harp and plucked at the strings as though they were the ventricles of my mother's heart. My mother's smile faded moments after the last guests left. I was baffled by how she could turn it on, then simply turn it off, just like that, the way one does a power supply. My mother with all her high-and-mighty-ness actually confronted my father the day after the party. My father claimed that anorexia made me ill in those early adolescent years and even added that I was delusional. The following day she threw my father out. He was left without any money and was shunned by everyone in high-society circles in London. While grandmama did not like my father, she admired his knack for doing business. I am still convinced that my grandmama did not really believe me but thought it a good enough reason to get rid of my father. She was more concerned with whether I would be a topic of conversation at the tea-and-scandal parties she occasionally hosted and regularly attended than with my physical or mental health. I remember standing at some distance when my mother told grandmama, dabbing that wretched scented handkerchief to her sniffling nose. My grandmama banged her walking stick into the furniture and demanded that my mother abandon my father, and to think of the marriage of her daughters and not herself. My sister, Cordelia, was only six at the time. During my teenage years I wondered whether my mother got rid of my father because she did not want her society friends to know that he had had his way with me—the man of working-class stock who was there first before the rightful upper-class one got his leg over. He was actually lower middle class, not that it mattered to anyone in my mother's family, because it was all the same to them. Five years later, on my twenty-first birthday, I was left wondering whether my mother threw him out because he had ruined me for the men she and grandmama had chosen for me—the kind who had sexual relations with their servants and expected their brides to act like virgins, whether they were or not.

Fortunately, it did not matter to my husband Albert, because he was not in the habit of looking at women's bodies, let alone touching them. I would not have minded, except ten days after our blissfully miserable honeymoon, smiling at fellow passengers aboard the *Queen Elizabeth II*, Bertie brought his boyfriend into our house and did not care whether the servants knew. Bertie mocked me at parties, and he invited his boyfriend to every occasion our family was host to. All his friends knew and young women would whisper to each other when I entered the powder rooms. I kept a diary, and when Bertie found it, he read it to his boyfriend. Betty came to my room in the morning, with the usual serving of tea and valium and one slice of toast with orange marmalade and told me that she had heard Master Albert read my writing to his gentleman friend, as she referred to whomsoever Bertie entertained in the room adjacent to his. I dressed hastily and when I stood at the door of the room he took as his private quarters, I heard them laughing, mocking my use of language and correcting my telling of events that I had endured.

After five years of living with him under those circumstances, I left. Actually, I was hospitalized first, and decided to leave later. The lacerations made by my suffering made their comeback in short, discreet lines at first, then grew to larger ones. Betty was there to help me again, as she did when I was a girl.

I saw my father a few times during that period in my life. He would come to the house and inquire after my health, mainly by speaking to Betty, who was now my housekeeper and in charge of the two younger maids under my employ. There were times when I actually felt sorry for him. He was a hard-working Liverpudlian who had managed to rid himself of the dreadful life he was born into for the grand upper-class South London existence with the mannerisms my grandmama would approve of, before he was announced as my mother's friend, let alone her fiancé. My father worked hard at the business my mother inherited and used his street smarts to bring the company to profits it had never previously enjoyed. My mother did marry beneath her, according to those by whose judgments she lived, and as a consequence won the sympathy vote of every woman who warned her against men of the lower classes. There were of course those men in our family who were relieved that her fortune would remain intact since neither my sister nor I was expected to need an inheritance; we were expected to marry high up into the military ranks my grandpapa kept company with. And so I did—to the son of a high-ranking officer who was as fruity as the passion fruit punch his mother served at parties.

Hearing Cynthia's mother extend herself to me on the phone in such a kind and knowledgeable way reminded me of how well I knew of the colour, creed, and class of men who raped women—all I had to do was look at the violence in *my* family. The trouble is that my father saw men in my mother's family take advantage of their daughters, and of the daughters of their high society friends, and he thought he could do the same. He did not know that there was a special code for men who were born into power and privilege, those born into high-society circles who raped and sexually assaulted their daughters and their family members and suffered no consequence, except the occasional awkward mention of female relatives who committed suicide, to whom the honorary Virginia Woolf status was offered.

I sat at Isabel's kitchen table resenting the fact that Jazz and the others, including my lover, Manjit, were in the living room and remembered how I met Manjit. The morning after my stay at Cynthia's

brother's house, she came to sit beside me, when I had the breakfast
her brother had kindly prepared, Marmite and cheddar cheese on
toasted whole wheat bread, accompanied by rooibos tea. I did not
want to put him out in any way, but he had insisted, and offered me
what they had in the house. I am not one for cereal or porridge, nor
have I ever indulged in the English heart-attack breakfast of bacon,
sausages, and eggs. Cynthia spoke quietly and intimately to me, noting
that both she and Esmeralda had decided that they would go with me
to the police station and that she was selfish to put her needs first. I
was moved by her goodwill; they were both so young and yet so
knowledgeable. We went to the police station close to where it
happened, a block from where I work. All sorts of details were asked,
but nothing happened. Nothing happened at all. I rang the station a
few times, and the young dapper-looking constable told me, firmly yet
arrogantly, that cases like mine often ran into dead ends. Imagine being
referred to as a dead end.

Cynthia and Esmeralda finished high school and were still seeing
each other a year later. They stayed in contact with me and invited me
to be with them for dinner on our anniversary, as they referred to it,
since they did not want me to be on my own. They had been to my flat
in Seapoint during the course of the year and knew that I had few
friends. Fancy that—remembering a rape a year later and spending it
in the company of the women who rescued me from a parking lot.
Cynthia's brother and his wife introduced me to Manjit during that
time, and I owed my recovery to them. When one divorces husband
number two, one knows that the invitations become fewer and fewer.
I never speak husband number two's name. So few marriages actually
work these days; those that do are preserved by not inviting unmarried
or unpartnered women like me to dinner parties. Manjit plays cricket
with Cynthia's brother and is a few years younger than I. He had come
to drop Cynthia's brother off at the door after a cricket match when
they asked him to join them for dinner. It is almost a year since, and I
only found out after we started seeing each other that Manjit was
Jazz's brother, and by that time I had already joined the writing circle.
He had just recovered from an arranged marriage that had turned out
badly and had involved several families in Cape Town and London. I

don't know why educated adults still allow culture and tradition to determine their happiness. They don't live in India; they were not born in India. Jazz grew up in England and Manjit studied there, yet families there and here seem keen to preserve a culture across the oceans that derives from a place none of them have ever seen. It is perhaps this particular view that has found Jazz and I at loggerheads. I find the whole matter quite dreadful—the reality of living in a modern world, going to university, yet holding on to old customs in order to prove that one is still of that ethnicity by following traditions intended for earlier centuries. Jazz still defends those customs, while it is common knowledge that she has had more boyfriends than birthdays.

I started tidying up the kitchen. I needed to remain focused and not trail off into my horrific history with men. Beauty and Amina came to check on me in the kitchen because they knew about my relationship with Manjit. I asked Amina whether she had telephoned her children and Beauty whether she had called her son. Amina was shaking beyond control. Beauty appeared calmer. They left the kitchen separately not to arouse suspicion, I think. I don't think anyone wants to be in Jazz's bad books.

The garage door was being opened by a remote; the sound interrupted my thoughts. The only person who had keys to the house, other than Beauty and Isabel, was her brother Robert. I quite liked Robert, he was always pleasant and friendly towards me. Beauty came to the door and looked over at me. I raised myself from my chair.

"Another visitor! What a night!" she exclaimed.

"Yes . . . quite," was my expressionless reply.

I accompanied her to the door as she greeted Robert. I could smell the whiskey on his breath, and the smell of spicy meat and smoke on his clothes. In spite of it, I could still enter the living room with him. He was a drinker, just like me, and had no interest in hiding it. Perhaps he'll pour himself a drink, I thought, in which case I would be offered one, which I desperately needed. We never drink alcohol in Isabel's house on Friday nights, on account of Amina and Jazz, who abstain due to religious reasons.

His greeting was short. He looked over our heads down the passage, and Beauty indicated with a side nod of the head that Isabel was in the living room. All three of us walked in there, Robert leading the way.

"Huuurh!" Robert exclaimed as we entered the room.

Isabel sat in her white cotton bathrobe; her hair was wet and looked as though she had gone at it with a rake and garden shears. Her eyes were red and her lips looked a bluish green, drained of life and colour.

She hugged Robert and cried into his body. He held her close.

I don't think I have ever heard anyone cry that loud. Isabel shook as she spoke, revealing the events of the evening, her voice going hoarse from the crying.

"It's okay. It's okay," he said and hugged her tightly.

Manjit looked at me. He had tears in his eyes. I wanted to be held by him. He knew it. He sat there, cross-legged and shivering, and held me with his eyes and burning breath. I swallowed his gaze with a loud gulp. I desperately wanted a drink and was hoping Robert would go to Isabel's drinks cabinet. I did not care if Jazz saw me drinking or if she made her usual remarks about women who drank alcohol and how dreadful she thought it was.

The buzzer at the front gate startled everyone. Isabel jerked forward and parted from Robert, looking frightened.

Robert frowned, then released a sigh. He said to Isabel, "Tom called me and said he got no reply from your cellphone. I told him Jazz had called and said it was urgent. That is probably Tom at the front gate. I take it no one has telephoned the police?"

We all shook our heads.

"Go and let Tom in," Isabel remarked, looking at Robert while glancing over at Beauty. Beauty lowered her head.

We fell back into our places on the two sofas as Robert walked towards the door with the keys and the remote attached to them. Beauty was twisting her hair, playing uncomfortably with it. I yawned then sighed into the palm of my hand, dreading the gathering of unexpected visitors. My body took the shape of an old ball as the sofa softened the blow of my disappointment. Manjit's eyes held me in a solitary grip. I soon grew tired of his empty offering and returned his gift by turning my back on it.

Beauty

The air in the house was suffocating me. I had no option but to stay. One does not abandon a friend who's suffering through an ordeal like the one Isabel was, simply because one feels stifled. I sat in the chair, scraping off the remains of my nail polish from my fingernails, one fingernail to another, too overwhelmed to look elsewhere. I had to be strong for Isabel, she needed me, well, she needed all of us, and we all knew that. The writing circle was a great comfort to me. As a sculptor I faced many challenges, and now, at my age, as I prepared to teach other young artists at colleges and art centres, I was faced with the task of having to write, and this task demanded more of me than I ever realized. I have never been much of a writer. Keeping a journal after Khaya died allowed me to talk to him, and to feel that each day I turned a new page I breathed life into a continued relationship with him—my soul mate and father of my child. He inserted his presence everywhere on the written page. I could feel his presence exerting itself between spaces, on those white pages—confronting colons. I could feel him push through the lines on the page. I could feel him challenge me from the grave, as I crossed my t's and clumsily constructed sentences that could never stand on their own; sentences that twisted the logic of language. Writing came slowly to me, as a reward for patience—a gift offered from the depths of emotions I did not know I possessed—but which, when tackled, first through speech, however quiet, came to my hand in the still of the night. Each word took its time; and with each passing day after Khaya died, more words filled the page, and I was able to spill then pour, then later engrave with greater precision what I felt for a man who had loved me with every inch of his body and who taught me to love the world I lived in—even if it did not love me back.

I learned to succumb to the written word through the loss of love for it was in love that I learned what words meant, and later understood what the written word could restore. I abandoned all forms of love, for it was in reconstructing love through words on pages that I learned to bathe my body in it, shower my pain with words that had been spoken in my ear, at the very earlobe which was nibbled and kissed by the man whose words soothed every inch of pain I ever felt. As I struggle each day with the writing I am now forced to call my own, in order to allow my body to heal itself from the suffering it has endured, I push myself to make peace with a past that still eats at the very core of my body. Sometimes when I sit down, faced only with a blank page, ink leaks from my pen, like clouds from a blue sky . . . there and everywhere. That big blue canvas I look up at, each day, looks at me with the ink it used to engrave each shape in the sky—to express its mood and its history while I struggle to inscribe mine. Kkaya always wrote me beautiful letters. I missed the occasion each of them marked, as he would slip them into my khaki backpack on campus, whenever the mood caught him. I reread his letters for days, weeks, months after his passing, growing more attached to them for they were not dated and would never be, he once told me, when asked—they would be forever. I would sit, huddled in a corner, anywhere, with my letters and ignore offers from friends or family members to join them at social gatherings. Before I knew it, there was only my pregnant belly, myself, and a bed full of letters in the room. I suffered terribly in those days, because I had isolated myself. I suffered because I saw myself as being separate from the family and the community I knew as my own. I suffered because I did not think that they felt what I felt—which was special and different. Isabel's suffering was now my suffering; I was in the house when it happened. I usually go to the gate but I did not . . . and it troubled me deeply. Perhaps I have become too attached to the violin, because the caution I carry within me, what others call instinct, had been seduced by the sounds of forbidden love which Vivaldi vivaciously portrayed and to which, in my nostalgic state, I had fallen prey. I blinked back the tears, but they fell in spite of my gallant efforts.

When Robert went to the front gate to let Tom in, I went to the kitchen to make tea. Tea is always welcome, no matter the time of day. Tea is one of those Cape Town treasures. Making tea is almost as pleasant as serving tea, then sitting down to take that first sip. Drinking tea with friends and acquaintances can be both pleasant and sombre an experience. People are always pleased when the pot is brewing; it flavours conversation and it sweetens the company one keeps. I needed both.

I was shaking as I walked about the kitchen trying not to think about the man I had just wrapped in black plastic and whose face reminded me of my brother's. Unlike the women in my writing circle, I had looked at him. I looked at him very carefully. I wanted to see the face of someone who was as desperate for a car as he was and who took the opportunity of extracting more out of his criminal activity than he had planned. Perhaps he did not intend to rape and possibly kill Isabel. What drives a man to those actions? I don't suppose I will ever know. The top part of his head was shattered and the lower part, its expression frozen, looked shocked and horrified that something he had planned had gone badly. His nails were clean, and so was his clothing. I could even smell the brand of powdered soap used to clean his clothes. Clearly, he must have come from a home where some care was given to his health and well-being.

I allowed Jazz the benefit of believing that I was unaware of her presence as she rummaged through his pockets. I had already closed his mouth and his eyes. She is very good at her job as a surgeon, certainly from what I've been told, and I don't expect her to understand my interest in letting a dead man go to a restful place despite his actions. I don't think Jazz has ever lost anyone, not the way I have, feeling for years later that I should have let them go and given them their final farewell out of the world as their soul was preparing to leave the earth. God creates humans and it is we here on earth who destroy God's creation because we want to enjoy power and privilege, which we gain through the oppression and exploitation of others. How would we know how he had suffered or what his needs were? Was he a frustrated man who had suffered in his Blackness because his oppression had put him there and nowhere else? Did he get any breaks

from anyone who had the wisdom and the courage to look at his
potential? Why fight back by raping women? Why did he choose rape
and murder when he had other options? I cannot be as cavalier as Jazz;
my knuckles bear great evidence of the struggles I have endured. Even
now, working as a sculptor in a society where freedom has meant that
more households want domestic servants than before and which
permits the continual exploitation of Black women, because although
there is no apartheid any longer there is its stepchild in its aftermath.
I looked at this man and saw in him a man who must have felt that he
did not matter to the world he lived in. My Khaya died in detention in
1989, and it broke my heart. He never lived to see his son, who was
born the following year. Kwame is fifteen, almost sixteen. I thank God
that my mother, who is sixty-four, and my grandmother, who is eighty-
one, and my sisters, both of whom are almost forty, all enjoy good
health. I have been raised and looked after by women in my family all
my life. My mother worked in Elgin picking apples, which is where my
father was born, and visited my father's family there whenever she
could. My father died in detention during the early 1970s, many years
ago—so long ago I don't even remember why he was there or what he
looked like. My grandmother looked after me when my mother was
away working. My grandmother worked for Mr Pirelli.

"Mr Pirelli is not like other people," my grandmother said one day
when I asked why she spoke so highly of him. "Look, look at all the
stuff he gave us."

He was retiring to some fancy cottage he had bought with his wife
along the eastern coast, past Durban, close to the Blood River area.

He had sent me pens and sketching pads when my grandmother
boasted of the little talents I had. They were expensive items, bought
from exclusive art shops—the kind I would be turned away from; the
kind where I could not afford to shop, at whose window display I
would stand smitten. He seemed proud, or so my grandmother said,
that I was thinking of going to university.

"She'd be darn lucky if she got into UCT," I heard him say one day,
when I had stayed away from school to help my grandmother finish off
cleaning the shop—like all good children who assist their parents and
grandparents who work as domestics in White homes and cleaners in

White businesses. My grandmother took the train and the packed taxi home, as she usually did. I had to go for an interview with three staff members of the Fine Arts Department at the University of Cape Town. Mr Pirelli said that he could take me to UCT as it was complicated to get to by bus and train. At age seventeen I had never been in a car before. I had only taken jam-packed taxis and was relieved that the offer came from a man who showed so much interest in me. No one I knew, no one in my family or in my circle of friends, had a car. I packed all of my drawings, my paintings and the little sculptures I had made in an old brown leather satchel my grandmother had given me, which Mr Pirelli had given her several years ago.

He drove all the way from Sea Point to Hout Bay, to take the remains of his shop to the man who had purchased it from him. Imagine that: there I was, a seventeen-year-old Black girl from Kheyalitsha, in the car of a White man, in the front seat, in 1987, and thinking that I was being treated, for once, as his equal. He talked endlessly about how he was all packed, and how he could not wait to leave the following day. I sat there beside him, listening to every word he uttered, lavishly illustrating the victories of his grand existence. I must have smiled and even laughed at some of his corny jokes, despite lending an ear to FM Radio, because I remember he commented on my teeth. When we arrived at the farmhouse in Hout Bay, he told me to stay in the van. The man and his wife came out and greeted me, their trip to the car made out of curiosity, not interest, like going to a museum to see the peculiar offspring of some new species. One of the men, who worked as a labourer on the farm, came to the car and started talking to me. I had changed the radio station to listen to my kind of music, and the sound of familiar tunes must have drawn his attention. He actually opened the door and was about to put his hands on me. I pulled away to the driver's side and ran towards the house and rang the doorbell. Mr Pirelli was annoyed at the man and said it was good that I had got myself out of the situation.

"You are not his type," he said. "You know that, don't you?" He posed his question like a command, with condescending eyes, attempting to share with me, for once, the portion of superiority he owned over people like the labourer.

The farmer apologized. His workers often became overly amorous when they saw women of my kind, he said without blinking an eyelid. His wife, who had only seen the top part of me when I greeted her from the car now looked me up and down and commented on my clothes, remarking with great alarm in her voice on how nice they were, and that I was very well dressed and very slim, and so well spoken for a girl from Kheyalitsha. I did not respond but held onto my brown satchel as dearly as I could. Mr Pirelli mentioned to them that I had an interview at UCT and they were impressed, they even allowed me to use their bathroom—the one they had refused me moments before.

When we were back in the car, Mr Pirelli told me that he felt proud he had paid my grandmother all those years and he was so happy to see that she had put the money to good use.

He drove hastily, checking his watch to ensure that I would be on time for my interview and exclaimed, after sighing, that he would cut through some road because it was very important that I not be late for my interview. He headed for a path he referred to as a shortcut; I did not even think it was a road. He looked at me and assured me that it was the fastest way and he had taken it many times before. Within minutes I saw his face transform itself from soft, fleshy friendliness to hard, taut resentment. He asked me to get out, and pointed to a secluded spot where several trees were clustered together. As I cried, he told me I had nowhere to go and would not know how to get back, he'd done our family so many favours over the years and why would I not grant him this one.

"I know you people like to do it . . . and I just want to do it with you once . . . I promise, just once."

Despite my protestations, he forced himself on me, saying I was making a fuss over nothing, when fifteen minutes ago I had been solicited by an uncouth farmhand who would have been very different with me. He was a nice man, he said, and he had asked nicely, and he would not be mean or violent and would still take me to UCT for my interview. I had never had sexual intercourse before. I knew that I did not want to have sexual intercourse with him, even though he tried to convince me that it would be my only time with a White man, and that

I should see it as a learning experience.

"Black men will not appreciate you the way I do," he said, in that patronizing, colonial, overbearing sort of way I am now old enough to identify. He did drop me off at UCT. I got out of his van as fast as I could. I ran to the nearest toilet and asked one of the women to help me clean my face and sort out my work. She stared at me as though she knew what had happened and had been there before. She caressed my face and straightened out my eyebrows, as though they were the only two things that mattered to her. Through it all, she did not once look at me, but bit her lip and blinked back the tears. I used the liquid soap in the toilet to clean myself up and wash his smell off me as much as I could. I had no time to prepare for my interview. I presented all of my work, all my paintings and sculptures that showed various women at different stages of sexual and physical abuse, the kind my mother was accustomed to and the kind I had witnessed at the hands of her boyfriends. The panel loved my work, and loved the way I presented it. They looked at me from head to toe as though to verify that I was worthy of the sculptures and drawings I claimed as my own. The younger lecturer of the three asked me about the firing of my sculptures, their texture, and where I worked. When I explained that I used the facilities at Community Arts Project in Woodstock, she smiled, and nodded to the rest of the panelists, ensuring that they all shared and took credit for the White helping hand that was extended to Black underprivileged girls like me. "You have a lot of passion," the older lecturer said, "and your work shows that very well."

If only they knew what had happened to me just minutes before.

I spent six years at UCT, working, studying, scrubbing tables at restaurants, later serving food when it became trendy for Black women to be waitresses and not just work in kitchens or public bathrooms. During my first year I met Khaya, but he was taken from the world so young. I struggled after his death. I closed myself off from the world and friends who offered me comfort. When I completed my degree, and my work started being reviewed, I began to feel as though I mattered to the world again, because I saw the world differently, and I had Khaya to thank, even if he was not present in the flesh. I had my young son Kwame to look to for the kind of sensibility I always thought I lacked. I knew that I mattered to my family and my friends, but I had never felt that I mattered to the world, not the way that reviews of my sculptures made me feel. There was much more emotion put into actually making the work, but so much pleasure when I felt people relating to it.

Isabel's attacker could not have felt he mattered to anyone, why else would he do what he did? And because he felt he did not matter, nothing mattered to him. He was perhaps in his late thirties. Although I did not know him, my thoughts were with his mother. How would his mother feel when she discovered her son missing, and worse still, that he was killed in the act of raping and hijacking a woman in her car, right in her own backyard, in the nice and friendly grey suburb of Observatory? How would she mourn her son?

I filled the kettle to the brim as the water thrust itself out of the tap. There would be eight of us now. I settled for one big teapot and several mugs from the cupboard and placed them on one of the many trays Isabel owned. I don't like mugs; I find them awkward and a bit distasteful but the occasion called for them. Tea cups on saucers have to be served, and I was in no mood to be serving a certain person, especially considering the lateness of the hour. I could serve my friends at any hour because they would do the same for me. There are some people, no matter whose friends they are, that I can never serve. Serving tea is by invitation only, not by obligation or circumstance. I opened the bottom cupboard and took out the biscuit tin. Isabel was not the kind of person who kept home-baked goods and my choice was limited to store-bought items. I placed several Eat-Sum-More, Tennis biscuits, and Choc Crust on a plate, then laid out several paper serviettes on the tray. That should do, I thought, as I rearranged the tray to accommodate all the necessary items.

I could hear Isabel crying as Tom hugged her. I did not have to see the hug; her muffled voice suggested they were in close proximity. I did not want to witness it. Isabel is very dear to me. I could hear her voice above the cries and him hushing her, as one might with an overanxious child, afraid that they will become distraught. I could hear Tom talking to Isabel in that English feel-good sort of way he had about him.

I poured milk into the milk jug and popped it in the microwave for a minute. We Capetonians like to have warm milk in our tea. I realized that Isabel might prefer rooibos tea; one pot of rooibos and one pot of earl grey, I then decided, hoping that no one would disturb me until I was ready to take the tray into the living room. I counted the sugar cubes and sighed to myself in quiet disbelief. There was clearly not enough for eight people. White people don't take much sugar in their tea anyway, so counting Carmen and Tom out, I hoped eighteen cubes would be enough for six people. I looked through Isabel's cupboard in search of condensed milk and found a tin. Although I myself do not enjoy it in tea, someone else might, in case the tea was not sweet enough. But I decided against it. It reminded me too much of my days as a young girl in Kheyalitsha when we had condensed milk on white bread when there was nothing else to eat.

My thoughts were soon interrupted.

"Good evening, Beauty," Tom greeted, as he came up behind me.

"Good evening," I replied.

"We don't have to hide our friendship from Isabel, you know," he said to my back, in that cool I'm-an-English-liberal-not-South African sort of way.

"We are not friends. And there is nothing to hide," I said, as I looked at him. I turned my back again and kept my hands under the tap running with lukewarm water.

"You can't ignore me. You can't just ignore me, you know," he said in a softer tone but still with a touch of superiority.

I opened the tap further, allowing the water to run in the sink with no intent for it. My actions did not deter him.

"Isabel is going to need you now more than before. I am . . ."

"Dr Livingstone, I presume?" I remarked, pronouncing every word with a raised brow and with a comical gaping mouth. Tom lowered his head and sighed.

"Do not try and tell me how to have relationships with my friends. I don't need your guidance or advice. Now, if you don't mind, I would like to return to the living room with this tea tray, and I hope that you'll have the wisdom to keep your mouth out of my affairs. I thought the days of colonial governance were over, but I see they've returned. Cchhht," I said, all at once, sucking the air out of my teeth as

I passed him.

Tom walked into the living room two minutes later, with a list of telephone numbers instead of a map. Isabel looked drained. Robert was sitting beside her and rubbing her feet. I poured her rooibos tea, with three sugars and no milk, the way she took it. She clutched it with both her hands. Robert winked at me when I poured his; the wink indicated that he was expecting me to fetch Isabel's whiskey or brandy and pour him his usual tot, which went with any drink he consumed. I had no intention of succumbing to his winks or aiding him in the pursuit of his vices. Everyone else came to the table to pour their own tea, including Tom. I turned my chair towards Carmen and Amina; each time I looked over my shoulder Tom was staring at me. Amina must have been to the bathroom again, for when she stroked my hand she left traces of her perfumed hand cream on my fingers.

I telephoned my mother and grandmother shortly after Isabel's condition became known to us, and told them that I would be staying at Isabel's for the night. I knew they would be calling my flat and did not want them to worry. I telephoned them morning and night, every day. I often stayed over at Isabel's, and given the circumstances tonight, Isabel would want me to. Kwame was already asleep. I checked my messages on my cellphone, indicating to Jazz that I would be quick about it, and received Mary's message to telephone her, even if it was after midnight but not later than one in the morning. It was typical of her; she often worked late, doing paperwork and writing reports for the various charities she was involved in. I called Mary, my adopted godmother, hastily explaining that I was still at Isabel's house and would speak to her another time. Mary was the first Black woman at UCT I met who was a professor, and a linguistics professor at that. She befriended me during my first year and consoled me after Khaya died. She is more than twenty years my senior and is retired. Her husband is a cabinet minister and she assists him these days while busying herself with all sorts of community projects. She asked after Kwame, and it reminded me of how many people I had in my life who cared about my son.

Kwame does remarkably well at school and I thought, as I sat down with my tea, that I ought to spend more time with him before

Ludwig arrives from Vienna. Kwame gets along with Ludwig, for which I am grateful. He rarely gets along with any of my friends. His singing has become important to him and he is preparing for his upcoming audition with the Soweto Boys Choir. He knows how hard I work in order to give him the best. Ludwig is the first boyfriend I have introduced Kwame to in his teenage years, and because Ludwig is not intrusive, he has been able to win Kwame's affections without ever asking for them. My mother and my grandmother also like Ludwig; he is thoughtful and loving.

Jazz reeked of disinfectant and her feet looked bleached and cracked. There was hardly a trace of the beautiful hennaed pattern she wore on them. I noticed that the nail polish from Amina's French pedicure had been removed; her feet looked terribly white and bleached too. The smell of hospital was in the house. Tom walked about with his white coat and a stethoscope hanging out of the right pocket of his coat. He was, apparently, still on duty and had his beeper clipped onto his left pocket. The smells of hospitals frighten me; they remind me of Frank and collecting him from work. Those smells of disinfectant, decay, and death all melting together, and finding expression on the uniforms of nurses who care for the thousands who find themselves in hospitals every single day, is what I needed to capture and draw into the cloth models for the installation piece I was working on. As a nurse, Frank enjoyed great popularity. He was well loved by his coworkers and apparently by many among the male population, the details of which, until his private hospitalization, I was completely unaware of. Why do brothers hide things from their sisters? I looked over at Robert, who reeked of *dagga** and alcohol, but whose presence Isabel needed. Isabel loved him, actually adored him, and although Frank and I were close as children, we grew apart over the years.

There was silence in the living room, as the women from the writing circle sat huddled together on the two sofas and chairs, some of us with jerseys and cushions. I sat in front of the fireplace and could feel the outside air pushing in. I took a few logs from the wooden crate by the fireplace and placed them on the grid. Isabel gave me a small nod. I gathered the few logs together and I blew and fanned with my woollen cape until a crackle finally popped into a beautiful small

* cannabis

orange flame. Jazz and Amina sighed with relief. Within seconds the room had a warm orange glow to it. All eyes were on the fire and I observed the women as their bodies curved to rounder, softer, shapes and their muscles unclenched the evenings' events. Jazz stepped forward and warmed her hands over the fire. She was now wearing Isabel's socks, and she rubbed her stomach as she placed her head on Amina's lap. My attention was soon drawn to the quiet conversation between Tom, Isabel, and Robert on the far side of the room.

All of us from the writing circle were suddenly quiet as we looked on. Robert raised himself from the seat beside Isabel and stretched; we could hear all his bones cracking. He was a rugby player and quite a large man. He spread the fingers of one hand and cracked them with his other hand, then vice versa. I knew he would have something to say in no time.

It was Isabel who broke the silence, firmly.

"I don't want to go to the police, not now, not ever," she said, as she gazed up at Tom, then shifted her gaze to everyone else in the room.

There was an awkward silence and the women looked at one another.

Everyone's eyes moved back to the fire again.

Robert sighed and scratched his head.

"What would you like to do, Isabel?" I asked.

"Beauty, quite honestly, I would like to forget the whole thing. I wish a guardian angel would fly over here, collect that creature in my yard, and place him in an incinerator, but I don't know any pathologist or anyone who works near an incinerator."

I gasped, then sighed quietly, as I listened to her. Isabel looked at the fire as she spoke, then crossed her legs and chewed her fingers.

I have always known Isabel to be kind, often in very challenging circumstances, but what had just come out of her mouth caught me completely by surprise. My shoulders fell and I hung my head. I knew she had come face-to-face with her worst fear, but her response to my question left me speechless. There must have been loose pieces of wood in the fire, perhaps even wet ones that had been collected the previous night, for suddenly they burst and popped. Carmen and Amina shrieked. Isabel jumped up.

"Beauty . . . Beauty," she said and sobbed uncontrollably.

I kept my head down. Within seconds she was at my side and threw her arms around me. I could not stop myself from crying as she sobbed and tried to say her sister's name.

"Remember Dol . . . Dol . . . Dolores . . . who's going to believe me, who's going to believe me . . ."

She screamed, and I edged closer to her. I held her close. Carmen, Amina, and Jazz joined us. My face was the warmest, since I was sitting closer to the fire. For those few moments when we were huddled together, breathing and exhaling all at the same time, I was reminded of how and why we first started the writing circle. Jazz and Carmen kept their usual distance from one another, of course. After the release, we each found our places on the floor, the sofas, and the chairs. I glanced over at Robert and saw tears streaming down his face. He did not care to hide them. He brought his tea mug to his mouth and cried, without a twitch on his face or turning to look at anyone.

For a while I thought Manjit was going to leave, but he hovered about, wringing his hands, covering his eyes, pacing up and down the living room. He looked visibly upset. He was scratching his head, then twisting and fiddling with his fingers.

Jazz came to stand beside the fire again. She warmed her hands and sighed out loud. She appeared to be talking to herself.

As I moved away from the fire, I saw Jazz's face come to light.

"We need to bury him. We need to bury him before sunrise. It's the only solution," she uttered, with the usual confidence she carried in her voice.

"Where?" Robert asked.

"At a graveyard somewhere," Jazz replied. "We need to find someone who works at a graveyard and find a way to bury him. That's the only thing left to do."

"You can't do that," was Tom's taut reply.

"I don't have time for arguments or put-downs right now. If you don't have a better plan, then keep your comments and that list of telephone numbers to yourself," Jazz said, with enough disdain for Tom to fill the entire room.

Amina had hiccups and stood at the far end of the room; she

moved to the window and peered out of it without actually opening the curtains. Carmen went to stand beside her to see whether she was all right.

"Tom, I'm *not* going to the police," Isabel insisted.

"Is there really no way I can convince you, Isabel? I have a list of people we could call. Not all policemen take these matters lightly."

Isabel shook her head and kept her eyes shut.

"Please, Isabel, is there really no way I can convince you?"

"No, there isn't," was her firm reply.

"But . . ."

"Listen, Tom, this is not for you to decide," Isabel interrupted.

"I'm just concerned that you might regret this later, Isabel," he said.

"My life is full of regrets already as it is. Believe me, burying that creature outside will not be one of them."

"But that is taking the law into your own hands!"

Isabel burst out crying and ran to her room.

"I'm sorry . . . I'm sorry," Tom said. He got up from his chair, and cracked his knuckles, pacing up and down. He continued talking despite his earlier apology.

"Let's be frank here, you cannot go through with this. You cannot take this any further," he said, looking at each of us in that commanding sort of way he had about him.

"It's incredible how you like to take charge of things," I responded, without realizing that I was speaking aloud.

"Well someone has to. I can't sit 'round here and take part in burying someone without going through the proper procedures," he declared, as he moved his hair over from side to side. I looked at him in disbelief. He was red in the face, and even redder in his neck, with patches flushing themselves out from under his goosebump-dimpled skin.

"It's okay for you to say. We have lived through proper procedures and we have seen no result. Isabel and I lost a sister because of proper procedures. We don't need to be lectured to," Robert said. He was sitting upright and his face was fierce.

"Let's be frank . . . burying someone . . .?"

"Well, let's be frank. Let's talk about *my brother* Frank. You had no qualms in burying my brother."

Jazz stood by my side with her arm around my shoulders.

"Beauty, come on, it's really not the time. . ."

"Isn't it, Jazz? On what grounds, Jazz? When will it be time to talk about my brother Frank? It's not something I ever talk about, and why not? It's really not the time for silence . . . not any more."

I could not contain myself any longer. Amina's hiccups were fierce and grew closer by the minute.

Jazz lowered her head and walked over to Amina's side of the room. They exchanged glances and embraced. Jazz kept her eyes on me as I spoke to Tom.

"So, what is proper is your wonderful purchase of cocktails and other HIV medication which you can afford, and which your British government provides? Was it proper for you to fornicate with my brother without any protection for him? That is the proper word for it, is it not?"

I really did not want to cry.

"Beauty . . . ," Jazz said, as she held me.

"Beauty . . . I'm—" he started.

"You asked us to be frank, Tom, so here I am. It is what you want, isn't it? Your wish is my command!" I even managed a curtsy.

"Earlier in the kitchen you intimated that we were friends. Since I cannot be your friend, allow me at least the honesty to say so, and better still, demonstrate it. Being honest is almost the only thing we South Africans have going for us, so why stop now. You had a sexual relationship with my brother, knowing full well that he was HIV positive. You are HIV positive, from what Frank's best friend told me, but you have fancy cocktails and medication . . . oh, and that is the proper word for it . . . and the proper course of treatment you are following. My brother did not have proper anything. So don't you dare tell us what to do! We are part of your ethnic spice, your little bit on the side from the main course of roasted White privilege pickled with British Empire. It's why White people like you come to Cape Town—to lie in the sun like roast pork. We are the peppercorns who flavour your palate. Your only interest in us is how well we serve your purpose."

"Beauty . . ." He said my name in a rhythmical sort of way, as though he meant it, and even came close to me.

"Go to hell!" I said, with all the force I could muster. I left for the bathroom. I had to massage my fingers; they were stiff from clenching. I left the door open because I wanted to hear what else he would have to say. Carmen joined me in the bathroom moments later.

"Tom, I think you better leave. Isabel is my sister, and I know what she's been through," Robert said.

"I want to speak to Isabel," Tom insisted.

Isabel rushed into the living room, fully dressed and out of her bathrobe. Carmen and I joined her.

"Just leave . . . just leave," she said.

"Are you sure you want me to leave, Isabel?"

"Yes. Yes, I am. You told me about you and Frank and I never said one word to Beauty. I wanted it to come from her. I'm okay with men who are bisexual. What I am not okay with are men who tell women what to do. I may be pregnant right now. I may have to have an abortion. I don't know. I have not thought that far. I hope to God I don't have to. I will have to live with every decision I make, and all the consequences that go with it, but I'd be damned if I allow you to tell me what to do. So please leave now!"

"Isabel, there is the morning after pill and there are . . ."

I gasped in disbelief.

"Tom, just leave. I will decide on my options, not you."

Isabel stamped her foot as she spoke.

Tom grabbed his keys and bolted for the door.

Manjit got up from his chair. Most of us had forgotten about Manjit, except for Carmen, who now whispered in my ear just how awful she felt and how she just wanted to go home.

"Isabel, I'll be in the kitchen if you need me . . . if anyone needs me," Manjit said, looking particularly in Carmen's direction.

Isabel took the tube of cream from her bathrobe pocket and rubbed cream all over her hands; she tossed the tube to Amina. One seldom saw her hands without her gloves. I was almost expecting her to slip on a pair but she did not.

"Robert, Manjit needs company."

Robert looked at his sister and nodded.

"We'll take it from here," Isabel said.

"Sure. No problem. You know where to find me," was Robert's reply.

Isabel let out a loud sigh as she settled into one of the dining room chairs.

"Are you okay?" Carmen asked.

"Yes. I'm fine."

I was not sure how to approach Isabel, after what I had just said.

"Isabel, I'm sorry I lost it with Tom. And, sorry to all of you too, I really could not control myself. I know I should try harder."

"Beauty, don't apologize. He had it coming. Tom was completely out of line."

I looked at Jazz, Carmen, and Amina as Isabel spoke.

They all looked at one another, then at me.

I sat by myself and brought my hands to my face. I felt completely disappointed at my display of manners. I should not have resorted to such harshness. Mary would be equally disappointed if I told her how I had handled the situation with Tom. It is from Mary that I learned to control my emotions; perhaps not control them so much as find the right time, upon careful thought and reflection, to express myself and be able to do so with dignity—and never to succumb to the ill-intentioned sentiments of those around me.

The flames were now burning higher. The room had a glazed look about it and the smell of the wood had infiltrated the entire house.

Amina walked over from the window and rubbed her hands over my shoulders, then leaned forward and kept her head close to mine for a few seconds. I could feel the warmth on her face and glanced at her teary eyes momentarily. She dried her tears against my woollen cape then returned to the window.

Carmen came towards me.

"Beauty, we all knew. We weren't sure if you did," Carmen said.

I think for that brief moment I was tearful and completely overcome by a desire to see my brother and hold him. I wanted to touch him under that blue jacket he wore. I miss Frank so much. I think Isabel saw it in my eyes. My body jerked, as if a current had been sent through it—as if Frank was in the room, reaching into my flesh, under my skin.

Isabel touched my hand.

"Beauty, I love Tom. I've been in love with him for a long time. He can be very out of order. And there is no excuse for his rudeness."

I sobbed silently. There was silence in the room. I could hear Manjit and Robert talking and making another pot of tea in the kitchen.

Carmen came to sit beside Isabel and me. She held both of my hands.

"Beauty, we need to talk about this. I'm sorry for your loss. I have friends who knew Frank and they all speak very highly of him."

Carmen was sweet and tender, as always.

We sat quietly for a few minutes, with our tears. Then I left the room and headed for the kitchen. I needed a top up, since my tea was quite cold. Robert and Manjit were conversing quietly. Robert looked up and came towards me. He grabbed me and hugged me tightly. I was a little taken aback, not by his display of affection but by the suddenness of it.

"I need a *dop*," he said, and I looked at him, blinking, sighing, and shaking my head at the same time. Robert always needed his *dop*, which was really any alcoholic beverage he could lay his hands on.

"Beauty . . . babe," he said, in a drawn-out, seductive sort of way, the kind of manner which, in his mind, wins him favours with women . . . perhaps at the racecourse.

"Can you get me a *dop* from Isabel's cabinet?"

"Not now, Robert. Another time," I said and left the kitchen with my tea.

My entrance back into the living room broke the silence.

"The clock is ticking. Any ideas, anyone?"

Jazz's question was met with more silence. Amina stood in the far corner of the room.

"In our culture, we use cremation, so those of you who do burials, start thinking. It's 1:35, we have to get moving. I've got pen and paper ready, right here."

Jazz's comments were met with sigh after sigh by all of us.

Isabel was sitting beside me. Carmen had moved to the floor.

"We have to find someone where there is no risk involved. Not someone through any of our workplaces," Carmen added.

Jazz sat with pen and paper while we sat around in nervy meditation.

Amina suddenly went to sit in her chair, then got up from it and sighed. She looked flustered and very bothered.

"Amina, are you all right?" I asked.

She shook her head profusely.

"Oh God," she said, and sighed out aloud again. She held both her hands to her cheeks.

"I knew this was going to catch up with me one day, I just did not think it would be at a time like this."

We all looked at one another. She was shaking and red in the face. She was wringing her hands; wringing them as though they were wet rags.

"Do you know someone who works at a graveyard? That is the question right now, Amina," was Jazz's direct response.

Amina walked to the window, then pulled the entire curtain open, causing everyone in the room to exclaim, then she gathered all of it in her two hands and drew it together, closing it, and we wondered what she would do next. She kept undoing and redoing her scarf until Jazz just blew her top.

"For God's sake! What on earth is wrong with you? If you want us to put the fire out then say so!"

Amina walked to the opposite wall and turned her back on us.

"My sister's husband works what is typically known as the graveyard shift. The truth is, he works at the graveyard and is a gravedigger. The problem is, no one in our family speaks to him. In fact, I have not spoken to him in years. I see my sister outside of her house; I often take her to lunch at the Woolworths café in Cavendish. Of course her husband doesn't know. He is not allowed to come to my parents' house. It's really a very messy situation. I think my sister would understand if I spoke to her, but I just cannot bring myself to ask that man. He loathes me. I was young at the time when this all started. I had just finished high school and Fuad and I had just got engaged. Janup also became Christian so it's a big deal in my family. I don't think my sister's husband will lift a finger to help me. Oh, and they live in Hanover Park. My father will have an *adjal** if I ever spoke to my sister's husband. Besides, I don't know where Hanover Park is, and my mother would be mortified if she knew I even considered going there."

Amina let out a big sigh after all that.

I was stunned; everyone in the room looked bewildered. Amina had grown quite close to Jazz and even she was surprised. Jazz raised her eyebrows and crossed her legs; that sort of mannerism really showed her uppity-ness. She pursed her lips and stared at Amina, even though Amina's back was turned. Carmen's brows were raised. Isabel looked stunned. I could not believe that Amina would admit that she was related to anyone who did not drive a Mercedes or a BMW. Amina came from quite a wealthy family. Her father started off as a butcher, but soon owned a whole chain of butcheries and grocery stores, and more recently a chain of supermarkets. Amina lived in Bishop's Court,** for crying out loud. She did not come across as someone with a sister married to a gravedigger.

How perfect, I thought, yet how inconvenient for Amina. She would never have told us this, under any circumstances. Amina wore Fendi scarves and Gucci handbags and shoes. She got her hair and nails done every week. She frequently went for massages. She flew to Paris for Jean-Paul Gaultier sales, if one can ever call such an event a sale. She wore clothes designed by people whose names I could not pronounce.

Carmen had her old and familiar smirk on her face. Isabel was sitting cross-legged on the floor and kept her head down. Carmen moved closer to me and started rolling her eyes.

"Amina," Jazz said, quite calmly, then resorted to her usual demanding tone. "Turn around this minute!"

"Jazz, I can't. I simply can't," she said as she complied and faced us all.

"Well, I'm sorry to disappoint you, but this is not something you can choose to ignore. Your father will have an *adjal* if he knew you were in a situation and you did nothing."

"Don't!" Amina called out.

"Your father will have an *adjal* if he knows . . ."

---

* sickened   ** one of the richest areas in the city

"How dare you!" Amina shouted.

"Please, we are all adults here. You have called me on so many issues here, in this house, every Friday night. It is what we do. We challenge one another. You are bloody out of order and someone needs to tell you . . . Miss exaggerated-sense-of-self-importance! It is more than high time that you confront your father. Stop hiding behind your father when it suits you!"

"I hate you, you know that. You're unbearable!"

Amina was beside herself.

"I know that already. Besides, who cares? Pull yourself together. Please call your sister and ask her to speak to her husband. I assume that he must be at work. I am sure they have cellphones."

Jazz pulled up her sleeves and was ready for action.

Amina stood with her back to us for a long time. Carmen and I knew about Ebrahim; we had no idea that Jazz knew.

Jazz persisted.

"Amina, we are going to your sister's house right now. We are in this together. Manjit can drive. I will call a private ambulance company. I know someone who works for one and you will tell your sister to fake an attack of some sort so that she can go with the ambulance to distract the neighbours and we can head off to the graveyard. We'll sort out the payment for their service at another time. Either you call your sister or I will. Don't make me call your father at this time of night to get your sister's number, and you know I will, so you better start moving. While your brother-in-law gets us sorted . . ."

"He's not my brother-in-law!" Amina shouted.

Jazz continued.

"We'll divert attention by having the private ambulance there. I will call the man I know from the private ambulance service and he will meet us here and drive behind us. They usually come in pairs so there'll be two of them, and there will be three of us. We'll have to put our dead man in the car before they arrive. We'll have the private ambulance behind us so we won't get pulled over at any of the roadblocks in Athlone or Hanover Park by the cops . . . and they usually have them on Friday nights."

Jazz was speaking to herself mostly, finalizing the plan, and using her fingers to work through it.

"Make that call, Amina, before I do."

That was Jazz—the Jazz we all know. She said it all.

Amina

Why do some women marry for love? I wish my sister hadn't. How can any woman find a man attractive who willingly wears his trousers beneath his waist, exposing half his bottom? I did not mind Janup being Christian, but to see her with him in public made my stomach turn. Janup was very fussy when we were children. She was always well dressed and always looked so beautiful, even when we went to madressa on Saturday mornings, difficult as that is, with a long black dress and a long black scarf with not one hair showing and with her Koran in the black sling bag she wore over her arm, like all the young girls attending Muslim school. Young men were madly in love with her wherever she went. Many of them encouraged their parents to befriend ours, they even went to mosque to see my dad, and became our customers, simply to be in my dad's good books. Janup got more marriage proposals than I have silk scarves—and I have plenty.

My mother did not ask too many questions about why I was staying at Isabel's but said she would tell my dad and think of something to say, if he persisted. I could rely on my mother in that way; she always stood up for her children. Abdullah was in his room asleep, since he usually has his drama class on a Saturday morning and a rugby match later in the afternoon. The girls were asleep too, and of course, like in my time, they too go to madressa on Saturday mornings. Abdullah is of an age where he no longer wants to attend madressa and studies the Koran with one of the teachers at the Muslim school, after regular school, once a week for two hours. He is a very intelligent boy, sensitive and perfectly capable of tackling his schoolwork and his extracurricular activities. I telephoned my oldest brother, looking over my shoulder to where Jazz was, to ask him to collect my car. He was a little sleepy but said he would collect it with his oldest son, who recently obtained his driver's licence. One cannot leave a BMW parked overnight. The decision was not one my brother questioned. I could rely on them, on all my brothers.

I sat at the back of Jazz's overbearingly large SUV, the older kind, which looked like a hearse; it seemed to serve its purpose for the trip we were on. The car looked quite appropriate, even as Jazz and Manjit rolled the dead man into the boot, while I held my nose and could feel my cheeks puff up. Perhaps older sisters rule their younger siblings in Indian cultures because it seemed very much like that with Jazz and Manjit. I don't think I have ever met a man as keen to please his sister as Manjit. Jazz was in charge of everything, as usual. I am beginning to wonder why she became a surgeon in the first place. She looked like a cold-nosed one as she shut the door and shouted, "Okay, so we're off," then patted the car as though it were a dutiful pony. Since she had come to the writing circle from work, she was wearing her white coat and already looked like a doctor by the time we left, about to do her community service among the poor on the Cape Flats. She usually hung her white coat on Isabel's coat rack at the entrance of the front door when she arrived and collected it when we left.

I am one of those people who do not enjoy driving around in areas where there are poor people; I cannot bear to see poverty, especially in the form of women—those with snotty-nosed children who seem to run after them in droves. Running up and down in Isabel's house took its toll on me. If we were not running after her, making sure that she did not collapse, or cleaning up the cement floor in her yard, then we were sobbing or cursing the man who had kept her hostage and violated her in her own car. Jazz seemed to be the only one, for the most part, who kept her wits about her. Each time Jazz demanded something of me, I tried to avoid looking at Isabel. While she is brave and organized beyond my comprehension, Jazz's ability to stay in automatic drive frightens me. There was something peculiar about her manner; something that was not quite right and yet I could not put my finger on it.

My sister appeared calm when I rang her from my cellphone. I had no idea what sort of mood she'd be in at two o'clock in the morning, but she was a lot more pleasant than I would have been. Her husband starts work at midnight, so she was accustomed to keeping unusual hours. I had to remove myself from Isabel's living room to ward off stares from Carmen and Beauty. Isabel seemed in a trance and Jazz was too busy making calls, drawing maps, and working out plans to care how I spoke to my sister, as long as the job was done.

I have grown quite fond of Beauty—she is kind and sincere. I do not find Beauty or Carmen to be judgmental and I can be myself with them. Carmen is very sweet, although I often find her staring at my clothes. She dresses appallingly and I wonder where she finds the clothes she wears—perhaps it is the life she sought out in Cape Town, quite removed from the privileges afforded to English women like her who came from the uppermost of lapsed aristocracy. All of her friends are Black or Coloured. I don't know how she gets by since she has no family in Cape Town. She often looks as though she has cried. I cannot bring myself to cry over events in my life that might deserve my tears; tears followed by quiet moments or long periods of silence is not something that comes to me the way it does to other women. People expect me to be happy and cheerful, and so I am. I transmit this happiness to my son and my daughters, because they deserve to see me happy in order to be happy themselves. I do find Carmen's presence in the writing circle quite rewarding, since she challenges us in ways that I have never been challenged before. I have never been much of a writer; I design patterns and I cut fabric, but Carmen's presence in the writing circle makes me go places with words my mother and father would blush at, if they knew. They might even say it was *geraam!** Carmen has a way with asking questions, although I often think they are inappropriate, perhaps even too personal at times, because I cannot bring myself to think about half the things she poses questions about.

My mother is very guarded. She was instructed on what to think and what to say by her mother, both of whom raised me. Most girls I went to madressa with said their fathers decided everything in their house, which came as a complete surprise to me because it was my mother who made the major decisions in our house. My mother comes from a family where the women and the men go on *hadj***

* sinful ** pilgrimage

together; someone or the other in my mother's family goes to Mecca every year. My mother is proud of her Dutch heritage, and while she keeps her head covered in public, her light-coloured locks are her pride and joy. Many women of her generation have grandparents and great-grandparents from Holland and Malaysia, and when I was a child I did not quite understand it all. When the new government came into power we suddenly gained more cousins—although they were White, they were considered our poor relations, because despite their history of legislated White privilege, their parents had not done quite as well as my father.

My sister ran away from home to marry her Christian boyfriend and my mother felt the pain of her decision sharply. The Cape Town Muslim community was scandalized by Janup's behaviour and saw it as an opportunity to ridicule my father and mock his generosity towards those within the Muslim community who were less fortunate but wished to undertake *hadj* to Mecca, towards whom he made notable contributions. We were accustomed to hold our heads high, but Janup brought shame upon our family. Not only did she marry a Christian man but she sought to immerse herself in a lifestyle my mother thought was beneath us. We were expected to live up to our fair skin and marry accordingly. Janup dismissed her upbringing and mocked my mother. For the first year of her marriage my mother refused to acknowledge that Janup had a husband. But she sent Janup money clandestinely, without my father's knowledge, and Janup had the nerve to return it. My mother and father have no contact with her. My three brothers have been instructed not to speak to her either, and they have done as they were told. My family loved my husband Fuad, but they had no idea that he treated me with utmost cruelty. I could not possibly tell them; perhaps I did not want to. I look back on those years now with such regret, sometimes with a sense of shame, because I was relieved when Fuad died. My son and daughters lost their father and I felt very badly for them, but Fuad's death was no great loss to the world. Fuad's mother died shortly after; some say from sadness, others say because she wanted to be with her son and died to spite her husband. Ebrahim has always been very kind to my children and me. I love him dearly. I introduced Beauty and Carmen to Ebrahim one day when Carmen had a housewarming party at her new flat in Seapoint. She moved from one floor to another, to a bigger flat in the same building. I knew that no one I knew would be there, and I wanted Beauty and Carmen to meet Ebrahim. It was difficult to go anywhere as a couple because father and son resembled one another, and most people knew Ebrahim as Fuad's father or as my Dad's business partner. Fuad's death in a car accident allowed me to get safely out of a marriage I had dreaded, and to be with a man who cares for me more than any man I know. The only problem with having a relationship with Ebrahim, who is more than twenty years my senior, is that my father would disown me if he found out.

I sat in the back of Jazz's car, thinking through my life and the many ways I struggle with sharing some of my experiences with the women from the writing circle. There have been so many events in my life that have left me feeling hopeless; some are not worthy of my memory, despite Carmen's insistence, while other memories still determine the way I relate to men. There was a time when Manjit exchanged glances with Carmen; then there was a time when they appeared to come out of the bathroom at the same time. Beauty seemed aware of some situation, and indicated that I not disturb them as they talked in the kitchen. I thought then what if he was the Indian man she had mentioned she was seeing? The thought soon left my mind because she is quite a bit older than he. Manjit is a good looking man and out of Carmen's league.

The private ambulance arrived on time, just as Jazz had planned. They followed us as she had instructed them to. Jazz sat in the passenger seat of her car while Manjit drove. She kept her feet on the dashboard, with all the little maps she had drawn resting on her lap, and told Manjit what roads to take. There were many people still walking in the streets. It was late Friday night, or rather the early hours of Saturday morning. When we met a red light at the robot,* I couldn't believe the number of people at the street corner. They were drunkards, followed by loud and overbearing women dressed in short skirts and tops, and must have just come from nightclubs or places of that kind. Where on earth did they shop? Shabeens sold alcohol after hours but I didn't think they sold outfits that made women look

* traffic light

cheaper than they already were. I do not enjoy driving around in rough neighbourhoods; I find them utterly depressing. It shocks me to see how poor people live. I asked Manjit if we could stop for coffee at a better-looking neighbourhood. Jazz shrieked with laughter, scoffing at my suggestion. Manjit was not to stop under any circumstances, she said. Although she and I are friends I often feel she mocks me. I was exhausted, and before I knew it, Manjit had stopped and announced that we had arrived.

I looked through the window, and there he stood at the gate of their downstairs flat—big and bald, wearing jeans and some sort of pullover—which was hard to distinguish from its backdrop because it was one of those flats threaded together by grey cement, designed to throw as many people together in them as possible. He was walking up and down from the outside gate to the door, smoking and holding a mug in his hand. The front light of their house was shining ever so brightly onto my sister. Janup stood in the window frame, leaning on the windowsill. She disappeared from it before I had blinked. I looked over at the ambulance men who were talking to one another. I looked down at my Gucci shoes and wondered how I would make it up to them for the drudgery I was to put them through; there was grey and black sand everywhere on the ground and most likely mixed with sharp objects, which had arrived there due to the lifestyle people led who walked upon it.

Donny came to the car. Manjit got out and introduced himself. They shook hands. Jazz then followed and shook his hand too. I looked back at the window of my sister's flat. She had not reappeared. Jazz went to chat with the ambulance driver, each time looking over her shoulder at me. I was cold and I was tired. I could not bring myself to talk to that man.

"Are you going to sit there all night?"

Donny had opened the door and stuck his head right in. He sniffed and puffed on his grubby cigarette, gripping it in his clawed hand, bringing it to his mouth like a ravenous animal before sucking the life out of it. He talked to me as though I were one of his friends. No one spoke to me like that. I threw my head back. He simply sat in the driver's seat and started talking to me.

"You see, Mina," he said, "the way I see it, you were bound to come to me for help one day, I always told Jannie."

He called me Mina and my sister Jannie. I didn't know what to say. No one called me Mina, not even my parents. The big ape called my sister Jannie.

"Good morning to you too," he said, and blew smoke in my face. The smell of cheap tobacco made me ill.

He simply had no shame. He knew that I did not want to speak to him, yet he continued.

"You see, the trouble with high society people is that they think their shit don't stink. They think they don't need *ouens** like me ... but everyone needs an ou like me, even if it's just once in a while, hey."

I stared at him coldly.

"It's cool, I never worry myself. You don't have to talk to me. Jannie said you'd be like that. But never you mind. You see, I have a wife, and I have four children, and we are all very happy, all very happy with no secrets to our parents or to one another ... and look at you. You look as miserable as you were the day I first came to your house. So you have nice jobs, you and your three brothers, and you have a nice handbag and you smell like those people in the fancy shops you shop at, but you have no love in your life."

That bastard spoke to me as though I was some common woman he had just met at the bus stop, with warts and fat ankles, carrying plastic grocery bags. How dare he! They were hurtful words, and before I knew it, the tears rolled down my cheeks, down my neck, past my pearl necklace and down my chest into my beautiful Christian Dior bra. I hated him even more. I hated him for taking my beautiful sister away from us and bringing her to a place like Hanover Park. He had brought shame on our family and he didn't care. Donny sat there and stared at me with contempt. He sat there making all sorts of sounds as he puffed away. I think he even sucked food out of his teeth. I had forgotten what it was like to be in the company of an uncultured man. The delivery man who came to my building had more manners than Donny. He sucked some food out of his teeth again, this time sticking his finger in his mouth with a matchstick to retrieve something unsightly, which upon retrieval he flung through the window. I

* men

sat there, tears rolling down my cheeks, trying not to look at him or examine his habits. He sneered as he got out of the car and slammed the door.

I heard him talking to Jazz.

"She hasn't said anything to me, so I'm doing squat. Miss High-and-Mighty better start talking because I'm a busy man."

He spoke to Jazz about me as though I was not even there, while looking at the car, through the window, right at me.

Jazz, the bossy boots that she is, stuck her head into the car. "Amina, we don't have all day. Speak to your brother-in-law," she said, pronouncing the term as though it belonged to me. "He's the only one who can help us right now. You better speak to him. You better get yourself out of this car, right now."

Damn her, I thought. I moved around in the back seat. The leather seats were squeaking. I took my scarf off, then lifted my hair and shook it like a horse's tail so it would not look as flat as the unsightly dwellings I was surrounded by. I put my scarf back on.

"Come on! Come on!" Jazz shouted, in the kind of tone I imagine sergeants at military camps use on those of inferior physical capacity. I have known Harminder since high school and could not imagine a gentle soul like him being married to Jazz.

I gathered myself together and stepped down onto the mouse-grey sand, observing my shoes sinking into it, and found his eyes all over me. He was enjoying himself; he looked at me disapprovingly, as though I had chosen the wrong outfit for the occasion.

"Donny," I managed to say, before he interrupted.

"Oh, you still remember my name. How long has it been, Mina . . . mmm, let me think . . . oh, I remember . . . almost twenty years."

He had a comical side to him. He wasn't intelligent enough to mock me, but he taunted me. I could not look at him; he thoroughly enjoyed the torment he was able to inflict.

Jazz gave me piercing looks from some distance away. Manjit was leaning into the ambulance van talking to the men. He seemed very worried as he looked over in my direction.

"Donny," I started again.

"Yessss," he said, dragging it out so I could feel the word grind against my skin.

"Donny, could you help us?"

"Who is *us*? I don't know any *us*? Do you mean *you* ... would I help *you*?"

"Yes," I said.

"No, how it works is that you ask me."

"Donny, please. Please don't make this any harder than it is."

"Blerry cheek, hey. You think this is hard for you? What about your sister? Have you thought about how hard this has been on Jannie? All of you turning your back on her like that. You will ask me like you mean it. And you better make it snappy because my patience is running out. Oh, and don't look at me like that. I can speak der Queen Inglish if I want to. I went to high school. You people think nothing of people like me. You better start talking, woman."

I thought I was going to die. The man had gall. I went to Alexandra Sinton High School. I studied Art and Design in London and Paris. I have met top designers, men and women around the world of class and style, and he spoke to me as though I belonged to him and his world. The thought of my dear friend, Isabel, suffering because of my inability to speak to Donny upset me greatly.

I looked at my sister's flat and knew she was inside waiting for me. I uttered the words I had rehearsed. The small little tongue hanging from the roof of my mouth did the talking.

"Donny, could you please help. I need your help and I would appreciate it very much if you could help me. I am sorry for what my family has done to you, and for what I have done, by ignoring you and treating you so harshly."

He nodded and threw his cigarette butt in the sand.

"Ja, ja, ja, now if only you meant that. But, you know what, that's fine for now. I don't need you people anyway. You better go to your sister because she's waiting." He did not look at me at all.

I opened the outside gate to my sister's downstairs flat. I had never been there before. The cemented path from the gate to the door felt like a long walk. My shoes were heavy with black sand and I could feel Jazz and Donny staring at me. The minute I approached the door it opened, and Janup grabbed onto me and pulled me inside. She held me close. She cried. I cried.

"I'm so sorry I've never been here," I said.

She pulled me closer.

"I'm sorry. I really am."

My scarf came off with all of the hugs and kisses. My tears rubbed off against her.

She stroked my hair. She was my older sister and I loved her dearly. I loved her even more for always loving me.

Moments later, as we hugged, Jazz and Manjit came to the door.

Jazz extended her hand to my sister.

"Janup, is it?"

"My friends call me Jannie."

"Jannie, I'm sorry we have to intrude like this. As you know, we are doing this for a dear friend."

Jazz was like that; she was uppity but could also be humble and speak to people like my sister and Donny. My sister wiped her face as she spoke.

"You don't have to explain. My husband will help you and Amina. Don't worry about it. I will go with the ambulance. I moved away from the window when I realized you had arrived. You just leave everything to Donny. He is a good man. He will do whatever he can to help."

"Thanks, Jannie," Jazz said.

"That's okay," my sister replied.

"Now, the ambulance will take you to Constantia Private. I will come and check up on you in a couple of hours. You'll be discharged in the afternoon. It is best this way, so that there is no suspicion. You can tell your neighbours that you had some heart trouble and that your sister brought a private ambulance and no one will ever know."

"It's okay. I know what to do," Janup replied.

Jazz hugged my sister and looked right at her as she spoke. "These are trusted men. Believe me. They are trusted men whose work reputations I know. They would never do anything to harm you. Go and lie in bed and I will bring them in with the stretcher."

Jazz took out her stethoscope. Janup went to her bedroom and got under the covers. I followed along. Janup even had a bag packed for the hospital. I was surprised to see how nice their place was. Janup had done some very tasteful decorating, and the curtains looked absolutely fabulous. The kitchen was spotless; the smell of good coffee hovered over it. I was not expecting it and I was uncomfortable to ask her about the smell of the coffee. I peeped into the bedroom, where all four children lay asleep on the double bunk beds. I looked about the house and saw several photographs of our family, including quite a few of myself. We had none of Janup in our house, and I felt completely ashamed, so ashamed that the tears came flooding down again. She had not forgotten us. We were still her family.

I watched as Donny and my sister kissed, passionately, as though they were young lovers. I think after a few seconds we all looked at the linoleum floor. Their lips were locked in a kind of embrace I had never witnessed before. Manjit smiled. I don't think even he had seen two people kiss like that. Waiting for them to emerge from their embrace felt like hours, and it felt as though they were not going to stop. Jazz tilted her head, in an approving sort of way as she gazed at them; she even ooh-ed and aah-ed. She seemed very friendly with Donny. My sister had been married to this man for almost twenty years, and she still kissed him as though he was some handsome Hollywood hunk. If they kissed like that in front of others, one did not have to wonder for too long how they conducted themselves in private. I felt half uncomfortable, half envious, I think, because I have never kissed a man like that in my life. No man has ever looked at me the way Donny looked at my sister. He cupped her face in his hands and stroked her hair tenderly, and as I drew my hand to my mouth, and exhaled against it, I could hear the heaving of my own breath, wishing it were that of another. My sister was still very beautiful, even though her appearance was rather plain.

I suddenly felt overcome with sadness thinking about Ebrahim, then of my marriage to Fuad. I thought of my first boyfriend whom I had loved dearly, at eighteen, but then he married someone else. Ebrahim was sweet and very nice to me, but my intimacy with him was limited. He often commented on how he thought he was failing me, because I have never fully experienced the womanly joys I know exist, and certainly the women in the writing circle talk about them regularly. I could not tell Ebrahim that it was not he, but I. Fuad hit me so hard that I think it numbed the sensation in certain parts of my body. There were times when I blacked out—just before my pregnancy— and there were days when I could not remember which day it was because I was so distraught, attending to Abdullah, whom he hated, and avoiding the curious eyes of the maid we employed at the time. There were days when I could not feel the sensation in my own nipples, even when I was breastfeeding, but I did not utter a word to anyone, because I did not want to leave a marriage that cost my father his savings and of which he seemed so proud. For all of the five years of our marriage I was incapable of having womanly pleasures—the kind of pleasures I knew women had and which I read about in Mills and Boon books, and to which more subtle references were made in the Barbara Cartland paperbacks I read at airports. Ebrahim brings me comfort and joy; his love is the only love I know. I patted my face and fingered my eyelids in an attempt to erase the remaining traces of runny mascara from them. Donny must have been watching me for he joined me, stood right beside me, put his index finger to his mouth, and held my face in one hand and removed something from my face with the finger he had moistened. I was so shocked at the forward gesture that I stood still, gaping at him, as he looked into my eyes, without any care in the world. I closed my eyes. The touch of his skin, when it settled on mine, felt foreign—as though it belonged to some-one else. Surely he knew that I despised him. My silence surprised me, and as I stood still, without making one move to retreat from his touch, I felt completely under his spell.

When my sister left with the ambulance, he told her that he loved her and that he would miss her for the few hours she would be away. He called her, "my darling," and she returned his term of endearment by referring to him in the same manner. How did a well educated and well brought up Moslem girl get to express herself so freely, I thought, isn't that what poor people do? I was concerned for the young children in the house. The oldest one, Adam, was almost nineteen. Just then one of the neighbours came to the gate.

"Is everything alright?" the man asked.

Donny stepped in.

"Good evening, Mr Benson. Everything is fine, Mr Benson. This is

Jannie's sister, and this here is the doctor. There is a little problem with Jannie's heart and the ambulance just took her away."

Jazz and I nodded at the man.

"Oh my God!" the man exclaimed. He held onto the wooden railing in the garden.

"It is going to be all right, uncle, not to worry," Donny was quick to add as he extended his arm to the older man. He had used a term of respect offered to older men with whom there is no direct familial tie but who have age and community standing.

"Jannie's only going in for observation. The doctor wanted to admit her right away. Jannie called me on my cellphone at work and her sister called their private doctor. So everything's taken care of, Mr Benson; nothing to worry about at all, sir."

"Oh, I see. And the children?"

"Oh, we didn't want to wake them. Adam knows not to wake them or worry them. We're all going to the hospital now and I'll be back here by seven o'clock in the morning, not to worry Mr Benson."

"Well, give her our best wishes, son."

I watched closely as Donny said goodbye to Mr Benson, who patted him on the back. "You take care, boetie, take care, my son," he said.

"Thank you, Mr Benson," Donny replied.

Jazz followed on while Manjit went to the car.

Donny opened the passenger side of his van for me. Jazz told the ambulance men that we had another person to see who was in an emergency situation and that Donny and I would be at the hospital shortly. They both nodded and took off.

I sat in Donny's van, shaking and shivering. He actually had the decency to turn the heat up. The smell of coffee was inviting, the same smell I had inhaled in their flat. He offered me his smelly jersey but I declined on the grounds that I did not want him to be cold. I had their kiss on my mind and could not think of anything else. At one point he looked at me, as though he knew. I looked back to see whether Manjit and Jazz were following us and wondered what sort of conversation they were having now that they were by themselves.

"Listen, Amina, for whatever you think of me, you have to know that you will be safe with me."

"Oh, I was just checking to see whether they are still following us," I replied hastily.

"Oh, Manjit and Jazz know where we're going. It'll be a fifteen-minute drive at this time of the morning. Jazz said she'll go to the hospital with her brother after this, and then they'll drop you off at your friend's house in Observatory."

I nodded.

I was quiet for some time, thinking of something to say to him.

"You know, when Jannie called me on my cellphone at work, I could hardly believe it. I mean, you of all people needing a favour from me."

"Are you ever going to forget it?" I asked, looking at him and wanting him to know that I meant every word I said.

"Oh, I didn't mean it in that way. I mean it brought you to our house, didn't it? I know Jannie sees you. She doesn't keep anything from me. But I know that she's always felt heart-sore that none of you ever came to our house. She's so proud of that house."

I was silent. Not once did he ask me about the man in the blue windbreaker; nor did my sister.

My head fell against the windowpane and all I felt was my own coldness against it. I had never been to my sister's house because I thought that she would be ashamed. Instead, she welcomed me, and made me feel more at home than anyone I knew.

"Would you like some coffee?" Donny asked.

I sat up in my seat.

"Do you have any here?"

"Yes, I take a flask with me every night. I don't get much sleep when the kids are home, you know. Just bend, it is right under your seat. I haven't opened it yet."

I grabbed the flask with both my hands.

"Thank you," I said and poured the steamy dark and wonderful smelling beverage in to the cup.

"This is really good coffee. Really, it's very good," I said.

"I believe you this time, you don't have to try so hard," he said.

I was quiet and sat there, not knowing whether to drink it or pour it back.

"So, you're really a coffee drinker, hey," he said, in that male-buddy sort of way.

"Yes, I am, actually," I replied.

"Your friend the doctor doesn't want us stopping, so you'll have to drink it like that."

"This is really good," I commented again, after taking several short sips.

"It's the real stuff. We have a proper coffee machine at home. We buy it from Woolworths. It's the Italian espresso kind. I wasn't born in the gutter you know."

I sighed. There seemed little left to say to him.

The coffee was dark and extravagant—just what I needed.

He looked over at me.

"Your son plays rugby, I hear. Your girls must be all grown up already," he said, giving indication of the knowledge of my children he had acquired through Janup.

"They're fine," I replied, not quite sure how to continue the conversation. I had popped into the room where my sister's children where sleeping but I did not once mention it to Donny.

No sooner had I gulped down the coffee than we arrived at the graveyard. I saw several men walking about, perhaps four or five of them, in what looked like a vast area, which was pitch dark.

I looked around and Manjit and Jazz were behind us.

"Don't worry. I told my boys that I am fetching a family who wants to pay their respects before they go on *hadj*."

I frowned at him.

We drove through the gates, and it made me very nervous. Donny parked the car in an awkward position and I looked puzzled. I could hardly see my hand in front of my face. He must have felt my body jerking nervously, for he soon answered my unasked question.

"I've parked with the back facing the grave so that Manjit and Jazz can be behind us. In this way the boys won't see what's going on, and Manjit and your doctor friend can just slip it straight into the lot."

I nodded.

I looked at him, then glanced at the surrounding area. Clearly, he knew what he was doing.

"We are a strange group of people, us South Africans, aren't we? Do you know how many families don't speak to each other, among themselves? When there is death in a family, they don't tell one another about it. We often have families who come to the gate at night and want to know where their family members have been buried, because they only found out the day after and were never told. My boys over there think that I am bringing one of those families here tonight. In this country, Muslims and Christians live side by side, but we also still fight, old fights, because fighting is what we do best. It's all so unnecessary. We are all cut from the same cloth."

I didn't expect him to be philosophical and certainly not to make sense. He took a very different tone when he spoke on matters pertaining to his work. He seemed determined to speak better English when he was in my company and he certainly didn't curse as he did in those days, twenty years ago, when we first met.

Jazz and Manjit came to my side of the car. Donny went off to speak to his boys, as he referred to them, and he spoke to them in Afrikaans, although I am not too familiar with the kind of slang men of his background speak among themselves.

I was taken aback by Jazz's sudden tap on my window. She had removed her white coat.

"You have to come and help. Put Donny's black jacket on."

"What?" I asked, shocked that she would make such a request.

"Put the jacket on, Amina. We don't have time now to debate its ugliness, just put it on. We don't want anyone recognizing you."

My worst fear was actualized when Jazz asked me to help lift the dead body from the car. I had decided to forget about the dead man.

"Let's do it now, Amina. We can leave before Donny gets back, which was really his idea. It should take a minute. The longer we stay here the more suspicion we will bring on ourselves."

I stared at her.

"For God's sake," she said, rather agitated. "I thought Donny told you to wear the jacket."

I put the smelly jacket on and dug blindly into my handbag for my packet of gum. The cinnamon smell of the gum was enough to keep me from thinking about the overwhelming stench of nicotine. I walked to the back of their car.

Jazz gave the order again after handing out another round of latex gloves.

"You'll take the feet, Manjit will take the middle and I will take the head. I am the only one who knows how to keep his head upright."

I didn't bother arguing. I bit my lip, closed my eyes for most of it, asked Allah to forgive me, and did as I was told.

The lot was right there. Manjit came over to my side and grabbed the feet from me. Donny had placed two ladders inside the pit, on opposite sides, and Jazz and Manjit climbed down that dreaded path with the dead man and placed him six feet below at the bottom, which I could only detect by the slight slump I heard. Otherwise the pit looked bottomless to me. I have never been to a Christian burial and have no idea how the ceremony is performed. I handed Jazz the paper upon which Beauty had written a poem or psalm of some sort to give to Jazz at this moment. Jazz looked puzzled but read the words with her head bowed, then folded the paper and gave it back to me.

She wiped her hands by rubbing them together and so did Manjit, who then assisted her on the ladder before emerging at the top. Jazz took the latex gloves from us, then placed them into another plastic bag, which she shoved into her handbag. She seemed rather quiet and asked me to join her in the car and to save my goodbye to Donny for another time. I looked to see where he was but she insisted that we leave.

"Amina, it's what he wants. It has to be quick. He will take care of the rest. We have to get to the hospital and your sister as soon as possible."

I nodded. She stood close to me and sniffed.

"I see you've had some of your brother-in-law's coffee."

I did not protest her use of the term. I felt a slight hint of affiliation with him, for the first time, not only through my sister but because he had shown me more kindness than I had ever expected.

Donny came over to shake my hand as we left. He took his gloves off and clipped them under his arm. I had tied my scarf, but left it hanging fairly loosely with one small knot in the centre under my chin; it came undone as I shook Donny's hand. His hand was warm and firm, and had a strength to it that took me completely by surprise.

I was already looking forward to seeing my masseuse, whom I now see every Saturday morning at ten. Donny shook my hand another time, and pulled me towards him as though he wanted to hug me. I felt an electric surge of current pass through my body. I moved away. It started to drizzle. I suddenly looked up into the sky and swore I saw a flash of lightning as Donny held me for that brief second. My hair fell forward through my loosely tied scarf, and he touched my forehead, moving his fingers through the top of my hair, from my forehead across my cheek and around to my temple, then when he held my hair at the tip, he gently tucked it behind my ears, under my scarf. His hand was spread and his fingers were warm against my cheek. I kept my head down. I suddenly felt the desire to be close to him, which frightened me, because he was after all a man who did not fit into my life in any way, other than by being married to my sister.

Part Two

Isabel

On Saturday I stayed in bed the entire day. There was no need for me to leave my bed since it was better than being anywhere else. I unplugged the telephone after I rang Mum and Dad. Dad talked endlessly about the new heart medication he had been prescribed, the cost of which he reminded me several times. Mum was quiet at first, then tentative, after she heard my voice, and I tried to be a little more talkative since she expressed more than usual concern for what she described as my poor health. How a mother can tell her daughter, "You sound pale," beats me. Mum has always claimed that she is able to see the expression on my face by listening to my voice. I sensed a little hesitation in her voice as I spoke, as though she did not quite believe me when I said that all was well, and I heard her call out to Dad to fetch her coat. I certainly did not want her to come to my house and for those few moments, when she was deciding on the nature of my illness, I did my utmost to keep her at bay. Mum always spoke to Dad when I chatted with her on the telephone. It was as though she had to transmit everything I said to Dad, to include him so to speak—as though the design of the telephone was somehow inadequate and therefore robbing him of the conversation only she was privileged to enjoy. I convinced Mum that while all was not quite well, as she had suggested, I was not terribly ill but only mildly under the weather. Lying had its price. Mum insisted that I take tea with her at the ladies' church club later in the afternoon. I shook my head and sighed out loud as I declined her offer, thinking how impossible she could be at times, and I simply did not feel well enough to leave the house. I could hear her taking her coat from Dad and putting it on as she shifted the receiver from her left to her right hand. I assured Mum that it was just a body flu, which I needed to shake off by staying in bed. Within less than two minutes I had gone from being well, to not so well, to not well at all but not terribly ill, then settled for not well enough to leave my bed. I sighed out of sheer exhaustion, but Mum continued, telling me that she could tell that my throat did not sound too good either and that Charmaine, my sister-in-law, would be very upset if I did not show up for the ladies' tea club. How she knew my throat was sore beats me. I didn't think Mum could tell by the way I spoke. My throat was sore and she was right, as usual. It was a soreness I could not describe, certainly not to Mum because she diagnosed every ailment one described to her. It ached, but only at the entrance of my esopha-gus. It did not hurt when I spoke but only when something solid was placed in my mouth that I was about to swallow. Mum rattled off recipes for sore throat which included ginger and lemon, and one with lemon and butter, then another one Mrs Benjamin used, followed by the one Mrs Behardien swore by which consisted of parsley steeped in boiling water with sea salt, but none that would cure a throat that had held a gun in it. I could not bring myself to tell my mother; she had been through enough with my sister.

I sat in my bed surrounded by a tray of tea and biscuits even though it was past my tea time and I had missed lunch all together. With the tea, the biscuits melted in my mouth and their passage down my throat was secured. I did not bother to collect the *Times* from the corner store. I simply could not let anyone see me on the street or read about any local or world events. Jazz insisted that I keep my cellphone on and so I did. She returned to see me while I was desperately trying to sleep and exchanged a few details with me. I could not sleep that night; my body forced me to succumb to its needs, but I could not pay it the kind of attention it was after. Jazz's presence alerted me to a series of events which somehow became more and more disjointed as I thought through their sequence. I tried to get information from Jazz about the previous night's events, even details on Amina's sister and her brother-in-law, but she would change the subject. The theatrical manner in which she rolled her eyes gave me strong indication that she did not want me to speak at all—and so I remained silent for the most part. Jazz has a way about her that makes me feel safe, and I trust her completely, and for those reasons I agreed to the various tests she rattled off and claimed she needed to administer. She then proceeded to take a blood sample and insisted on doing a pap test, the results of which she would notify me about as soon as she received word from the lab. I stared at the unfriendly equipment she whipped out, but I was not prepared to fight her on any of her suggestions for tests and examinations. I had not mentioned the mammogram to her and did not want her to know that I had taken one. Each time I engaged her on the previous night's events, she urged me to lie still, then proceeded by providing all sorts of details about the tests and the statistics on my chances of contracting various diseases.

Although I worked at the same hospital as Jazz, I hardly ever saw her in the corridors. She had a good reputation and heads of departments talked about her work at meetings more than they talked about anyone else. I have known Jazz for more than ten years now, and it is still difficult to get her to talk about personal matters. I tried, we all did, but many in the writing circle thought she shared her experiences with us on a superficial level—it was all she could offer. Carmen and Beauty always commented on how they felt there was more to her; more to her than met the eye, but no one was bold enough to really challenge her, except perhaps Carmen, who paid dearly for it. Carmen was the one who pushed, lightly, then with more vigour, once Jazz provided an opportunity, however small. Carmen was very good at urging us to examine what we held back. Even if we insisted that our writing revealed all of what we felt, she would engage us in conversation and in so doing push the limits of our spoken words. After each gathering I would return to my journal and examine my writing more closely; this is what Carmen was known to do—urge us to examine the very walls we had built around ourselves with the absence of words. When Jazz sat up real close to me on the bed, she looked into my eyes, with her little optometrist torch, and she stroked my hair back and gently rubbed my head without once commenting on the bad job I had done in cutting it. She seldom showed tenderness and it made me cry. Tears were streaming down my face, and she wiped them, one drop after another, with her bare hand. "You'll be alright," she said, over and over, and I believed her. I believed her more than I believed myself. For that brief moment, when she packed her bag, I looked at her, and asked: "Have you heard from Harminder?"

"Yes," she replied.

"I saw him this morning at the Constantia Clinic. There he was . . . of all the people I should walk into. He was covering someone's shift. I have nothing to say to him. The sooner he realizes that I am not going back to him, the better. My parents are fine with my decision. It is not up to them, and they know it. I wanted to marry that man. No one forced me to. Why I married him in the first place, I still don't know. But I better not say that too loud because Carmen will make me regret it. You know what she's like, she'll unpack my unconscious in front of me and then I won't be able to put it back together again." Jazz chuckled—it couldn't be considered a laugh. She had offered me more than ever before. Jazz was not known for her ability to conduct lengthy conversations or disclose her concerns to the writing circle.

I think it was the first time I managed a smile and it was not for long. I don't think the rest of me was ready to accept a smile of any kind—it just did not cooperate with any other muscle in my body. My lips started to quiver because they smiled on their own, with no help from the rest of my face. I was both sad and relieved to see Jazz leave. Although I wanted to be on my own I enjoyed the comfort her caress had provided, however sparing.

"Have you spoken to anyone about what happened?" I asked, as she looked into my eyes while taking a blood sample from my arm.

"No, I haven't. I was going to ask you if you want me to mention the incident to my *friend*."

"No, I would prefer if you didn't."

I could not allow the details of my life to be communicated to some unknown man, her *friend*, whose existence I was privy to but whom I had not met and suspected to be a married man.

Jazz nodded without another word.

Beauty, Carmen, and Amina left shortly after eight. I don't think any of them got any sleep. Beauty slept in the bed with me, Carmen stayed in the study and Amina slept on the sofa after Manjit and Jazz had dropped her off, even though I told Jazz she was welcome to the spare room. I hardly go into the spare room. Beauty seems to use it when she is here, which makes me very happy since it needs people to live in. After Calvin left, that room has never appealed to me much. I hardly think of Calvin these days, and since the divorce was finalized last April, I think of him less and less.

It was almost five o'clock when Beauty rang my cellphone asking if I needed her to come 'round. Amina and Carmen rang shortly after, and so did Jazz. I turned my phone off soon after my brief conversation with Jazz. I often wonder where Jazz gets her energy. She was scheduled to work the late-night eleven-to-seven shift later that evening, which she did regularly for one week every three weeks. Where she gets the time for a love life, I don't know. Robert sent me several text messages. I told him not to worry about me and I had enough food in the house, which seemed to be of some concern to him. Many Capetonians believe that the consumption of excessive amounts of food aids the process of forgetting misfortunes. The thought of filling my emptiness with curry and cream cakes—a favourite South African pastime—made me ill beyond recollection. Besides, a fridge full of food was premeditated eating—I was horrified at the thought.

It was 7:30 pm when I looked at my cellphone again. It rang as soon as I turned it on. I had forgotten all about my arrangement to meet my colleagues for dinner and live music at Mannenberg's on the Waterfront. Veronica was quite annoyed. I explained that I was ill, to which she responded that she wished I had telephoned earlier and not kept everyone waiting. Everyone had arrived promptly at 6:30, she said, with the understanding that I was going to be attending and delivering the farewell speech for our colleague, Louise, who was taking maternity leave. I felt lousy, but I could not leave my bed. I could hear Leslie Kleinsmith in the background, and I burst into tears as Veronica continued to reprimand me. My tearful disposition disturbed her. She was silent for a while. I sniffed uncontrollably and she offered to come and see me. She was ready to leave the restaurant and jump into her car, but I managed to keep her on the phone. She apologized and said she was sorry and wanted to make it up to me by coming to see me at home. I told her that my flu was contagious but would most likely pass by the weekend. Veronica sighed and apologized for her manner and said she hoped to see me at work on Monday morning. My cellphone rang continuously after she hung up. Calls from Beauty, Amina, and Carmen were difficult to ignore. I sat in bed sipping tea and watching the cellphone flicker each time it rang. Sunday morning came and went. Monday morning came and I could not lift myself from my bed. The television in my room was no comfort either. There was usually something on the American war in Iraq, and I could not bear to see any more of it. My eyes were focused on the ceiling most of the time. I noticed a few water stains on it, some of which Calvin had vowed to attend to when he was still keen on doing renovations to the house. It is fascinating to observe ceilings closely, especially those with unusual patterns on which shapes of faces appear. Tuesday morning came and went, so did Wednesday. Tom had not telephoned once and none of the women in the writing circle inquired as to whether he had, except of course Beauty, to whom I lied. I am not sure why. She had Ludwig with her, and he no doubt had brought her and her family presents from Vienna, as was evident from Beauty's new jade necklace and matching earrings. Beauty wore only black, irrespective of the occasion, and the dangling jewellery gave her face and arms a radiant look. Ludwig is both beautiful and kind— neither quality bestowed upon Tom by any of my friends.

For most of the week I managed to keep everyone at bay, including Robert, who rang me several times each day. Each time Jazz rang she mentioned that Manjit had asked after me, and while I was certainly pleased that my family and friends showed such concern, I could not bring myself to let anyone see me in pyjamas, certainly not in the state I was in. I rang Dr Steyn, the head of my department, later in the afternoon and told him that I was still ill. I knew I had to submit a sick certificate after three days but could not remember which day it was. Dr Steyn's secretary mentioned that Jazz had already dropped off my sick certificate. Thank God for Jazz. I could feel my body getting weaker and I was less likely to see a doctor other than Jazz, or Tom, if he bothered to ask, because I knew all of the doctors at Groote Schuur, and they knew me. Jazz knew how I felt about seeing any of them.

Between the enamel ring of my toilet and the declining digits on my bathroom scale there was nothing else I saw in front of me that entire day, other than several glasses of water. I drank water and nothing else. I managed to drink it without looking into the glass, too afraid to see my reflection. The previous five days I had managed to drink water and tea with condensed milk because there was no sugar in the house, and I polished off all the biscuits in the house for breakfast, lunch, and dinner—effectively sparing myself the ordeal of walking to the kitchen, seeing people through the back window, and having to turn the stove on. My kettle had never been filled as regularly and my teapot saw the reflection of someone who could not face to look at anything else, not even a mirror. It's quite dreadful when tea gets cold; the little bits of oil that float on the top, especially from an Earl Grey pot, make the most peculiar faces. I suppose Bergamot oil allows the tea leaves when immersed in hot water to be projected like a work of art. Tea is certainly better than water. Tea is coloured, either red or reddish brown, and is not transparent, which counts in its favour. Water reflections have a fascination about them—they seem to stand still in time. But as soon as the water hit the bottom of the glass and I brought my mouth to it, I felt conflicted about it taking me over—washing me, drowning me, holding me under while I struggled and gulped, one thunderous mouthful after another. My weight was down to fifty-five kilos two days ago, I think, the lowest it had been in three years and I wanted to keep it that way, possibly lower, considering that I managed not to think of food at all. When Jazz finally rang and text-messaged me for the seventh time, I agreed for her to come to the house. I managed to get out of bed, have a shower, and get dressed before she rang the bell. The water that ran down the drain looked pavement black and smelled foul, and I had not once left the house. It occurred to me that I had not had a shower for some time—precisely how long, I could not recall. I had vague recollections of going in and out of the bathroom, and the past days had merged into one sequence in my memory, and became irrelevant once I got dressed. Jazz used Beauty's keys and remote, which she had kept after Beauty left on Saturday morning, to enter the house. I visualized her entering through the back; I did not meet her at my back door, I simply could not bring myself to undertake such a task. I had not bothered to go to my backyard or to see the inside of my car.

I could smell food as Jazz entered the house. She called my name from the kitchen as she entered through the back. I heard the rustle of shopping bags, then a thump on the table as she placed them down. When I heard her taking plates out of the kitchen cabinet I went in. She had taken two plates from my cabinet and piled food on one of them. She smiled when she saw me enter the kitchen, then frowned and examined me with her eyes from top to bottom. She handed me my mail, which she had removed from my letterbox. I took them and put them on top of the refrigerator, along with my gloves, which I removed. I noticed the discarded containers and realized she had purchased the food from Wembley's. I could smell samoosas, roti, and curry, though slightly, they were not as pungent as I am accustomed to. All Jazz wanted to do then was talk about my weight loss, which annoyed me because it was not her business. Jazz is petite and very slim, and if not clinically at least socially considered borderline anorexic by most people. She eats at the most inopportune times, none of which any of us in the writing circle have witnessed. She will occasionally mention eating dinner at some late night place with her brother or her *friend*, whom none of us have actually met, and will provide quite elaborate and unnecessary details of the food. Jazz is very secretive about her relationship with the man and is very hushed about matters pertaining to violence against women, claiming that her *friend* is working on new legislation pertaining to it. When I last weighed myself, the scale indicated fifty-two kilos, which was good. I could now try and fit into the jeans I had worn five years ago, I thought, as Jazz went on and on about something which I cannot remember. I did not say much, as I sat opposite her with my plate and helped myself only to the curry sauce. I opened one of the little brown paper bags and noticed that the parcel was further wrapped with newspaper.

"Ahh!" I exclaimed, and Jazz looked at me with a smile on her face.

"*Slapchips**," she said, like a true Capetonian. "I thought you would-n't be able to resist them."

I do love chips, and I could not resist them. The salt and vinegar

* French fries softened by salt and vinegar

taste was what I needed and I had more than I thought I could manage.

I was in no mood to eat much. I have always enjoyed samoosas and certainly roti and curry, but neither appealed to me. The smell was peculiar, a bit odd I thought, although Jazz did not seem to mind at all. I was repulsed by the manner in which she scooped the vegetable curry sauce with roti—the process seemed rather unsavoury as she coiled her fingers around the roti and the sauce dripped down her slender fingers into her mouth. Everyone gushes at Jazz, even little animals on the street. I looked up at the ceiling and observed the images that appeared; they were not like the ones in my bedroom, but larger. Jazz carried on licking her fingers.

My cellphone rang again, and Robert asked if he could come and see me. I told him that I was fine and Jazz was with me. He put Sarah, my fourteen-year-old niece, on the phone, since she wanted to chat with me. She was getting ready for her first teenage dance party on the coming weekend and she was excited and told me that she was wearing the low-cut jeans I had bought her three weeks ago. My body started to shake and all I could think of was my sweet little niece and whether she would be safe. Of course she would not be safe, what am I saying. Her father was planning to drive her to the party and would make sure that enough parents were present for him to feel that he could leave her. He knew all of that: he and I had discussed it, and I had gone over all sorts of procedures with Sarah and Susie, my younger twelve-year-old niece, so many times, making sure each time that they understood that young girls their age were prone to sexual assault. Their mother was from a small *dorp* in the interior and knew little of such matters. "Make sure you go to the toilet with someone, never on your own . . . make sure that you're never alone . . . don't walk to the bathroom alone . . . anywhere, even if it is in someone's house," and after a while, I could hear an endless hum as she responded to each of my directives with great speed, already anticipating the order in which I gave them. When Jazz gave me a strange look, I realized I might be upsetting my niece. I hung up the telephone after some pleasantries. Jazz looked at me and I kept my eyes focused on my plate. She gestured that she wanted to tell me something. When she had consumed a mouthful, she finally blurted out, with great excitement, "I spoke to Amina this morning and she said the twins each got their menstrual period this week, three days apart. Isn't that incredible? Two girls born on the same day, with slightly different body types, and even the internal mechanisms of their bodies are in sync with one another. Amina has two young ladies now. How time flies."

I could not eat the curry sauce and within seconds I broke down crying, tears dripping down onto my plate and on the curry. Curry is not supposed to swim in tears. I dragged myself from my chair and dropped the plate in the vicinity of the sink, which was already stacked with other dishes. How could I sit in my house for six days, worried about my young nieces, unable to give them any hope of being free of this horrible situation, of always having to look over their shoulders and live in fear of rape and sexual assault? I knew it would possibly happen to them, and there I was, listing all the things Sarah should not do, when all she could think about was that it was the first party she would go to on her own, the first her parents were not invited to. How could I prepare her for possible sexual assault when I did not have the courage to report mine, not even when it had happened in my marriage. What do mothers like Amina tell their children? Those beautiful girls, Faiza and Faroza, were young women at the tender age of twelve. I began to cry and scream hysterically, and Jazz looked at me calmly, then came to stand behind me, holding onto me as I let the roof and the walls have it. Every wall in my kitchen could smell my breath. My curtains were drawn, the lights were off in most parts of the house, and I felt completely horrified at my seclusion. There were tissue papers strewn all over the house, clothes on the floor, empty flavoured water bottles in my bedroom, biscuit boxes and paper cups everywhere on tables and other surfaces. It bothered me that I had no recollection of how they got there. I had not done the dishes and simply had resorted to plastic cups when all the glasses were in the sink. There was a smell emanating from my body that was not mine—probably his—and it was foul. The more I screamed and cried, the more I seemed to feel as though something was being poured inside me. I was filling up with a rage I did not think I possessed. My fists were loaded, and I used them to bang on my kitchen wall as fast and furiously as I could, even though Jazz tried to hold me back. Why have I allowed my life to be ruled by men who have never cared for me, but cared only about themselves? Cedric, my first boyfriend, then Calvin, whom I married, and now Tom, each of them had something in common— they did not know the first thing about love. Calvin had an affair with a woman at work and gave me the excuse, when I found out, that I was too busy mourning my grandfather even to notice him. He was tired of me pining over my grandfather, my wonderful grandfather whom I loved dearly, and whom apparently I could not mourn after the three-week period he stipulated was sufficient. He wanted to have supper at a certain hour, I was meant to cook it, and I couldn't, most of the time, and therefore I was not worth the comfort a husband offers a wife. I could not serve him, and after a while I did not want to. I lived under the assumption that his love for me was not only of carnal pleasure but also of expressing emotion. How wrong I was—how very, very wrong. I cried into the wall, mourning the years I had served him, and how he left anyway, and how I vowed I would never do the same for another man. After the wall had received adequate pounding, I sat down and held my head on the table. Jazz waited for me to say something, but I was looking at something on the wall, a spot I had not noticed before.

"Have you been outside yet, Isabel?" she asked.

"No, I haven't," I replied.

She came to sit beside me and cleaned the blood off my hands then bandaged my hands with white gauze. The stinging sensation of the surgical spirits did not bother me as much as it had before, and I could smell my own wounds. The mark was still on the wall and irritated me. How did it get there? Jazz shifted my attention, talking to me as I gazed up at the ceiling.

"Isabel, I would prefer to go to the car with you, while I am here. Let me know when you're ready. I can come by tomorrow, Friday, Saturday, Sunday, whenever you want to do it. And if you need any food shopping, then please allow me to do it for you. If you need to go for a walk, please call me. Call Beauty or Carmen, or even Amina— they have all asked after you."

Jazz's words were kind but her observation skills were poor. The spot was still there. It did not matter from which angle I stared at it. It had developed a mouth and a pair of eyes. When I moved back to gaze at it from a distance, its eyes grew large. It was quite high up on the ceiling of my kitchen and I would need a ladder to reach it, which Robert could bring but I was in no mood to have him in my house. Robert would, no doubt, bring food and alcohol, which I did not want to see or smell. The thought of either made me feel sick to my stomach. As Jazz talked, I ran to the bathroom and hurled furiously. Tears were ejected from my eyes, fat and loaded, and I decided then and there that I wanted to see my car. There was no reason for me to delay matters any longer. That bastard was winning. I grabbed my keys and opened the back door with the remote. The smell of guavas greeted me and the wind was chilly and cold, but I walked onto that bare cement floor anyway, avoiding the guavas that had fallen on my property from the nearby tree. Why shouldn't I go to my car? I had paid for the house and there was nothing left for me to lose any more. I could not let that bastard get away with it and maim me, keep me hostage with the memories he had forced onto me.

"Are you sure?" Jazz asked.

"Of course I'm bloody sure," I replied in haste.

Jazz walked behind me as I walked about the backyard, inspecting every spot on that cement floor, with the light on, of course, and could not see any trace of his blood.

My car was spotless. Jazz and Manjit must have shampooed it when they dropped Amina off, because I had noticed the carpet shampoo bottle in the bathroom. My mind was racing, and I managed to put some thoughts together of what Jazz and Amina had done that night, and how they had managed to clean up the horrible mess that bastard had left behind. When I had done enough walking about, I opened the door of my car and sat at the driver's seat. There were no newspapers on the back seat, as there often were. Jazz sat beside me in the passenger's seat. I put the key in the ignition and the sound of *Freshly Ground* played joyfully, without interruption. I listened to the last song on the track and removed it. Jazz sat quietly beside me, for a change, and did not utter a word. The car did not smell of disinfectant, as I thought it would. Only Jazz had the wisdom to replace the smell of violence with the smell of jasmin.

When I walked back into my house, I hardly recognized it. It did not look like my house at all. I walked about from room to room. Jazz followed me and finally got me into my bed by the time ten o'clock rolled around. I noticed the time because she looked at her wristwatch several times as she sat at the edge of my bed, stroking my hair. I knew she would have to leave shortly to do her shift at work. My hands had been bandaged, and I could see spots of blood seeping through the white gauze she had securely wrapped around my palms and fingers.

"Are you still taking your annual leave next week and attending your cousin's wedding?" I asked.

"Yes," she replied.

Just as she was about to leave, I asked, softly, "Jazz, what happened to the gun?"

"Manjit has it. I think it is best if it stays with him. He said he would have it melted."

I nodded.

"I hope they catch the bastard," I said.

She frowned at me strangely.

She looked at her watch again, then back at me, then muttered something about me going to see some therapist whom I loathed. I closed my eyes, as she rambled on about all the therapists I had introduced her to and how I should see one of them. I yawned for the duration of her little speech.

Her cellphone rang.

"Isabel, Beauty is here. I think someone should stay with you. Beauty has been very worried, everyone is."

I nodded.

"I'll give Beauty the keys and remote," she said, grabbing her bag. She kissed me on my forehead, sweetly and tenderly, and I was reminded that Jazz had more love in her veins than I had given her credit for. A wave of discontent came over me as she left. Despite Jazz's constant talking, she was caring and always knew what to do. I exhaled my bad thoughts in my bedroom and waved at her, as she stood at the gate and looked back at me.

Beauty stayed in bed with me the entire night, holding onto me from behind, as we slept. She stroked my hair each time she turned to make herself more comfortable. We did not talk much. She was quiet. I knew Ludwig was back from Vienna but I did not ask.

On Thursday morning, I decided that I had cried enough.

I rang Robert at work after Beauty mentioned that he had telephoned her, claiming that he was not able to get hold of me. He reminded me that he had spoken to me the day before. I assured him that I remembered our conversation, although I only had a distant memory of it. I asked about Sarah's party on the coming weekend and he released a deep sigh of irritation.

"They'll be fine," he said, drawing out the word, as though trying to convince himself or steer the conversation into another direction. "Charmaine is a bit strict with the girls, and I know what she's trying to instill in them, but what can we do, we have to allow them to go out with their friends?"

I sighed, resigned to shelve the matter and not speak to him any further about it. There was little need for me to talk to my clueless brother.

Beauty watched in silence as I emerged from the shower; I had cut my hair again. She looked at me strangely, the way Jazz did when she visited and brought food, and when she asked if I needed any more help.

"Oh, I just evened it out a bit," I said, as she looked at my hair with the worst sort of unspoken disapproval. Sculptors have the sort of gaze that can bestow beauty on an object they find fascinating and bequeath ugliness on another without blinking an eyelid. Beauty had the ability to scrutinize everything without saying a word—she and Ludwig were perfectly suited in this way. I had spent quite a bit of time while I was in the shower inspecting my genital area, which looked unsightly and peculiar, and with the help of the many mirrors I kept in the bathroom I was able to examine myself much the same way as my gynecologist did. I had found my first grey pubic hair; I could not possibly tell Beauty about it, considering her mood. I nicked myself shaving it. Thankfully the music drowned out my cries, and the remains of Jazz's small first aid box, scattered everywhere in my bathroom, aided the process of covering the unsightly wound and stopping the blood.

I walked about the house while Beauty remained in the spare room. When I went in, I heard the soft sound of the violin, which troubled me greatly. Beauty wrote in her journal and did her most intensive work while listening to the violin. I looked at the table and there, still partially wrapped, was the case of the disk, glistening with Ludwig's name in bold print. Beauty had her work spread over the two oak tables. She was occupied at her computer, putting together the notice for her upcoming exhibition. I opened all of the windows despite her protestations that she was cold. "Put a jersey on," I said, as she rubbed her bare arms. She looked at me hesitantly. I walked into all of the rooms and opened all of the windows and drew aside all of the curtains. The late May morning sun was kind, and I wanted to enjoy its small offerings. I dressed myself as well as I could and bolted for the door. Beauty followed me and asked where I was going.

"I'm going out," I said. "I won't be long."

"Are you driving?" She looked very concerned.

"No, I'm walking. I'm just going up the road."

"Are you sure you don't want me to come with you?"

"Yes, very sure," I replied, without looking at her.

My black trousers were quite loose but the matching jacket covered them well. I tied my red scarf to my neck and threw my big black bag over my shoulder. I brushed my hair, as best I could, given the fact that it did not have any particular style to it, and applied some light makeup. My face looked rather pale and I went for the heavy eyeliner, which I think suits my short hair. I had everything I needed, including my red velvet gloves, and hurried to the door. I wished Beauty and Jazz did not have to watch me like a baby.

I felt fantastic. I needed to get a few things done and could not remember how long I had been inside my house.

"Do you know how long you'll be?" Beauty asked, her eyes doing more of the talking.

"I'll be an hour or two," I replied, feeling a little pressured to give an account of how I intended to spend my time. I was not about to do so.

"I'll be here when you return, Isabel," she remarked, as I locked the door behind me and used the remote to further lock up and secure the electronic gate. I looked back at my house, relieved that I had left

Beauty behind. What a nag pot she'd become.

It was a little breezy when I took the corner on Station Road. Thinly layered cirrus clouds hovered around Table Mountain and were descending, fraying as they merged with Groote Schuur hospital up on the hill. There was that yellowish glaze all around the mountain, the colour that seems to embrace it this time of the year, as autumn moves towards winter. I walked briskly, looking through shop windows, and observing young women and men on the street engaged in conversation. Older women carried their shopping bags close to their bodies, as the wind circled in and out of their light jackets. The men up on the corner on Station Road and Lower Main Road were selling their usual African artifacts, and the young Congolese men whom I had spoken to before asked whether I wanted to purchase some of their new African masks. I hesitated then decided that my house needed some new items; it looked very drab. Both the young man whom I spoke to frequently and his brother had been teachers in the Congo, but now, as immigrants in Cape Town, sold curios on the street. They packed my few items well, and I paid them. The younger of the two was a little shy and did not speak much. He asked if I spoke French, and I laughed at the suggestion. The older one asked why I had cut my hair, and I replied that it was getting to be a bit of a nuisance. The little things men notice and the obvious ones they fail to notice never ceases to amaze me. I ran a few errands, looking at shop windows to amuse myself as I scurried in and out between them. It was after three o'clock in the afternoon when I returned home, feeling very pleased with myself. The delight in my step faded as I entered the house and was greeted by Beauty who looked grey with worry. She gasped when she saw me. I had hardly put my shopping bags down than the questions came flooding.

"Are you okay? Why didn't you answer your cell? Carmen and Amina called several times. Jazz wants you to call her. Veronica from work asked why you didn't show up for your lunchtime date with her? Dr Steyn wanted to know whether everything was okay and whether you'd be at work next Monday. He mentioned that your clients were being seen by your student and several colleagues . . . there were court dates that needed to be taken care of . . ." She rattled on. Clearly, she had plugged my telephone into the wall and now expected me to give an account of my whereabouts to people I had chosen to ignore. I could not be bothered to return telephone calls. I unpacked my purchases and started decorating my house.

I am not sure what Beauty's problem was, but she kept staring at me throughout the remainder of the afternoon as though something were wrong. She hovered around me until I finally told her that I could hang the decorations without her supervision, and that if she wanted to stay in the house with me she needed to get her work done and leave me to do mine. She retreated to the spare room where I heard murmurs of her conversation with Kwame, her son, to whom in a lowered voice she insisted that I was ill in bed and not able to speak to him on the telephone. I had the goodness to stay out of her conversation with him, even though I wanted to speak to him. She telephoned her mother and her grandmother, then later had a lengthy conversation with Ludwig, during which time she turned the volume up on her radio. Her voice was softer when she spoke to him; she managed a giggle, which surprised me, for I had been the recipient of her cutting tone, the reserved, aloof face she wore when she was fed up. Shortly after, she took a call from Mary, her adopted godmother, whom she promised to have dinner with, without so much of a mention that she was with me. I gathered, when she used the phrase "us" that she meant Ludwig and Kwame and that the dinner would be at Mary and Sipho's lavish house in Bishop's Court—an exclusive neighbourhood now inhabited by people who, during the apartheid years, would not have been allowed to live there. I dusted all the surfaces in the living room and the dining room and decided where the two new masks would hang, leaving a mark with my pencil and measuring with my hand, from thumb to pinkie, the distance between them. The candles I bought at the Waterfront two months earlier now came in handy and I placed them diagonally opposite the Ostrich egg collection I received from Charmaine and Robert as a birthday present last year. At the time, Calvin's departure had forced me to recoil and as a result the house received little attention. My cellphone rang and I ignored it; it was in the kitchen and simply too far away. Imagine my surprise when Beauty handed it to me and told me that Jazz was on the phone.

"Are you okay?" Jazz asked.

"Of course I'm okay," I replied. "I wish everyone would stop asking me that."

"Isabel, I've postponed tomorrow's writing circle until further notice," she said, as though I was expected to agree.

"What on earth for?" I asked in a raised, curious tone.

Jazz seemed hesitant to offer an explanation.

"We're meeting here, as usual, at eight o'clock, and I have already bought the food. I popped into the small Woolworths at the garage on my way home. If you've telephoned Amina or Carmen to postpone, then you need to attend to the matter and let them know that we're on. I am quite looking forward to tomorrow night and the food in my fridge needs eating."

"Isabel . . . ," Jazz called out, as though I were being unreasonable.

"Jazz, what is the problem?" I ground my teeth. "We have decided to meet every Friday night and why should we postpone this week's gathering? We have never missed one since we started; even when one of us was on holiday."

Jazz was rather stroppy. I hung up the phone and continued decorating. Beauty stayed out of my way until I was done. I fried some of the smoked snoek in the pan and toasted some bread. We ate in silence for most of the meal, except for the tentative reply Beauty offered when I asked how the preparation for her next exhibition was progressing. She appeared rather distant, but bestowed the occasional stolen glance in the direction of my jeans.

On Friday morning I turned off both my house and cell phones after I had spoken to my student assistant and made sure she did not bother me the rest of the day. She was in her final year of social work and had to cope on her own. People were starting to annoy me. My brother was behaving badly, asking me ridiculous questions about my health as though I were a child. He drinks like a fish and smokes like a chimney and has the nerve to tell me that I do not sound well. My mother spoke to me in that dreary sort of way, as though it was my cheerfulness that was the problem, and not her desire to squash it. Beauty walked in on me; given the fact that the bathroom door was open I couldn't exactly blame her. I did not expect her to enter it just as I got off my bathroom scale, which now indicated a favourable fifty-two kilos. She frowned at me again; this habit was also beginning to annoy me. Later she walked to and fro, talking to Ludwig in hushed tones on her cellphone, then checked her messages on her laptop computer, and finalized some of her small rag models, some of which she had sketched and cut from gauze-like linen, which I thought was quite an unusual texture for a model which was meant to represent a woman's body. She would make these rag dolls, dozens of them, in various shapes and sizes and dress them up, then work from them to mould sculptures. The dolls were models of women covered in bandages, in various stages of recovery, and looking a bit like accident victims. Some of them looked like corpses, and I hated them. I hoped silently they would die instead of suffer through recovery. My attention was drawn by the process she was putting them through, which involved removing the strips of gauze and writing the women's histories of violence on them with black ink, then wrapping the bodies again and bathing them in water, milk, then flour, then a spice which would represent them. She used various selections of spices. I thought the whole procedure quite peculiar. The dolls looked like mummies, wrapped in written words and gauze, as though they had wounds, and for a second they came to life, just like that, after she told me she had named them, and I was appalled. They were hideous and very intrusive. They were already trying to sit on my chairs but I stared them down, away from my freshly polished furniture. I just wanted them to go away; there was no chance that I would invite them to the writer's circle . . . not women like that.

Beauty and I remained in our rooms the entire afternoon: she in the spare room and I in my bedroom, where I continued to clear my cupboard and sort out my underwear drawers. I hadn't realized just how disorganized my cupboard had become and could not remember where I had bought half the clothes in it. I got rid of clothes and stacked them in plastic bags with the intention of taking them to the woman at the charity shop on the first floor of the hospital. I looked for one particular set of black underwear and realized that I had not done any washing in days. I collected a few items of underwear, which seemed strewn in odd places around the house. I still could not find my favourite black pair. Perhaps Biscuit had played with them and dragged them somewhere between the furniture. I opened my front door in the hope that I would see Biscuit. I fetched her pink porcelain saucer with tuna and rattled it on the cement floor, hoping I would hear those little bells around her neck, but there was no sign of her. Mrs Applebaum brazenly walked over to my front door and spoke to me. I had no interest in seeing her. She looked dreadful, as though she'd been crying. She muttered something about Biscuit, but I simply walked back inside. I did not need her pity and slammed the door in her face. She must have talked to Jazz, since she stared at my clothes, the way Jazz did, and looked at me as though she too was about to make comments about my weight loss. Beauty must have been watching at the window, for she left her room and spoke with Mrs Applebaum, who started crying into her soggy handkerchief which, when not in use, she kept under the sleeve of her cardigan.

Shortly after seven o'clock I prepared the living room for the writing circle. I decorated the table with food I had bought at Woolworths—the patés went in the centre along with some of the cheese and crackers. On a separate plate I stacked the smoked salmon, scattered a few slices of halal sausage on another, put the sliced biltong and a few nuts in bowls and prepared a vegetable plate. I wore my old jeans, the ones I have not been able to fit into for more than five years and draped several necklaces around my neck to make a contrast with the white silk shirt, which made me feel quite frivolous and excitable. If only Beauty shared my sentiments. She looked rather glum. Beauty looked concerned when she looked at me, but when she was doing her work, inking and milking and writing on her newest collection of rag dolls, she looked content. The contentment turned to sadness after Mrs Applebaum left. That woman can really dampen one's spirits. I wished Beauty would leave and go back to her flat instead of coming and going. She spoke to Kwame about their upcoming trip: he was auditioning for a spot in the Soweto Boys' Choir. Ludwig does not stay in Cape Town for long periods, yet for some reason Beauty has decided to spend her time with me, which I find rather peculiar. She spoke to Mary again, and I was relieved when she ended that conversation, because I think Beauty's irrational behaviour merits concern. She was making excuses to people all the time about not being able to see them.

I was happy when everyone arrived. I had stacked several small plates along with serviettes on the table, and began to feel awkward when everyone stared at the table then at me, or was it at my jeans? My jeans seemed to capture their attention more than the food I had laid out. They all seemed rather cross with me. I was the excitable one, for a change, and no one seemed to care much for what I had to say, as we went around and did our usual weekly check-in. I knew my hair was short, and I had cut it without going to the hair dresser, and for the entire time that I spoke and read my writings on what I saw on the ceiling, I was stared at by four sets of eyes, which simply engraved their disapproval of my body onto me, and expected to respond to endless questions about my health and welfare. I was excited, I was happy everyone could be there, although there had been talk of postponement, and here I was, being scrutinized and given disapproving looks because I had managed to lose a few pounds.

I felt relieved when the bell rang at the front gate. I raised myself from my chair; everyone else got up too and tried to keep me from answering the door in my own house; I ignored them. There were questions about whether I was expecting anyone, since all our friends knew that we had the writing circle on a Friday night and no one had called on me before. All four of them stood behind me as I opened the door. There was a collective gasp from them when the two policemen at the gate took their hats off and asked to speak to me. I recognized them both and invited them in. Jazz looked at me with fury and agitation on her face. Amina was beside herself with anger. It appeared as though the four of them were ready to strangle me on the spot. I asked the policemen to take their shoes off at the door, as everyone did who entered my house. They were a little reluctant but complied when it was clear that it was the only way they could enter my house. I didn't see why they should be exempt. I had my wooden floors done a few months before, and the front portion especially, with the special oak, which the supplier had ordered from Ceres, had been waxed. While the two policemen removed their shoes I offered them tea and made sure they each had a cotton serviette. There were to be no crumbs on the floor, I asserted as they stared at me. I cannot stand crumbs on wooden floors. Carmen, Amina, Beauty, and Jazz hissed at me. The two policemen, sipping their tea, began to explain their purpose. They were both Afrikaners, one a fairly young constable, and his partner an older man, both of them rather pleasant.

The younger one asked me if I was comfortable talking in front of my friends.

"Yes, of course. Why wouldn't I be," I replied as I sat down opposite them on my sofa. "Please ask whatever it is you've come to ask me."

He then proceeded.

"Madam," he said, to which I smiled. I love it when they call you Madam.

"My partner and I wanted to get more details from you about this man who attacked you."

"I gave you all the details I could yesterday."

Carmen's gasp nearly swallowed the room. Jazz was hissing at me with her nose; Amina's mouth flew open and Beauty's face was flushed.

"Yes, but yesterday you said . . ."

He took out his notepad and flipped it over to the page where he had written down my statements.

"You said he was almost six feet tall, and that he wore a blue windbreaker. You also said you didn't see him and that after he had . . . he had . . ."

"Raped me! After he raped me!" I shouted, pulling a face, as both of them stared uncomfortably at Carmen, Jazz, Amina, and Beauty.

"Please, go ahead. These are my friends and they know all about it," I said.

I don't know why everyone was so worked up; their gasping created quite an orchestra.

"Well, Madam, you gave us a description and I'm afraid my partner and I have some concern, because you see, it doesn't all add up."

"What do you mean it doesn't all add up?"

"Well, first you say that he was over six feet tall, then you described him, when asked after the first break, remember when you had some tea . . ."

"Yes, of course I remember talking to you. Do you think I'm stupid? I would appreciate it if you would just get to the point. I find you quite rude. Don't they teach you manners in that training school of yours? Stop treating me as though there is something wrong with me. Just get on with it!"

They never saw that coming.

"Well, I asked whether you remembered if he gripped you and how big his arms were and you said his arms were short?"

I'd had more than I could bear from them about my condition; I was fed up.

"You described him as tall at one time and then at another time you described him as someone with medium build. There was a time when you said he was dark, then close to the end when you described how he got away after he uhm, mmm . . ."

"After he raped me!"

One would expect policemen to be better trained to talk to women.

"Yes, Madam, as you say, after he raped you."

He looked at his notes again.

"You said it was too dark for you to see, then later you said you saw him, and you gave various descriptions of this man, and they all seem a little confusing. So you see the problem we have in putting together a profile of this man for our team, possibly even a picture, is that your descriptions are not consistent."

I had had enough by now.

"Of course I reported the bastard," I shouted. "How dare anyone expect me to let this man get away? He raped me and got away. I want the police to catch him. I don't want him to get away with what he did. He could do this to another woman—perhaps he has already. What about my nieces! My nieces!"

The younger one had the nerve to speak down at me.

"Calm down! Calm down!" he said, flagging me down as though I was a driver in a speeding car.

"You want me to calm down? Who the hell do you think you are? You get paid to do your job, so go and do it! I report a rape and you tell me that my descriptions do not add up. You do the math. Don't ask me to do it. I don't know why men do such senseless things. Go and do your bloody job. Don't you dare come into my house and question my statements."

"Ma'm . . ."

"Don't you Ma'm me." I picked up my keys and was ready to throw them at him. Jazz intervened and grabbed them from my hand.

"Isabel! Isabel!" she yelled.

Carmen and Amina were standing behind me. Beauty had tears in her eyes. I know that she did not like it when people raised their voices, but these policemen were out of order.

"Now, this is my house. If you cannot speak to me in a decent manner, then get out!"

Jazz was trying to intervene again.

"Jazz, don't speak for me. I don't need anyone to speak for me. I just want these policemen to leave."

Jazz had given the younger one her card, and I took it from him, and tore it up. He had his eye on her from the moment he came into my house. Jazz was the most petite of all of us, and men like him were attracted to women like Jazz. He was, of course, unaware of the fact that she had a bad temper and had little traces of womanliness. If he wished to speak to her about me, or she to him, then they had to do it to my face, not behind my back. I asked the policemen and the women from the writing circle to leave at once.

Jazz

For those few hours after I got off the telephone with Isabel, during which time she insisted on us meeting for the writing circle, I knew something was not quite right but I could not bring myself to believe that she of all people had gone over the threshold of her own agony and retreated to a place of imagined circumstance in order to sustain her sense of reality. She was quite beside herself when we entered the house, looking haunted and beastly. The smile on her face was manufactured with various selections from her Lancôme blusher palate, which on a troubled face produced a masklike appearance quite unmatched to the face I knew. Isabel's face and body appeared to be in opposition to one another. Her face was smacked with various layers of compressed makeup powder and its muscles appeared trapped, which in turn produced various veneers of madness. Her eyes bulged with destitution, her body cried out wanting to be seen and heard, her temperament, teetering on schizophrenic. My limited knowledge of psychiatry does not allow me to venture such a quick diagnosis, purely through limited and situational observation, but the symptoms she showed convinced me of her condition. Her interactions with us were cutting, despite the smiling face, and at times she seemed bewitched by the evil which had infiltrated her life, quite against the better judgment for which she was known and of which she seemed now completely oblivious. Isabel was, of course, one of the expert therapists in the field of rape and sexual assault in Cape Town, she evidently needed peer counselling but refused, despite the long list Carmen and I compiled or the suggestions offered by Beauty and Amina of all the women we knew, to whom we had been introduced as a consequence of Isabel's work relationship with them and of whom she had such high regard. She did not see the need to go near her peers and scoffed at the mere suggestion. Beauty had whispered in my ear in the kitchen before the police arrived that Mrs Applebaum had managed to come to the door, shaken and distraught, to inform Isabel that Biscuit had been killed by a driver speeding in a silver-grey Volkswagen, who did not bother to stop despite the screams the children had let out on the street. Isabel had apparently refused to see Mrs Applebaum on the grounds that Mrs Applebaum had examined her physique and expressed sorrow towards her by the manner in which she stared and by her tearful state. Beauty did not have the heart to tell Isabel that it was Mrs Applebaum who needed sympathy for the loss of Biscuit. Beauty, who was not exactly an animal lover, had gone to Mrs Applebaum to express her apologies for the treatment she had received from Isabel, and fabricated some story about Isabel taking medication which made her drowsy and lethargic. Biscuit had brought many in the neighbour-hood a lot of joy, and Mrs Applebaum was, apparently, inconsolable.

That night Isabel's manner was abrupt, her tone was callous, and she strutted about the house like a neutered pussycat whose litter had been whisked away. She threw all of us out of her house when we tried to reason with her, after she instructed the policemen to leave. Beauty refused to leave and managed to argue her way back into the house. Minutes later, as I was on my cellphone to Manjit, momentarily observing the manner in which Carmen and Amina sat huddled together in Amina's car, beside mine, we could hear Isabel sobbing and shrieking intermittently all the way from her house to the train station where we were parked. We looked at one another and shook our heads. I continued talking to Manjit, filled with anger towards Isabel for the manner in which we were exposed to the policemen in her house. Perhaps I was a little annoyed at myself for not keeping a closer eye on Isabel, for I could certainly have prevented her from going to the police station to report her rape. It is the report on the rapist, already dead and buried, which concerns me. I cannot speak for the others, although it is clear that Beauty, Amina, and Carmen feel the same way as I do and fear the repercussions. I have great affection for Isabel but am not known for my patience. Beauty was very dedicated to Isabel and very patient with her. After the police left, I looked inside Isabel's bathroom cabinet and saw no evidence of tablets anywhere; I whispered in Beauty's ear to keep me updated on Isabel's condition.

Because of the circumstances that evening, I had no time to tell Isabel that her test results were clear—that nothing out of the ordinary had come up and there was nothing to be concerned about, but she should take the full dose of the morning-after pill I had handed her. Beauty made it known to me that Isabel had taken the tablets I brought her, everyday, and kept them on her tea tray permanently. She, like I, was aghast at Isabel's anger when I spoke to the policemen. Isabel's behaviour was akin to that of a jealous lover. I had no interest in the younger Afrikaner policeman. I found him, in that dreadful uniform, with that lower-class humour and slow wit, as desirable as a plate of Brussels sprouts. The older policeman was more interesting and certainly quite attractive, with age, experience, and grace on his side. Apart from everything else, he knew how to observe women, and kept his words few and his glances, however plentiful, discreet.

Although I had met the younger man before, I hoped that he would not recognize me. When I first moved to Cape Town from London, nine years ago, Interpol was investigating the murder of a Hindu medical doctor from London Central hospital, where I did my internship, and he sought an interview with me in my family home with Manjit and both my parents present. His timing could not have been worse; he came to the house when one of our relatives from England had been killed in a bomb blast in India and both my parents were completely beside themselves with grief. The lengthy list of revolutionaries in my mother's family back in India, where they fought the Hindu elite, especially supporters of the late Indira Gandhi, made every member of my mother's family vulnerable to police harassment in India, and even in London. The young Afrikaner policeman had written to me once, shortly after our first meeting, to inform me that the interview had been written up and sent to Scotland Yard, but no developments had occurred and the murder remained unsolved. His manner was at first rather disconcerting, for he demanded evidence of my identity, especially my age. He insisted that I looked younger than thirty-eight, when in fact I was older, and I gladly presented every piece of identification I could lay my hands on. In my caste, men have the middle name of Singh, and my mother had removed her last name from both my passports, the Ugandan and the British one, and this made the policeman suspicious. He scrutinized every piece of identification I handed him, looked at the photos and examined me with narrowed eyes from top to bottom.

I did not know anyone when I first moved to Cape Town and spent most of my time with my family. Isabel was one of the first people I met. While a job at Groote Schuur would be the best move for my career, I was worried that my application would be declined. Dr Singh, a cousin of my father, refused to give me a reference even though I had worked under his supervision for three years; he told my parents when confronted by my Dad on the telephone that he did not think I had the necessary skills to work in neurosurgery despite my qualifications. One of my father's friends at the hospital had reported to him that Human Resources had not received Dr Singh's reference letter, only Dr Govinder's. What Dr Govinder, my father's brother whom I had lived with and whom I was instructed to always address formally, failed to tell my father was that his friend Dr Singh had sexually assaulted me when I was nineteen, then blamed it on his drunken state. Dr Govinder's wife, Auntiejee, treated me horribly. She accused me of playing tricks on Dr Singh in order to get attention, and did not believe me when I told my uncle that Dr Singh harassed me by sending me letters, and even followed me about at Medical School. During my last year of school, he regularly waited for me in his Mercedes on the street, pretending that he was in the neighbourhood and would offer me a lift home, which I always refused. Many men of Dr Singh's age scouted around for possible brides for their sons. When he heard that I was born in Uganda and not England, he thought that I would be subservient enough for his son and desperate enough for a British passport, the latter which I had already obtained. Dr Govinder, my uncle, as a result of an arrangement between him and my father, had claimed me as his daughter, thus allowing me the possibility of living with them and going to private school in England, and being eligible for a British passport. Since we had the same last name, no one posed any question about the arrangement. Sikh men, especially those who wear turbans, look alike to most people, though my father and my uncle wore turbans only for religious ceremonies and formal photographs. Dr Govinder generally spoke well of my father. Once inebriated, however, he depicted my father as the younger brother who was less fortunate and who needed his financial help in order to take care of his family. He claimed to have paid my school fees. Auntiejee regularly gossiped about me to her women friends at the temple, the contents of her talk relayed to me by her daughter. Despite all this, I did not have the heart to tell my father that his family members had treated me with utmost cruelty.

One Sunday afternoon, my parents were dressed to the nines and had the taxi ready for their trip to the airport. I was taken aback by their mention that my uncle Dr Govinder would be visiting us for two weeks. My parents insisted that they had told me but I had no recollection of any such conversation with them. The thought made me ill beyond comprehension. I despised the subtle suggestion by my mother that my memory was selective or that I was pretending. My mother knew I was vulnerable to these sorts of accusations, since I had spent two years in a sleep clinic working with a dream specialist, attempting to get to the bottom of my insomnia, my sporadic sleepwalking, and my wealth of haunted dreams, which always involved some animal being hunted then slaughtered in a sea of red blood—not the kind of dream a vegetarian cherishes or cares to remember.

I was fortunate enough to have obtained my annual vacation. But that year my mother played a nasty trick on me—of this I am sure. I could not bear the thought of being in Auntiejee and Dr Govinder's company. Auntiejee was completely under Dr Govinder's command and had nothing to say for herself when I lived with them, except for the occasional reprimand she directed at me. That was for a good eleven years, before I left and lived in residence, asserting to my parents that it was better for me to be close to the university and get to know the doctors and be known by name and face when I applied to London Central and for specialization in neurosurgery. Dr Govinder and Auntiejee had apparently arrived in South Africa three days prior and were visiting friends and family in Durban. Shortly after hearing of their visit, I found myself with a severe stomachache, unable to get any relief despite the large quantities of water and apple juice I consumed.

It was late in the afternoon when I finally left my family home in Rylands to attend an afternoon tea party for the bride, which was organized by the bride's aunt on her mother's side. Surpreet, the bride, was to attend with the groom, Pram, with their respective parents. Surpreet's father and my father are cousins; her mother was born in England and had an arranged marriage with my uncle, who was born in Uganda. Pram's parents were both born in Durban. Surpreet's mother's younger sister, Sunita, had married an Englishman named Paul. The tea party was at their house in Constantia. The bride and the groom are usually not seen together before the wedding, but modern times, and ascent in class often gave rise to a reverence for English culture—thus, this event was hosted in the heart of Constantia. Indian ceremonies, which smeared and practically bathed the groom in turmeric before adorning him with colourful roses to the rhythm of the sitar, were not a Constantia delight; they were reserved for the actual wedding ceremony the next week in colourful Rylands. Tea parties for the bride and groom a week before the wedding, for select guests, are not customary in Indian cultures either. I muttered my disapproval to Manjit as he drove and I blew on my manicured nails.

"You've only met these people once, Jazz," he asserted.

"Yes, but the bride's celebrations do not include a tea party in Constantia among English people or those who imitate their unfortunate habits."

"You've lived in England for a large part of your life," Manjit said, throwing me a puzzled look.

"Oh, I like England. It's English *people* I don't like," I replied, with a giggle.

Manjit was heaving; he was quite cross with me for some reason. He stared at my feet on his dashboard.

"Besides, the England I like is the little India part . . ."

"Jazz," he interrupted. "It is only one afternoon, one bloody afternoon of your life, and it is about the only family gathering, apart from the wedding next week, you are expected to attend for the year, perhaps even for the next two or three years."

I sighed and drew the window down, annoying Manjit further, since it drained the strength of the air conditioner, which he preferred above the somewhat chilly May wind.

"I know this is not the kind of conversation you'd like, but I am going to tell you anyway."

His face was red and I sat up with bated breath for the speech.

"I don't appreciate the way you treat Carmen. You don't have to like her. You don't even have to be nice to her. The only thing I ask is that you be civil to her. I am not giving up my relationship with her and I don't see why you insist on lecturing me on Sikh respectability considering that you've had your fair share of girlfriends and boyfriends, not to mention your *friend* who, I am almost certain is a married man, since why else has no one met him?"

I was flabbergasted by this outburst.

I shifted my body in my seat.

"You do not speak to me like that. I forbid it! I am your elder. Who I choose to have relationships with is my own bloody business!" I shouted, quite beside myself. I was quite a few years older than Manjit. I was about to proceed with my tongue-lashing, when suddenly, speeding right past us, was Amina in her blue BMW, and beside her in the passenger seat was her much despised brother-in-law. I hastily moved my hand to the hooter, alarming Manjit, and got a quick wave from Amina, her back firmly behind the wheel, her face pointed at the driver's mirror, and her left hand in that quick, impersonal, royal wave she has managed to master.

"Was that Donny with Amina?" I asked, but Manjit's stern look meant that no reply would be forthcoming.

Could I have imagined that I had seen Donny with her? It was almost four o'clock in the afternoon and surely she would not be with him in a car, her car, if it were not absolutely necessary? I realized that she may not have recognized Manjit or me since we were in my father's Mercedes and may have just waved in response to our hoot. My father had insisted we use his car, while he collected his brother and his wife at the airport in a limousine, which he intended to use for the entire day. It took a while for Manjit's sour face to break, and when it did, he frowned, for he had just realized what we had seen. He was silent, but bothered, and the frown on his face remained for quite some time. He turned to glance at me occasionally as he drove.

"She does live in Bishop's Court, doesn't she?" Manjit asked. "This is her neck of the woods."

"Yes, I know. Precisely!" I said and nodded to myself, convinced that I had uncovered something.

"Why then would she be with Donny . . . mmm?" I asked.

Manjit shook his head and continued to look ahead. I looked out of my window, which seemed the most natural thing to do, considering the approaching neighbourhood. We passed upper Claremont, so different to Rylands, and admired the abundance of trees, which always beautified Cape Town and made it adorable and endearing, especially to foreigners. The area was beautiful, there was nothing like it anywhere in the world. The clouds were thick and frothy, and the mountain had that mistiness about it that drew us in the closer we got to it; it practically brushed my cheek as I leaned against the window. Despite my silent absorption in the view, my mind raced back to Amina with the most rotten thoughts, which I cannot reveal for they shame me somewhat.

I had promised my mother that I would keep my cellphone off for the occasion, but since we had not arrived at our destination I rang Amina; I could not resist it. I got her answering machine, and left a brief message asking her to return my call. I rang Beauty and got her answering machine too. I knew that she had planned to spend the morning with Isabel, who had apparently agreed for Beauty, Ludwig, and Kwame to visit. Isabel adored Kwame. I sent Beauty a quick text message indicating that I had just seen Amina and a man in the driver's seat who resembled Donny, her brother-in-law. Beauty of course had not met Donny but I had filled her in on the situation the day after Isabel's ordeal. As I looked up from my phone, I stared right up at the mountain, which now appeared as though at the head of a table, flanked by two rows of trees. Manjit took a left turn and glanced over at me; he received a cold stare in return, for the inappropriate manner in which he had spoken to me concerning my behaviour towards Carmen and the manner in which I conducted my love life.

We arrived at our destination, a lavish Constantia house, at the same time as my father, who was smiling from ear to ear and looking rather pleased as he drove into the driveway right behind us. He had taken it upon himself to drive the limousine, having dismissed the chauffeur.

We were directed to a marked parking spot by a uniformed paid subordinate. He nodded in a dutiful sort of way, quite befitting his station, and having directed us collected our keys, like a valet. Before we took our next step, a round woman in a black and white uniform escorted us to a lavish garden plump with flowers, cast-iron antiques, a large swimming pool beaming with blueness, and three luxurious sets of tables each set for six guests and adorned with red tulips, which bothered me slightly. There were several two-tiered cake servers with a selection of cakes, and what appeared to be crustless cucumber sandwiches with lashes of smoked salmon and cream cheese, stacked on a mahogany tea trolley, which bore evidence of the style the hosts cultivated here in Cape Town, right at the bottom of the continent. For each step we took, there appeared a servant of some sort and for a brief moment Manjit and I looked at one another, mindful of the manners with which we were raised, as we both reluctantly looked in the direction of the parking area, expecting to greet our parents and their guests.

"I will escort you through the double doors, Madam. Your parents will be joining you shortly."

The woman's voice had an organized tone to it—as though she had been trained for the occasion. I nodded at her awkwardly and followed her lead as she pointed towards the double doors. I fiddled with my scarf, a long silk blue Indian scarf draped over my shoulders, which went wonderfully with the dress of the same silk fabric, and found myself staring uncomfortably at the confident display of wealth. The lawn was impeccable, and the smell of cleaning agents scented by the thick locks of pink bougainvillea draped around the brick wall which framed the large house was suggestive of the labour each servant had performed, under organized instruction, of course, for the property bore great evidence of eloquence, charm, and a strained yet generous portion of English coloniality. There were no dogs, thank goodness. For a brief moment I imagined a handful of Great Danes, possibly grey, leaping about on the vast lawn, but my imaginary barking dogs were hastily replaced, upon surveying the area, by stone carved Dobermans, strategically placed on either side of the large stone pillars, which framed the back exit of the house leading to the expansive veranda where large potted plants, in cast-iron pots, were neatly arranged. I caught a glimpse of a grey box, a flashing small red light at the top of it, possibly part of an alarm system, and observed, as I looked about, similar grey boxes scattered in every enclosed area.

I looked over at Manjit, who was also surveying the grounds, inspecting it with narrow curious eyes and wrinkled brow. I saw my brother nodding, as though he approved of the proportion allocated to each piece of landscaping, then observed him shift his gaze upon the house, pursing his lips as though he was about to kiss it, all of which disturbed me greatly. The hosts then availed themselves to us, each immaculately dressed and utterly charming, the kind of charm one could not reject or scoff at but merely tolerantly observe in the hope that it would eventually fade in the Cape Town sunset. Sunita was dressed in a dark blue Chanel suit with matching hairstyle, while her husband Paul wore a modern Indian suit. She looked like an Indian goddess, or close to it, although her carefully orchestrated appearance shouted French or at least Continental. She strutted about like an expensive little cat—the kind princesses in fairy tales keep on their laps. Paul was tall and quite stately-looking; his face, although slender, as English as Winston Churchill's.

"How do you do? Very pleased you could come," he announced, quite loudly as though he was deaf, with a hint of an affected Indian accent, which caused my mouth to drop and my eyes to perform their slow and irritated roll, the kind I performed on English culture vultures who annoyed me with their liberal cultural appropriations.

"Welcome to our home. Nice to see you again," Sunita said, keeping her head low and her brows high. Her face was pointed, as though her movement was always directed forward, and she withdrew her hand after shaking mine, brought the left one from behind her back then held them both close to her face, rubbing her thumb over her fingertips as though she was removing gold dust off them. She directed Manjit and me to the table she had allocated for us, then turned to direct my parents and Dr Govinder and Auntiejee to the same table after greeting them. The second table was reserved for her and her husband, his two sisters and their husbands—the geriatric table, as it were. The third table was reserved for Surpreet and Pram and their parents. Manjit and I were about to walk over to greet the second table, when suddenly the woman who had ushered us into the garden stood before us and informed us that we were to be taken on a tour of the house. Manjit and I looked at one another and nodded our agreement. Sunita had a benevolence about her that smacked of arrogance, and I immediately sought to retrieve the little traces of my English public school accent, which remained hidden and controlled at the bottom of my gullet, reserved for occasions where I was expected to succumb to ridiculous displays of Englishness. Her husband's relatives came to our table and introduced themselves, and evidently they were well informed about our professions and seemed keen to converse on matters relating to them.

My parents and Dr Govinder and Auntiejee joined us and we greeted them. They were pleasant and addressed both Manjit and me cordially, without the usual song and dance they performed when they had an audience. Perhaps the occasion elicited that kind of behaviour. There was no time to pursue this speculation, for Sunita and Paul had also joined us. She led the way, with Paul at her side, and took us up the long winding staircase into the library, which was stacked with the classics, travel books, a few historical tomes, and a selection of encyclopedias, all in all a fine literary collection. I nodded, while others made favourable remarks about the room and its contents. We were then directed down the passage where select Indian and Persian carpets were scattered in well chosen places, and glimpses of their travels were revealed to us by the display of photographs of Sunita posing proudly in front of important European landmarks. Paul was the proud photographer, for it was he who commented on the day and the time when the photo was taken, and other details, while Sunita talked about the actual city and its attractions and the flight which brought them to it from another European one. We were taken to one room after another, before the hosts showed us the rooms their children had occupied when they were in Cape Town.

I tore myself from the organized viewing party, and gazed at the curtains and paintings, which ranged from Impressionist to Modern Art reproductions, then several African and Indian pieces, accompanied by select African sculptures, all polished to perfection. I peeked over the balcony on the far side of the house, closest to the kitchen area, and for the life of me thought I smelled boiled beef, which I hoped was reserved for *their* supper. There is nothing more English than sliced boiled beef. I continued to look at the paintings as I heard in the distance Sunita nattering on about her three children at university in England and in other parts of Europe, her monologue obviously rehearsed, littered with comments of their vast accomplishments and how the children simply loved their home in Constantia and considered it a great perk to be in Cape Town during their breaks. I yawned and Manjit looked over in my direction, just as I brought my hand to my mouth. He motioned with his head that he wanted me at his side. I refrained at first, despite the stares both he and Sunita issued in my direction. I thought if any conversation ensued on my failed marriage and the collapse of Manjit's arranged one, I would rather not be present to furnish Sunita with the necessary details. Sunita stood still and waited for me with an inquiring smile on her face, and so I decided that I might as well join them. The fierce look my mother wore took me right back to my childhood, and I could almost see myself in plaits, sucking my thumb in my bed as I awaited her decision on the kind of punishment I would receive.

We went from room to room, while Sunita laboriously and attentively noted every detail of the house and told little stories she'd accumulated, laughable misfortunes of those in her employ, purely for repeating on occasions like this one. Manjit was utterly charmed by her, I could tell, and enjoyed every detail offered on the original design of the house and its shortcomings and the subsequent alterations made to it, which had brought it to its present glory. I feared that my shoes might have carried some of the grit from our house and the garden, and shuddered at the thought of some old woman on her hands and knees cleaning the traces I left behind on the beautifully kept marble floors. I looked about and steered away from the group again, and saw, in a small room leading off from the main passageway, a photo of what appeared to be Sunita's parents. I tip-toed inside. It was quite a beautiful room and I wondered why Sunita had not taken the trouble of showing it to us. There was something regal about her mother, clearly a wedding photograph, and the look on her father's face was familiar, yet I could not put my finger on who or what the face reminded me of. Outside again, I was joined by my parents and other guests, the hosts following on. At this time, the same man who had collected my car keys made an appearance and nodded at Sunita. I noticed that he now wore on his black waistcoat a little gold pin that bore the name, "Mr Phumelo."

"I'm afraid your tour has come to an end. Tea is to be served shortly," Sunita said, as she swept her long, thin fingers across her hair, ensuring that it retained its impeccable shape.

I stood back and allowed my parents and their guests to venture over to our designated table while I tugged at Manjit to stay behind. We then walked behind them slowly, each occupied with our own thoughts.

"Jazz, I think you're right. I think it was Donny. I got a quick glimpse as they passed. I actually recognized him, and I did not see the driver, since she overtook us, but I did recognize Amina's car and saw the back of her."

I stood still and looked at Manjit. I had already told him of the policemen at Isabel's house, which made him very anxious and quite worried.

My mind was racing back and forth. That photo of Sunita's parents, the look on her father's face, reminded me of another; and the sighting of Amina with Donny left me uneasy.

"Where are you off to?" Manjit asked.

"I think it's more than high time that I got a proper bloody drink from one of the servants. I don't intend to sit through this event for the purpose of eating cake and drinking tea."

"Are you mad!" he screamed. Heads turned swiftly, smiling, a quarrel between brother and sister furthest from their mind. I smiled back, as I have been taught, and reprimanded Manjit under my breath, cursing him in a manner appropriate to his outburst and to the setting.

Manjit, whose masculinity must have been pressing against his embarrassment, tugged at my arm and dragged me to the table.

Lo and behold, before us, inside that half circle of three tables was now a small platform upon which a quartet sat. The woman had thought of everything! I sat, bemused by it all, Manjit sitting close by, and the eyes at my table all upon me, as my parents and their guests tried to ascertain whether I approved of the house and the quartet. Strangely enough, my parents and aunt and uncle had tried to keep me away from music, yet sought to engage me on its appreciation each time we were before musicians. I could now feel myself raging against the restraint they had imposed on me. I kept my gaze away from them and asked Manjit about the conversation that had developed when earlier I tore myself away from them in the house.

"Did Sunita ask Mum and Dad any personal questions?"

Manjit's eyes moved but he did not answer.

"Did she ask them any questions about us?" I persisted.

"Don't be ridiculous," he replied. "People like her never do."

I raised myself from the table and Manjit followed suit. Before I knew it my parents and their guests had raised themselves from their chairs too and the four of them followed us. I walked over to Surpreet's table, although I had not intended to do so right away. She looked lovely, in her dark suit, and so did Pram, fashionably dressed in an Italian suit with matching shoes. My uncle, Surpreet's father, came to my side and put his arm about my neck.

"This is Jasminder," he announced, pride beaming from his face.

"She's a neurosurgeon up at Groote Schuur Hospital," he remarked in a raised voice—even the servants turned their heads. Pram's mother and father got up and shook my hand, after brushing their clothes with their hands, as though they were too old and dusty for formal presentation. After all hands had been shaken and other polite exchanges made, we returned to our table. I sat in my chair thinking of Beauty and Ludwig and how they might enjoy such a quartet even if it was in a house whose owner I found overbearing and pretentious. Although I have not been witness to Carmen playing the harp, she has mentioned it and I am sure she would have found the event entertaining. I chewed a peppermint, which I hastily dug out from my handbag, as I pondered the moment at the table with Surpreet's parents, where, in a rare eye-to-eye contact I found Dr Govinder smiling at me, taking credit for the compliments showered upon me by my uncle and aunt. My father did not take credit for me the way Dr Govinder did. Those cruel spasms in my stomach made their presence known by my emitting the foulest breath. The mint seemed insufficient. I hastily sought the help of another.

I may have been too preoccupied with my condition to notice that Dr Govinder was now sitting beside me, having taken a chair previously occupied by my father, and staring at me. He stroked my hair, in a manner one would describe as loving, if the receiver were a child, and I withdrew my personhood with a slow and tormenting gaze, which did not seem to affect him at all. I observed the manner in which he stared at my mother, then shifted his gaze to me, then back to my mother, whose glowing face he obtained the desired validation for his gawking. I looked at my father and offered him a smile, and commented on how smooth our ride had been in his Mercedes, as I noticed the proximity between Dr Govinder and my mother, his head bent and his eyes pegged to every movement she made. My father's alertness alarmed me, for I did not know him to be a jealous man, and certainly his brother would be the least of his concerns. Manjit nudged me with his elbow and I staggered back a little in my chair, quite unaware that I still had my vexed eyes fixed on Dr Govinder. Upon gaining my equilibrium I saw a glint in his eye; his lips were pursed, matching his eyes, and his nose held his entire face up in a conceited, victorious sort of way, giving him a kind of masculine dominance. He was a few years older than my father, but his manner was younger and much more commanding and he certainly did not steal glances from my mother, but took great liberty in bestowing them upon her, boyishly, unashamedly, and the old lady seemed keen to bathe her vanity in the showers of affection he bequeathed upon her. My heart was racing. Something was not quite right. My mother and Dr Govinder were up to something. The spasms in my stomach now turned into rebellious contractions. I knew that it could not be my menstrual period, I had already had it for the month. I sat looking at my shoes, afraid that I was going to faint. I held onto Manjit's arm but his attention was elsewhere. When I looked up again, I saw Dr

Govinder and my mother looking at one another, while my father sought to conduct some irrelevant conversation with Auntiejee about the exchange rate between the British pound and South African rand. My mother would lower her eyes, then raise them slowly, her eyelashes opening up like daisies freed from a throttling hand. Dr Govinder and my mother transmitted their desire in an amorous, licentious manner no one at my table seemed to notice. I saw an occasional glance from my father in the direction of the two doves and realized, as I saw colour take to his face, that he was trapped and had no tools at his disposal to prevent the vulgar exhibition.

I sought the assistance of the woman who had led us into the garden, who now wore her gold pin with her name on it which indicated that she was Mrs Phumelo.

"Yes, doctor," she said, and directed me to the ladies' room.

I entered the beautiful and delightfully scented ladies' room and within seconds the contents of my stomach were voluntarily released in the toilet. Tears ran down my face and I found myself crying, for reasons I could not openly declare. I was upset at myself for attending the tea party, for being in the company of Dr Govinder, even if it was in honour of Surpreet. Indian ceremonies are so much fun and leave so much more room for movement and possibility to avoid people one detested. I could have been walking through rose petals, dried and hand picked, scented and scattered in the shape of a presumed pathway, instead of sitting on a lawn with two stone Dobermans and a host who was bursting with English pride. For those few moments, as I attempted to erase the thoughts of Dr Govinder and my mother, I allowed myself the privilege of being at an Indian wedding, participating in a ceremony of bright colours and traditional, dignified gestures. Tears were streaming down my face as I took myself out of the moment and into another, with all of my fears, anxieties, and recollections from the past. I could not move. My legs were numb and my body shook violently. My mind was flooded with images, moving steadily as though across a screen. It was like being at a cinema, invisible to others because it was only in my head. I regretted my observations as I hurled against the wall, then collected the glass of water I had been given and splashed it over the unfortunate excretion. I was breathless and gasping between each flash of memory. I saw red, the green of the grass, the white of my panties, then red again. I was eleven years old. Dark. It was dark. Humid. Hot. Night. Breathing. Fast. Old house. Uganda. Gabieba. Maid. Away. Weekend. Friday night. Dad smelling of drink . . . on his bed. Mum put me to bed. Did not tell Mum about the blood. I was scared. Mum would be cross. Shouted at me to close my eyes and go to sleep. Manjit in Mum and Dad's room. Manjit small. Manjit asleep sucking on his bottle when I peeped through the door. Yes. I remember. It was red. Everything was red. It was after supper. Still early. Very light outside. Unclejee, I called him then. Unclejee visiting with the red car. The red station wagon. I snuck into the outside toilet after Mum left. I left my room after I called out at her, only to hear my father groaning down the hall from his room, where he lay inebriated and half unconscious on his bed. I went look-ing for my mother. I called out in the yard and got no reply. I sat in the outside toilet for what seemed like hours. I was eleven and I had cancer. How would I tell my mother? I had blood dripping from my genitals, what else could it be? My mother had not looked in on me to see whether I was asleep, as she usually did. I called Gabieba again, the servant, out of habit. The call of her name always produced her pres-ence, and an attentive one. Unable to stop the blood and aware that I might die, I recited some passages I remembered from the Holy Book. I walked in the yard, past my uncle's red station wagon. The chickens had been put in their pen. I observed a bump and went closer. It was dark now. The window of the car was hazy. I could not see through it. There was a cloth tucked inside the windows, from the inside. The cloth looked like my mother's scarf, the same burnt reddish orange colour. I went closer. It was my mother's scarf. The bump was more obvious. My mother was on top of Unclejee. She was breathing loudly, her mouth open. Her eyes upon him. He was breathing loudly. He would not stop hurting her. I put my hand to my mouth. Why would my mother let him hurt her, I thought. I moved away from the car. I looked again. They were both breathing heavily, looking at one another, smiling. My mother wasn't hurt. I was about to bang on the window, but she was not hurt. My mother dug her nails into him. They were both laughing. She dug her hennaed hands into his back.

She was not in pain but enjoying herself with my uncle. They were laughing, rubbing the accumulated moistness on their bodies and aiding one another. When Mum came to my room, she saw the look in my eye. I was crying. She knew that I knew. I was ashamed that I knew what they were doing. She had never talked to me about what husbands and wives did when they were alone. Gabieba told me, and told me not to tell Mum.

I had never before gone that far in the path of recollection; memory had not previously allowed me to reach that far, for colour, the colour red always acted on its own to numb me and take me out of the moment. I stood contemplating how I could, under the circumstances, return to the tea-party. I cried uncontrollably, shaking and shivering as I thought of my father. I detested Dr Govinder with every part of my being. I drank water from the tap, using my hand, which shook vigorously, refusing to be cupped. Isabel! Amina! Beauty! I called out, quietly, between breaths. Red showed itself again and the same series of images as before revealed themselves to me. I could not bear to see them again. I shrieked. Mrs Phumelo, the woman who had previously ushered me to the ladies' room, made an appearance and asked whether she could be of any help.

"Get me some brandy, please," I asked.

She looked over both her shoulders and smiled uncomfortably as she shook her head without saying a word.

"Can I get you a penardo, or an aspirin, Madam?"

"Get me some brandy or vodka, or both . . . anything, just get me something to drink, please. I will reward you for your kindness. No pill or medication is going to help me now." I gave Mrs Phumelo one hundred rands and saw her eyes bulge. She looked at me with raised brows and offered to clean my now partially soiled handbag. I declined her offer.

"I'll be back now-now, doctor," she said, as she scurried off. I fiddled around in my pockets, rubbing my damp hands against my scarf, shaking and shivering. I grabbed my cellphone and rang Carmen. Oh, God help me, I wanted Carmen. She knows about these things. She does psychotherapy . . . and drama . . .and her kind of stuff. I panted. I breathed out, more than in. There was too much air in my mouth, in all of me, and I exhaled, louder and louder. Carmen answered and was surprised to hear from me. I managed to greet her as calmly as I could, when suddenly a shriek, beyond my control, came out from me.

"Are you all right, Jazz?"

"No. No. No," I said.

"Do you want me to fetch you?" she asked.

I remained silent, leaning against the wall, and heard Carmen calling my name urgently. If I continued with the conversation she would have attempted to drive to the house to see me.

Mrs Phumelo appeared with a small bottle of brandy and a glass.

"Shall I call your brother, Madam?" she asked, a concerned look on her face.

I shook my head as I lifted the bottle to my mouth and returned the glass.

I took a long and breathless swig, then wiped my mouth with the end of my sleeve, then exhaled before responding to her kindness.

"No, I am all right," I said. "I need to be alone now, and thank you for your help."

"As you wish, doctor," she replied, before nodding and walking away.

My mother was going to hear from me. I was going to give it to her. My bloody first period, in Uganda, and she removes her dress and scarf, and wraps him up with her legs and her reams of silk as though he were a present! Lying wrapped in redness on top of my uncle, in his red station wagon, with a red face flushed with passion, and I am dragged to my room, half conscious, for I had not eaten all day and had fed my food to the dog under the table. I fainted in her arms—I must have—and the next day when I awoke, she spoke not a word of it. When I asked about how I fell asleep, and told her that I had a memory of someone in a car, she yelled at me that I had a lively imagination, and I had gone to bed when she put me to bed, at my bed time. I cried in my room the following day, and when Gabieba returned, she told me that I did not have cancer but that it was my menstrual period. Idi Amin's announcement came days later and a week after her romp in the red station wagon, I was put on a plane with my uncle and his wife and dragged off to England. "It's for your own good, for your education," my mother said.

I stood against the wall, heaving, wishing I had a cigarette in order to take those rebellious, forbidden draws I had taken as a teenager—which elevated me above the rules and regulations of womanly composition imposed on me by my uncle and aunt.

I intend to kill him. To kill him and make him pay for what he did to me and to my father.

Carmen

It was Saturday morning when a knock sounded on the door. I had had a terrible night and hardly slept a wink. Isabel's state troubled me a lot. Beauty and Amina had joined me at the flat after Isabel dismissed us like badly behaved children. Too distraught to return to her flat, where she had to prepare for her travels to Johannesburg with her son Kwame in the coming week, Beauty collapsed on my couch, exhausted after a terrible screaming match with Isabel. Amina raced home after she drank some of my herbal tea and rang me when she got home, worried and very upset. I whipped out my packet of Gaulloises, a gift from Ludwig via Beauty, who asked if she could ring him, and he joined us half an hour later. Kwame was apparently occupied with installing some newly acquired software on his mother's computer and did not want to be in the company of adults, despite his mother's request that he join us. The three of us smoked and drank a few glasses of wine, then I rang for a taxi, on Beauty's suggestion. Beauty was very tired, and Ludwig did not enjoy driving in Cape Town.

I heard the knock again and looked at my clock. It was later than I thought, and not morning any longer. I grabbed my robe from the floor, hopped on one leg and looked through the peephole. The image was rather blurry and I think the person had moved away from the door, for I could not obtain any image of the face. I stood with my back against the door, too tired to be bothered. The previous night's events were fresh in my mind. I lived in an apartment building where no one was allowed onto any of the floors unless a resident let them in, when they rang from the foyer. My neighbours would often open the door for Isabel, Beauty, or Amina, and I thought, as I leaned against it, that it could only be one of them. Although no one from the writing circle stopped by to see me without telephoning, it occurred to me that it might be Beauty, who could possibly have returned to collect her car. I opened the door just as the knocker approached it for another attempt. Nothing and no one could have prepared me for the sight I saw. It took me all of twenty seconds to recognize the person, tight-lipped and gaunt, with no expression on his face. I brought my hand to my mouth and let out a loud gasp, which startled him somewhat.

"Albert? Albert?"

My response came out as an outburst, to his dismay and my own, and it was posed as a question rather than a greeting. He fell back against the wall behind and I leapt forward to ensure that he had not hit his head. I saw his eyes glaze over, then he fainted.

I looked up and down the corridor, then grabbed his two suitcases and brought them into my apartment. I tried stirring him, but he did not move. I placed his body on my rug and dragged it with great force until he was safely inside my flat. He was still for quite some time, even after I had placed my lighter to his nose. I held his head in my hand, feeling the surge of an unknown, childlike, attraction. I knew something dreadful must have happened, for when he opened his eyes, he blinked and closed them again. He seemed keen on being in my arms, for he held on to me with desperation. I was uncertain whether he recognized me since he had not uttered a word. He was very, very frail. I sat back on my heels, looking at the man I had married and who had mocked me as he frolicked in our marital bed with lovers, many of whom were barely within the age of consent. It occurred to me that my appearance was not quite presentable and I rushed to my bathroom and washed my face and gargled as fast and efficiently as I could. When I returned, he had still not opened his eyes. My loaded, unsettled heart drove me to my wicker chair where I sat waiting for him to come to, in his own time. I crossed my legs on the chair and rocked back and forth, pondering over all sorts of reasons for his sudden appearance and how he had known where to find me. When he finally came to, I was even more taken aback, for he rolled over and attempted to raise himself. Tears dropped from his eyes, and his face remained expressionless, as though they came from another source.

"Carmen, oh Carmen," he muttered.

I got off the chair and joined him on the carpet.

"Albert, what are you doing here?"

He shut his eyes again.

I dashed off to the kitchen and fetched a small pitcher of water and two glasses and placed them on a tray beside him. I poured one for myself but then handed it to him as I noticed him looking up at me, shaking somewhat. He gulped it down.

"I've come to ask your forgiveness," he muttered, looking over-wrought with sincerity.

Before I could say another word, he collapsed.

I could not be angry with him, even if I tried. There was something in his tone that was urgent, apart from his looking and sounding poorly. His appearance bore testimony to a life which had gone from splendour through vice to ruin. If I ever wanted revenge, I now had the privilege of exacting it and the occasion brought sadness rather than elation. Albert, the man I had met, was friendly, loving, and jovial; Albert the man I had married was selfish, cruel, and egotistical.

He had two suitcases with him and I had no idea whether his visit to Cape Town was to see me solely, or whether he had other plans. My sister's husband is a second cousin of Albert, but she had not once mentioned him to me. I left him on the floor because I had used all of my strength to bring him inside. I put a pillow under his head and ensured that he was breathing before covering him with a blanket. My heart was racing; I looked over at my grandfather clock and subtracted an hour as I picked up the telephone to ring my sister Cordelia in London; it would be early lunchtime for her, I thought, sighing wearily, wondering whether the usual summer lunch followed by a tea party would find her in her beautiful garden, far away from the one and only telephone she kept downstairs in the drawing room. She has refused to use a cellphone and found the phone in her bedroom and the one downstairs sufficient for the large house they lived in with four young boys. These days we spoke to each other a few times a year, usually late at night. Cordelia was excited that I rang and she spoke with the same animated haughtiness she had cultivated when we were children. I could hear several voices and lots of laughter, not the family setting I remembered, and so early in the afternoon too.

"I am so glad you rang, Carmen, darling, and mother will be ever so pleased that you remembered her birthday. Our guests have not arrived yet, but Auntie Dolly and the Colonel are here."

"Her birthday?" I asked, surprised that she referred to my mother, knowing full well that we did not speak. "What are you talking about?" I was bewildered at the manner in which she spoke to me and alarmed by the unfamiliar sound of a joyful family gathering—where my mother was present. Apart from the laughter, there was that familiar, slurred, inebriated speech, and she sounded just like my mother when she had had one too many.

I asked if she had been drinking, which annoyed her.

"Good God, Carmen," she shouted. "You're one to talk. You've been known to kick back more than a bloody army. Now shut up, darling, and tell me that you rang to speak to mother. It's her bloody birthday, after all, and we're having a party."

I could not bring myself to converse with my mother. I had quite a close relationship with my sister, I thought. Cordelia inquired after my health regularly and showed great concern on occasions when depression set in. Of course, her solution to everything was Valium, and for what it's worth, those little yellow pills worked for her, as she regularly remarked, though they had lost their ability to sustain me outside of the coldness and repression of the British Isles. I wrote to my mother occasionally, as seemed reasonable, since she continued to send me cheques, percentages of the inheritances from deceased relatives most of whom I had never even met. Since she was the head of our household, all the inheritances for her children were sent to her. There were days when I opened my mail and would immediately ring her, fed up and annoyed. She would insist, above her inebriated state, that I was entitled to the couple of thousand pounds left to me by some mean-spirited colonel or his equally contemptible wife, blood relations, as she referred to them, precisely the kind, I thought, based on my experience with so many of them, who turned their noses up at English people like me for still living in the colonies. I could not bear to have their money, or their pity, since they all knew what my father did to me and they knew of my mockery of a marriage to Albert, even the second one, which turned sour in Cape Town, to the fool whose name I refuse to mention.

I heard a loud bang and the clatter of porcelain, then several screams.

Cordelia shifted her attention without once announcing to me that she was now no longer talking to me—it is such a bad habit and I find the manners of women who speak to their children while they are on the telephone with an adult completely and utterly deplorable.

"Cordelia . . . Cordelia," I called out again.

"Yes, sorry darling," she replied.

"What on earth is going on?"

"Oh, Douglas just broke one of the cups to the punch bowl. Michael is attending to them."

I was surprised to hear that Michael, her husband, was home and mentioned that.

She detected the tone of surprise.

"Yes, of course, dear. The war in Iraq does offer him a few perks, you know." Her husband was a colonel in the military and often absent.

"No servants then, today?" I asked, pointedly. I simply could not resist.

"Oh, good heavens, no! These are modern times. One gets caterers for these things and they do so detest the servants. It's a mutual hatred. Besides, the servants do enjoy the weekend off. I should have asked one of them to stay. The children can be quite unbearable at times."

I asked her again if she knew whether Albert was ill, or if she had heard anything about his health being poor.

"Oh, for heaven's sake, look in his pocket for clues, if you must. I haven't seen old Bertie in years. He's fallen out with so many people. He's against the war, you know, and his views are not well received among military families. I remember that he was diabetic, but other than that, I don't ever remember anyone saying that he was ill . . ."

"Of course," I sighed.

"Later . . . later!" I called out, while my sister called my name out to my mother. I put the receiver down hastily and rummaged through Albert's suitcases. The larger one was locked, and I found the insulin within seconds in the smaller one. I washed my hands then returned to him, slapping him lightly on the cheeks as I administered the injection. I was pleased to hear that Bertie was against the war, as I imagined he would be. Moments later, he came to, and managed to raise himself from the floor. He stumbled to a chair, and refused to accept my assistance when I offered it.

He took a handkerchief from his pocket and wiped his mouth. He stood tall and frail, attempting to look more commanding than his frame allowed. I was surprised that he had so many grey hairs. He was still quite a good-looking man, but had lost the fleshy firmness in his face, which he once carried with such allure when he was a younger man.

"I suppose, you think me foolish, coming here, asking your forgiveness, and then having to care for me, on your living room floor, as a result of my condition."

I looked up at him from my chair.

"I remembered that you were diabetic. You've never referred to it as a condition before," I remarked, a bit puzzled by his choice of words.

"I haven't eaten all day. Well, I arrived early yesterday morning and checked into some ghastly, noisy hotel near the city centre . . . near the harbour somewhere. I needed to pluck up the courage to come and see you."

He fumbled through various papers in his pocket for the address.

"I should have eaten this morning, but I drank some juice, and waited for hours before a taxi arrived."

"Bertie, I don't know why you had to come all this way to ask my forgiveness. You couldn't have done so on the telephone?"

He sat down in my wing chair and looked at his shoes, and occasionally up at me with pressed lips.

"You mean you haven't heard?"

"Oh for heaven's sake! I don't maintain contact with anyone in London other than my sister."

"I'm ill, Carmen. Quite ill. For the longest time I've wanted to see you, to talk to you. To express to you, possibly convince you, that I am sorry for the harm I caused you."

"That was almost twenty-five years ago. Why do you care whether

I forgive you? Your life was filled with the pleasures of your class and the benefits it afforded you. You were young. We both were. Why come here? Why to me? Surely you must have offended others equally, or have you sought their pardon before mine?"

"Carmen, I obtained your address from your mother. I have been through a spiritual journey and have, to my recollection, recognized all of the harm I have inflicted on others. I don't expect you to believe me and since almost twenty-five years have passed between us, I thought it best to try and see you here, where you now live. One of my father's friends has a small cottage on his property where he lives with his wife in a place called Hout Bay, which I have rented. It is small, from what I have heard, and judging from the photographs he sent. I hope that while my request for forgiveness is untimely and perhaps an intrusion, you will find it in your heart to consider it."

I remained silent, unsure what my next word should be. Albert asked if he could use the telephone to ring the family whose cottage he would be renting. As he paged through his little book, I noticed a photograph of the house. I glanced at it momentarily. It hardly looked small to me. Someone answered and informed him that the family was expecting him the following day, and they would most likely be back in the evening.

He sighed and repeated the conversation to me, without realizing that I had heard every word.

I offered him a room to stay in and told him to get some rest.

I remembered that I had an uneaten sandwich in my refrigerator and offered it to him. I made each of us a cup of tea and sat down at the table with him. He ate in silence. I wrapped my hands around my cup, desperate for its warmth.

"I appreciate your kindness, Carmen. I shall never forget it. I shall be out of your hair in no time. As soon as I hear from them tonight, I shall be out of here. I hope you will allow me to visit you. I intend to stay in Cape Town for three months."

"Have some rest, Bertie," I said quickly, changing the subject, and proceeded to the second bedroom, which I then made available to him. It was quite suitable for a short stay. I shut the door behind him and sought the comfort of my couch to recuperate.

Three months, I thought. Three whole months he will be in Cape Town and expecting to see me. I shivered, and felt a palpitation in my chest. I sat upright, wondered whether I could be having a heart attack, for I now also felt a sharp pain.

I stretched, carefully, and before I reached my phone, it rang. I was so pleased. Beauty was on the line, and before I could say anything more than my usual greeting, she reported to me that Isabel had agreed to see one of her colleagues for peer counselling, a woman named Helen, of whom we all had such high regard. Helen was in fact at Isabel's house and had been there since midday. Beauty, Kwame, and Ludwig had spent the morning with Isabel and found her in a much better mood, although not herself. I was pleased that Isabel had agreed to see Helen but may not have expressed my jubilation sufficiently, for Beauty noted that I was quiet, and I confessed my uneasy state of heart and mind, and a concern that my chest pain was troubling me.

"Stay where you are," she said. "I'll call a taxi."

"Don't you have packing to do for your trip next week?"

"It can wait!" she shouted. "Ludwig has taken Kwame shopping and I am meeting up with them late afternoon, before we go to Mary's for dinner."

By the time Beauty arrived, my chest pain had subsided. She sat opposite me in the chair, looking beautiful and very elegant in her long crossover black dress. She looked a little surprised at the two suitcases that were stacked together at the entrance of my flat before commenting on the redness of my face.

My breathing was still unusually fast and I heaved as I spoke, which brought her off her chair and at my feet. Perhaps it was the manner in which I broke the news to her.

"Albert is here?" Her eyes grew bigger and bigger. "Albert? . . . Albert, from England? . . . Your Albert?"

"Yes! . . . Blimey," I said, the remains of my association with Bertie now surfacing.

"He arrived this morning," I whispered. I looked over at the clock. "Well, earlier," I said, only then realizing that it was already after four o'clock.

"No wonder you have chest pain," she said in a low voice, looking rather concerned.

"I'm fine, though. I thought, for years, as I cursed him, that I would be angry and that all the hatred I had harboured against him during those years would surface, but I feel nothing like that at all."

"What is going on today?" Beauty asked, sighing, and crossing her legs she made herself comfortable.

"I got a text message from Jazz just as I came out of the taxi to tell me that she and Manjit had seen Amina with Donny, driving right past them. Amina at the driver's seat, of course, in her car, and Donny beside her."

Beauty was shaking her head as though trying to make meaning out of Jazz's message.

"I've never met this man, and I am shocked that Amina could be bothered to be seen with him. You know, perhaps she was forced to rethink her position, considering the kindness he showed her . . . well, all of us, really. If anything, I hope this whole situation has brought her closer to her sister and her sister's family," I added, thinking through my own situation.

"Are you all right?" Beauty asked. She came closer and sat on the carpeted floor, crossing her legs. "No comment, not even a hint of interest, as I mentioned Manjit's name?"

"Argh!" I sighed, like a Capetonian.

I returned to the whispering tone Beauty and I had adopted on account of my guest.

"A part of me just wants to kick him. He's never going to be able to stand up to Jazz or his family. I'm fed up with the crumbs he feeds me, and the worst is, each time he does, I go running to it as though it's a feast."

I lowered my eyes out of shame, embarrassed at the undignified way in which I conducted my relationship with Manjit, feeling for the most part that I wanted it more than he did. My eyes were moist, but I prevented them from flooding with tears, and Beauty came to sit behind me and massaged my shoulders.

"Carmen, so much has happened to all of us in the last week. I have nightmares about what's happened to Isabel. Each time I see her face, I cannot but think she must feel some anger towards me. We were all in the house when it happened."

I grabbed the sleeve of my shirt to carelessly wipe my tears. Beauty handed me a tissue.

"Yes, I know," I replied.

"Beauty, I have a confession to make," I said, softly.

She frowned and tilted her head.

"I hypnotized Isabel in order to remove the gun. I feel badly for not having told her or anyone. I wanted to tell her last night, to tell everyone, but there was no time. I rang Dr Fitz yesterday, before the writing circle gathering."

Tears suddenly came forcefully to my face.

Beauty bent forward and squeezed my hand.

"Remember him? Remember Dr Fitz?" I asked

Beauty rocked her head and raised her shoulders, a sign of her uncertainty.

"He specializes in hypnosis. I booked an appointment for her, for both of us to attend. Now I'm not sure when or if she will listen to me and take my advice on this matter."

"I don't think anyone would hold it against you. You did what you thought was best."

She moved forward again and squeezed my shoulders.

"I saw Isabel this morning. She's got a long way to go still. Helen arrived just as we left. I didn't want to leave Isabel alone. Helen is great. We'll see how it goes. She may need a lot of time to recover from this."

We were both silent for a while, just looking at each other.

"Do you think we've been too harsh on Amina? She did go out of her way to help Isabel, and she did do something quite out of character, and she has, until now, said very little about her relationship with Ebrahim, other than bringing him here so that we could meet him."

No further word passed from our lips for some time as we stared at each other, disturbed by the unasked questions on our minds.

Beauty dragged me into the kitchen to make me eat something. I told her that I had given the one and only sandwich I had to Albert. When she realized that I had not eaten all day, she looked worried. I did not have much in the refrigerator other than bottled water and alcohol, and Beauty refrained from shaking her head disapprovingly, as she often did when she came to my flat. She offered to purchase food from the small Woolworths one block over from my building, and I handed her my keys and my debit card.

I sat at my kitchen table with the window open, blowing cigarette smoke out. No sooner had I nodded off beside the window, my head hanging loosely against it, than my cellphone rang. I attended to it, and although my call ended rather abruptly, confusingly and peculiarly, I was surprised when Albert walked in, clearly unable to sleep.

"I heard voices. Has someone been here?" he asked.

"Yes," I replied. "A friend of mine. She's just gone to pick up some food."

"Oh, thank goodness. I am ill, but not that ill. If I hear voices I always have to check their source."

There was an awkward silence between us. We must have each held our breath, for no sooner had I attempted to release mine, in recognition of his humour and at this preposterous meeting after twenty-five years, then I found myself bursting with laughter, and moments later, he joined me.

"Oh God, I'm sorry. I know you're ill. You look very ill. And I don't mean to mock you. For a moment I got caught up in the humour of it all . . ."

He grabbed me and kissed me on my lips.

I yielded to his advances—the forceful manner in which he pulled me towards him—drawn to the stirring sensation of pleasurable necessity. I kissed him with a gaping mouth, and exhaled both shock and pleasure into his. I was overcome by my participation, then annoyed when he withdrew before I did.

"What on earth are you doing?" I asked, breathless and trembling.

He took a step back.

"This is madness. You've walked in here, uninvited. You've not asked me one personal question and then you successfully charm me and kiss me. I happen to be in a relationship with someone. How dare you?"

Before Albert could answer, Beauty opened the door with the set of keys I had handed her, two shopping bags in each hand and a newspaper tucked under her arm.

"Oh hello," she said, looking back and forth between Albert and me. "I'm Beauty."

"Is that your Christian name?"

"It's the only name I have," she replied, quite sharply, as she bent to put the shopping bags down.

"Albert," he announced, stepping forward to shake her hand as she raised herself to take his.

"Forgive me for being so rude. I don't think I've ever met someone with your name," he said, with a slightly reddened face, gazing back and forth between Beauty and me, quite determined to attend to his ignorance and restore the little faith I had in him.

"It's not unusual, not here in Cape Town, especially among the Xhosa people, my people," Beauty commented, as she took her shoes off and walked into the kitchen with the food shopping. Albert looked awkward and held his hands out in order to assist her, but she overlooked them.

"Ohhhh, I see," he said, as he followed her into the kitchen and walked passed my flustered face.

"You did that click; that click sound when you said that. I won't attempt it. I feel ridiculous already," he added.

Beauty unpacked the smoked snoek, biltong, cheese, ham, bread, bagels, cream cheese, smoked salmon, olives, several bottles of fruit juices, a salad pack with tomatoes, a pack of sweet corn and one with beets, several packets of shortbread biscuits, plain and chocolate, and a few tubs of yogurt. The fruit and vegetables she unpacked in the basket I kept on the refrigerator. She removed the newspaper from her armpit and placed it on the table, then handed me my keys and my debit card.

"Has anyone ever told you that your name suits you? If you don't mind me saying so, you are very beautiful."

"Yes. I've heard it before," she replied, as she kept her head down then gazed at me, her eyeballs still and enlarged.

I was left with a small tinge of jealousy. Beauty is my friend and I don't begrudge the attention men pay her. Men and women both pay her that kind of attention, all the time. Apart from her obvious physical beauty she is also beautiful in mind and in spirit. For a brief moment I began to resent Albert's inappropriate manner. He looked at me, and I had to remind myself that his intentions might not be wicked. He looked at me adoringly and induced a chill down my spine.

"I got a very strange call from Jazz. She's at some tea party, I think, some sort of family tea for a cousin who's getting married next week. She'd been crying, and when I asked whether she wanted to talk about it or at least give me the address, she hung up."

Beauty sat down instantly.

"Jazz? Jazz crying? Jazz, calling you, and for a matter that has nothing to do with the writing circle? What on earth is going on today?" she asked, in a low and drawn-out voice.

Her body was hunched forward, her mouth was as open and as still as a fish's, and her posture was frozen in the moment, as she pondered the significance of the events of the day.

Albert looked at Beauty, then at me, then back at Beauty, then at me again.

"Are you part of a writing group, Carmen?" he asked, looking somewhat surprised.

"Yes I am," I replied. "Surprised?" I asked, attempting to take a quick stab.

"If you need some privacy, let me know, please. I don't want to be in the way," Beauty said.

"No. No. Not at all," I responded, as I looked at Bertie and he looked at me.

My eyes fell on the food Beauty had just brought. "Let's eat. I'm famished."

I set the table and took my linens from the small cupboard I kept in my dining room. I used the dining room for my formal occasions but soon found myself setting the table, transferring the porcelain plates from the kitchen to it, then decorated it, much to Beauty's surprise.

Albert remained in the kitchen, perusing the newspaper.

"Good God!" he exclaimed. "There is an awful lot of violence here. A little baby girl killed? A nine-year-old girl gang-raped by young thugs who broke into her grandparents' house . . . what is the place, Kuil . . . Kuil, Kuilsriver? The deputy prime minister facing rape charges? Good heavens!"

I walked into the kitchen and found him staring at me then back at the newspaper.

"What? They don't have rape and murder in England?" I asked.

I continued to move plates and food around.

"You've got a beautiful view of the ocean, Carmen."

"Yes, I do, don't I?" I replied, casually, as I laid out the cutlery.

Beauty, bringing the food into the dining room, looked at me with narrowed eyes.

"Are you all right?" she whispered.

"I don't know," I replied, in an equally soft tone. "I feel glad somehow, glad that he found me and came to apologize to me. I feel strangely happy to see him. I cannot quite explain it."

"He's pulling on your heart strings, you know. He seems quite confident that you still have feelings for him."

I stuck my hands in my hair, holding my head at each side, not quite sure how to respond to Beauty's comment. I am known for interrogating others and myself, for urging everyone in the writing circle to pursue questioning as part of a process which writing requires, for it was in questioning myself that I had come to accept the unfortunate twists and turns my life had taken.

I looked at Beauty, and we embraced for a short while before I called on Albert to join us at the table.

Albert and Beauty chatted more than I did, and I recognized that, despite Albert's state, he was still quite capable of intelligent conversation. Beauty seemed particularly pleased by his interest in her sculptures and the methods she used to produce them.

A knock on my door was the furthest from my mind, but there was one, which brought silence and raised brows.

I answered without even bothering to look through the peephole.

"Your friend, the artist girl, has parked on the line of my parking spot," Mr Bromwell asserted, without offering any greeting. "That car has been there all night. It's parked very close to mine. Do ask her to remove it or park it on the street. I suppose she could repark it and perhaps you should direct her, so that it does not touch my line."

"Good afternoon to you too, she's not a girl she's a woman. Now bugger off," I said and slammed the door in his face.

Beauty laughed and Albert looked somewhat bewildered.

"I had forgotten how fierce you can be," Beauty said as she collected the plates and brought a plate of chocolate biscuits to the dining table.

"He's a horrible old man who has nothing better to do with his time than watch for little human errors and then report them to anyone who's daft enough to listen to him."

Albert had taken the liberty of placing his hand on the small of my back. He rubbed my back, as he had done when we were friends, before we were married. His gesture seemed natural somewhat, and I did not ask him to remove it.

I walked into the kitchen in an attempt to make tea and observed Beauty, who had seen Albert's gesture of affection, arranging various cups and saucers on a tray.

"You go and sit down," I said. "I'm so glad you're here."

"I have a confession to make," she said.

She stared at me with a peculiar look on her face, her teeth showing without a smile.

"Go on, then," I said as she waited for my response.

"I know, I'm not supposed to like him, but I do."

"He's English, he's upper-class, privileged," was the clarification I offered, reminding her of the faults he had acquired at birth.

"He does not seem to possess the lethal colonial combination of ignorance and arrogance. He's ignorant but not arrogant."

Beauty was very sharp and a good judge of character, but I could not compromise my knowledge of him for the sake of the present.

"Yes, but English upper-class ignorance is always at the expense of others," I added.

"You've told all of us what he did to you and the way he treated you. He's witty, sharp, very amicable, and with great sensibility," she said, as she offered substantiation for liking him.

"Yes, and he's also gay and has no business showing me affection. It's all twenty-five years too late."

Beauty stroked my head and followed me into the dining room.

No sooner had we sat down than a knock on the door silenced our conversation again.

"I am going to lock that man in a cupboard somewhere, I swear," I mumbled under my breath, quite beside myself with annoyance at Mr Bromwell. All other visitors had to call from downstairs and I opened the door with the intention of belting out further atrocities.

Manjit stood there, not Mr Bromwell. He had Jazz with him and had his arm about her waist, as though she needed it in order to remain upright. A strong smell of alcohol circled the pair of them. I frowned. Jazz stood face down, leaning against Manjit, completely unaware that she was at my front door. She was completely and utterly drunk.

I had never seen Jazz take a drink, and had felt the brunt of her disapproval when we went out to dinner as a group and Beauty and I ordered a glass of wine. I must have stood there for some time staring at them because Manjit's question alerted me to my lack of manners.

"May we come in?" he asked, rather sternly.

"Yes, of course," I replied, remembering that I had given him the downstairs key on the Friday night of Isabel's ordeal, in her bathroom, on the agreement that he would use it later that evening, which, as usual, he did not. As Jazz lifted her face, it was clear that she had been crying. She staggered towards a chair, then let out a loud cry as she sat down and lowered her head into her folded arms. Manjit assisted her as best as he could and removed her shoes. Beauty and Albert were leaning uncomfortably against the arch of the dining room and saw it all. Several awkward glances were exchanged before our eyes returned to Jazz.

Beauty knelt down beside Jazz and put her head against Jazz's in an attempt to comfort her.

I was faced with Manjit's unusually cold stare.

"Can I get you anything?" I asked

"No, thank you," he replied as he looked at Albert.

"Oh, I'm so sorry," I said, realizing that I had not introduced Manjit or Jazz to Albert.

"Albert, this is Manjit, a . . . friend, and this is his sister, Jazz," I continued, as I pointed to her in the chair.

Manjit did not move. Albert stepped towards him and extended his hand. Manjit hesitated before shaking it.

I was anxious and troubled by Jazz's presence in my flat, and curious as to why Manjit had brought her in the state she was in.

Jazz was sliding down the chair, incapable of sitting up, while Beauty held on to her and looked quite concerned.

"Let's put Jazz in the spare bedroom," I said.

Beauty and I held her at each side and took her to the room Albert had occupied. I moved his jacket from the bed as Beauty and I released her, then we draped a small blanket over her, which I took from the cupboard. Manjit stood in the doorway and observed us without lifting a finger.

"I'd like to see you alone," he said to me in a rather commanding manner.

I looked towards Albert uncomfortably, then back at Manjit. He returned my look with cold eyes.

I could not imagine for the life of me what had transpired between Jazz and him, nor how I could have had anything to do with it. Why had they come here?

I cleared my throat and managed to attract Beauty's eye, as was my intention. I motioned with my eyes, and she came towards Manjit, keen to engage him on Jazz's condition.

"Manjit," she said, holding her hand to her chest and looking very worried.

"What on earth is the matter with Jazz? What happened? I've never seen her like this."

"Argggh!" he sighed. "Long story."

He ran his fingers through his hair.

He put his hands on his hips and looked at both Beauty and myself.

"I need to speak to Carmen in private."

I had never seen him act that bold.

"Oh, I'm sorry," Beauty said and stepped aside. She walked over to Albert in the dining room and began talking with him.

I walked into the centre of the kitchen and Manjit followed.

"Your friend! Your friend! Now, I'm your friend. After everything you've said, you invite that man here and call me your friend!"

"What are you doing here?" I asked, quite put out by his manner and his line of questioning.

"Oh, now I need a reason? I've had one helluva day, and so has Jazz, and I ring your phone and it's turned off, very conveniently I see, and you're here, having a wonderful time, with the queen's dishes, and introduce me to *him*," he emphasized, with disgust, pointing to the dining room, "as your friend."

I fumbled about in the kitchen and found my cellphone. It was turned off. I looked at it peculiarly, and realized that I must have turned it off after Jazz rang.

"I don't know where I stand with you anymore," I replied. "I introduced you as my friend, which is not untrue, we are also friends, and besides, you have been the one who has been unable to tell your family about us, so why object now?"

"What the hell is he doing here?"

"I'm still not sure."

"You're not sure?" he said, dragging his words with scrunched nose and face to convey his contempt.

"He showed up here with the intention of staying in Hout Bay, where he's renting a cottage. He's waiting for the owners to call, since they're out at the moment."

"He rocks up here and you don't know why?" Manjit asked, as though he was speaking to someone of feeble mind and intelligence.

"He wants me to forgive him, for everything he's done in the past."

"I see," he replied and nodded, but not convinced, judging by the look on his face.

He let out a deep and troubled sigh.

"Manjit, what is the matter?" I asked, quite sure that something dreadful had happened which involved both him and Jazz.

"Oh my God," he said, as he brought his hands to his face.

"What am I going to do? What am I going to do?" he repeated, exhaling into his hands.

He lifted his head and rested it on the back of the chair.

I got up and went to stand behind him. I stroked his head, without saying anything, and saw tears run down the side of his face.

"Manjit, what's the matter?"

"I don't even know where to start," he said.

"Start anywhere," I responded, with as much support in my voice as I could muster.

"Jazz and I started the day off on bad terms. We had to attend a tea party for my cousin, a small family gathering that is part of the celebration for her upcoming wedding. Jazz and I had a row in the car about you, and she was very annoyed. I should not have put her on the spot like that. When we got to the tea party, my uncle and his wife, who have come all the way from England to attend the wedding, arrived with my parents, and Jazz had a hard time being with them. She regained recollection of an incident that she witnessed as a child. Then she got drunk in order to confront them all. She confronted my mother first, and my father got involved, and my uncle, my aunt, everyone. Jazz held a knife to my uncle's throat and my mother slapped her down to the ground. I don't think I can go back to my parents' house tonight, not after what's happened. Jazz has been thrown out of the house and she cannot go back."

"Your father threw her out?"

"Well, let's just put it this way: there is so much going on for Jazz right now, for both of us, that we cannot possibly believe anything my parents tell us. My father did not say much, all he did was to try and hold Jazz back."

"I had no idea that you or Jazz had problems with your parents."

Before my words had time to resonate with Manjit, Jazz was standing in the doorway of the kitchen, smashed out of her mind.

"Well, what do you want me to do . . . shout it from the rooftop? Is that it? You want me . . . to air my dirty laundry . . . so that you can see me as needy . . . as you are? English people keep their feelings to themselves . . . not you . . . not you, Carmen," she said, slurring and staggering.

There was no way I was going to engage Jazz under the circumstances.

She moved from the doorway; I could hear Albert talking, but there was no sound from Beauty.

Jazz stood right in front of Manjit.

"Why did you bring me here, Manjit?" she asked, her eyelids folding over more than once.

"I wanted to see Carmen," he replied.

"Oh yes, I remember, you were giving me lectures on how I treat Carmen. Carmen, Carmen, Carmen. She doesn't want you. Her English husband is back," she said, all at once, slurring as she spoke.

"Manjit, I'm not putting up with this," I asserted, looking at Jazz, who paid no attention to me and hovered about the doorway then stumbled back into the room where we had taken her.

Manjit looked at me fiercely.

"You have no idea, do you? I feel responsible for what happened to Jazz today. I should not have pushed her so hard. She lost it. I am her support. I am the person she relies on the most, and I wasn't there for her, because I was so wrapped up in how she treated you." He sank his head and shook it.

"Oh, so this is my fault, then? I am supposed to feel guilty about what happened between you and your parents?"

"I come here, and you have your ex-husband here, who, incidentally, unlike others who come into your flat, has not removed his shoes!" he exclaimed, gritting his teeth.

"You came here of your own free will, and used a key I gave you a week ago, when I was expecting you, at your suggestion, silly me, and you haven't bothered to give me one explanation why you did not show up!"

"I have to give you explanations? What for? You were there. You knew what had to be done. You knew the situation. Did you expect me to give you an account of every step I took? Jazz has been to hell and back over all of this, and you have no idea of how things are in our family?"

"You can at least let me in. How else would I know?"

"I don't do touchy feely stuff. Not like you people," he remarked, with disdain.

"I see. You're jealous. You're jealous because Albert is here. You couldn't be bothered otherwise. All this nonsense about talking to Jazz about me is just a way for me to feel guilty about entertaining Albert in my house, while you were breaking your back, defending my presence in your life. Well, you don't have to any longer. I'm fed up. You can leave. I don't want to see you anymore. The only time you make an effort is when you believe your relationship with me is threatened. So go. Don't come back here again."

Manjit rose from his chair and looked at me with absolute hatred.

"You should wear your glasses!" he exclaimed then bolted for the door.

Jazz came staggering into the kitchen again.

"Carmen, do you know what happened today?"

"No I don't, Jazz," I replied and turned away, casting my eyes towards the ocean.

She grabbed me by my arm.

"I remembered . . . you know, I remembered," she repeated.

I suddenly felt a pang of anguish, for I have always suspected that Jazz must have experienced some trauma as a child, both with her parents in Uganda and with her relatives in England. There was no other explanation, I had concluded one day as I sat opposite her in the writing circle, astounded by her desire to constantly be in control.

She came towards me and reached to hold on to me.

"You're all right, you know, Carmen. You're all right."

Jazz hugged me, and I returned the gesture, feeling quite horrid. I was concerned for her, but the circumstances did not allow such concern to be expressed.

Manjit looked at me, and there was nothing further to be said. He took Jazz by the arm, greeted Beauty heartily, and Albert only slightly, and left my flat.

Beauty

I left shortly after Jazz and Manjit. My head was bursting with information, and bumping into old Mr Bromwell in the parking lot took my mind off things a little.

"I have a niece who's up there at the Art College, you know," he called out.

"So much African art being studied, these days," he added, determined to get my attention, in his drawn-out, old Seapoint accent. The new Seapoint accent is more Nigerian than South African. Mr Bromwell has the habit of eliminating greetings and plunges into conversation as though we were intimately acquainted. He is a short, stocky man and lives on his own. The passing of his wife several years ago left him determined to ruin the days of those who find themselves in his company, even if only by occupying the parking space beside his that belongs to Carmen. Most of the residents have two parking spaces allocated to them. Mr Bromwell rents his second space to a young man who lives in the adjacent apartment block and sees it as his most treasured investment.

"Yes, Mr Bromwell. No, Mr Bromwell. I don't have any sculptures for you to buy, Mr Bromwell. I don't have time to see the collection you brought from Swaziland on your holiday, Mr Bromwell," was the order in which I responded to his questions. I got into my car, bolted all four doors and headed for the Waterfront, where I was to fetch Kwame and Ludwig, before going to Mary's for dinner. I was overtaken by several young people on the highway, in very fancy cars, and cringed when I looked at my speedometer and calculated the speed at which they must be driving. As I reached the bottom of the underpass to approach the circle, I was caught by the red light at the robot. It gave me a moment to think about Jazz and the condition she was in. Something must have happened to her; she would never allow anyone to see her in a drunken state. Something quite out of the ordinary must have happened. I drove around the circle, then into the entrance of the first tower at the Waterfront, and was completely beside myself when I realized that some music event must be underway since there wasn't a parking spot to be found. There were people everywhere, a young music crowd. I sighed hopelessly. Fortunately, my cellphone rang.

"Hello. I thought you left your phone at home?" I said, remembering that I had seen Kwame's cellphone on the table earlier.

"Ludwig bought one," he said, giggling.

"Put Ludwig on please," I said, quite surprised.

"Hello, my dear! Welcome to the twenty-first century," I said when Ludwig came on.

He laughed. "Yes, I caved. This city is too fast and too busy to be without one."

"Told you so."

"How are you?" he asked.

"Bothered," I told him.

"Bothered?"

He sounded surprised, perhaps due to my earlier cheeriness.

"Well, I will have to tell you about it later. Put Kwame back on, please, so I can tell him exactly where I am."

I gave Kwame the details of where they should meet me, as I looked about to determine my location.

I was bothered. I had spent quite some time talking to Albert. He was easy to talk to, and attentive, given the fact that he must have been somewhat jet-lagged. I thought Manjit's presence had aroused a certain sentiment within him, a realization that he should consider Carmen's company more precious than he had previously anticipated, because he looked in the direction of the kitchen for quite some time, attempting to gauge the intimacy between the two.

He tried to disguise his interest in Manjit by referring to him as Carmen's friend, knowing full well that they were more than friends, and that Manjit's presence, accompanied by Jazz in the state she was in, and the manner in which he spoke to Carmen, was that of a lover. Manjit was contemptuous of Albert, as was clear from his reluctance to shake his hand or even attempt conversation with him. Albert is no fool, and he knew that Manjit's jealousy towards him would enrage Carmen, and he was spot on. The conversation he pursued with me was too personal, I thought, especially for an Englishman. I attempted several times to change the subject and introduce less personal ones, like the nature of his trip and the weather in England, but he ventured back to the topic of HIV and AIDS.

It all started innocently. Albert was keen to know about Carmen's life in Cape Town and I furnished him with details, casual ones, nothing of a delicate nature, and when the opportunity arose for me to talk about my family, I briefly mentioned, being South African and having no qualms talking about the matter in public, that I had lost a brother to AIDS. He pulled his chair closer and began talking to me about his own condition. My palms were sweaty, and my face was hot with discomfort, but he proceeded, despite the loud and rather distracting exchange taking place between Manjit and Carmen.

"I'm here to spend my last days with Carmen," he said, adding hastily, "if she'll have me," sounding rather convinced that he had already secured her agreement.

"Does she know any of this?" I asked.

"No, not yet. I haven't gotten to that part yet," he said, losing none of his confidence.

"And are you convinced that these are your last days?"

"My dear woman, I am HIV positive," he replied. "I have what is considered full-blown AIDS. The doctor, or rather the team of specialists whose care and expertise I have benefited from over the years, told me that I don't have much time left."

My mouth flew open, and I had the inclination to pinch myself for fear that I was imagining something quite out of the ordinary. He was candid in his deliverance, prepared to reveal the entire story.

"I've had more boyfriends than I'd like to admit, and I am approaching forty-seven, and cannot mourn my sins in England. Believe me, I have plenty. AIDS is treated with silence. It is a painful, silent death, and one I cannot undertake on my own. Perhaps for the lower classes it is a different matter, I don't know, I suspect so, given their close proximity to one another . . . well physically, in how they live. You have beautiful oceans, wonderful weather here, and Carmen is about the only woman I have ever loved."

"I see," I commented, uncertain what to say next.

"So you see, contrary to your initial reaction, and I don't blame you for it, we have a lot more in common than you think."

"I beg to differ," I quickly replied. "I do not consider being gay a sin, which you clearly do. My brother was gay, but I do not consider his life, the choices he made, or how he conducted his love life as sinful."

My voice was raised and my temples were flaming. I was not going to allow him to take that tone of earned self-flagellation. I absolutely detest those who equate gayness with sin, and am least tolerant of those who place condemnation within the argument, as though punishment, like illness and death, is the obvious outcome, a deserved one at that.

"Oh no, good heavens, no! That is not what I meant. I have several cousins, many friends, who are gay, and they are not HIV positive nor do they have AIDS. The sin I speak of is the overindulgence, the ruthlessness with which I conducted my life, the treachery, the deceit, the betrayal I openly and willingly committed against others. I was not a kind man, I can be, but I learned from my elders that the best way to express my masculinity, to compensate for the fact that I was never very macho, was to be horrid. In that way, people who did not like me because I am gay would at least fear me, and would focus on my ruthlessness and not my sexuality. Carmen knew I was gay when I met her. I did not hide it. Carmen knows that I can show tenderness, for she was herself a recipient many many years ago. When she began to hate my gayness, I began to punish her for it."

He was very clear about his feelings and appeared very solidly focused on them. I feared for Carmen, that she would have to make a decision about her closeness to him under the current circumstances, for she had a relationship with Manjit to consider, which seemed to have gone terribly wrong right at the moment of Albert's arrival.

My thoughts were interrupted by a thump against my door. I looked up and saw Ludwig and Kwame. Ludwig was carrying a bouquet of flowers and so was Kwame. They each had several shopping bags with them.

I opened the doors with the remote and they climbed into the car, laughing like two schoolboys.

"This is for you," Ludwig said, as he handed me the flowers.

"Ohh, thanks Ludwig." I kissed him on the cheek. Kwame was at an age where open displays of affection made him uncomfortable.

Kwame notified me that his bouquet was for Mary.

"I'm so pleased you got the flowers. Auntie Mary will be very happy," I said, proudly.

"I got some of the vintage port you like," Ludwig said.

"You mean, you like," I replied jovially.

We made some pleasant talk and my mind was taken off the conversations I was anticipating with the women from the writing circle. The highway was busy. Fortunately the cars were bumper-to-bumper in the opposite direction, all heading towards the Waterfront. At least they have a beautiful view to keep them occupied, I thought, as I drove along the mountain to Bishop's Court. Within fifteen minutes we had arrived at our destination. Bishop's Court is a lovely neighbourhood, except one hardly sees anyone on the street. There are no buses to it, and one has the distinct impression, judging by the generosity the property owners show in driving their employees to the closest train station or bus stop, that they prefer it this way.

Mary and Sipho are the most wonderful hosts and take the utmost care when they have guests for dinner. Unlike other people, they do not invite large groups to their house, and they cherish the occasion, for it shows in the manner in which they spend time with their guests.

Their gatekeeper was expecting us and waved us through. Upon our arrival at their house, Doris, their housekeeper, made an appearance and was as usual very happy to see me.

"Oh Miss Beauty," she remarked. "You are such a lady now."

"I will never be a lady, Doris," I replied playfully, as she held onto me. "I don't want to be lady. Being a woman is tough enough."

She laughed and shook Ludwig's hand. She grabbed Kwame's arm and spoke to him in Xhosa, which allowed Ludwig to join me.

Doris always comments on how tall Kwame is, which makes him

very happy since he is not particularly tall and often hints that he suffers socially because of it.

Mary made her appearance. She looked gorgeous, as usual.

She was thrilled when Kwame offered her the flowers and very pleased to receive Ludwig's gift of vintage port.

She offered Sipho's apologies for being on the phone but added that it was an urgent matter and that he would join us shortly.

We walked into the living room and were offered a drink each.

Mary has a beautiful house, a comfortable one. It is not ostentatious, by any account, since Mary makes every effort to keep it cozy and welcoming. Mary had humble beginnings and never forgets it. She's come a long way from Langa and is never boastful of her accomplishments. Sipho comes from a fairly wealthy family in Johannesburg, where most of his family still live.

They have a son and three daughters. Their children all live in Cape Town.

"Are Patience and her husband coming tonight?"

"No, he's away on business and she's at the Waterfront with the kids."

"Oh, we just came from there, I couldn't even find parking," I remarked, as I brushed my feet against the bristles of their welcome mat and winked at Kwame to do the same. Patience, their oldest daughter, often joins us with her husband and their two children. Thandiwe and Lillian, the two younger daughters, are also married and have a child each. They are charming young women and often go out of their way at events to greet me.

Just then Sipho joined us.

He was, as the expression goes, tall, dark, and handsome.

He greeted all of us and seemed quite comfortable with Ludwig, whom he had met several times before. He is a cabinet minister and yet hardly ever speaks about his work. He also plays the saxophone and is the kind of man who merits every compliment given to him. He has a soft heart and treats Mary like a queen, and his children like little gems.

Ludwig handed him his latest CD and Sipho kissed it, then made two fists and thrust them forward, as men often do when cheering for their horse to hurry to the finish line at the Kenilworth racecourse, on their television set, of course. Ludwig is always a little uncomfortable with the way men express themselves in Cape Town. Among South African men there is touching, patting, punching, shoulder rubbing, knuckle banging, and grabbing—mannerisms which Ludwig considers a bit rough. His Jewish, Viennese sensibility prevents such close proximity with men and he often expresses his discomfort at being punched and grabbed—the kind of behaviour men of a certain age in Cape Town regard as signs of friendship.

After we all had had a drink and were comfortably in our chairs, Mary and I enjoying soft saxophone music in the background, I noticed that Sipho did not quite look at ease.

I hesitated to ask, and saw him looking over at Mary, who lowered her head with a soft sigh. There was an openness about them that allowed a certain degree of inquiry. They were not insular people and while we were not related by blood, I have never been made to feel as though any question I posed, however awkward, was overstepping the hospitality they offered me.

"Is everything all right, Mary?" I asked.

"Oh, well. These things happen," she replied, as she uncrossed her legs then crossed them again.

"What things?"

She let out a sigh and looked over at Sipho.

"Peter, our oldest, has been missing now for a few days, possibly a week. He's never in one place to begin with, and the woman he saw on and off, more off than on, telephoned last Wednesday to say that she had not heard from him in a while. As for Patience, she does not speak to Peter much. I think his sisters are all fed up. People often say that the oldest child is the most organized and the overachiever in the family, but with Peter, we just don't know where we went wrong," she said, looking at me then around the room.

"You must be quite worried? Do you think something terrible could have happened?"

"I've had a strange feeling, since before that woman called," Mary said, looking over at Sipho for confirmation. Sipho nodded and raised himself from his chair.

"Peter and I had many disagreements but he did stay in touch," Sipho noted, as he flipped through his vinyl record collection, enclosed in several glass bookcases on the far side of the room.

Kwame squinted at them, looking rather amused by the collection of records. Sipho called Kwame over.

"I finally took them all out of the spare room. So, now you know where the expression, *you sound like a stuck record*, comes from," he said, his arm around Kwame's neck.

They had their backs turned and were laughing merrily.

"Sipho was never close to our boy like that. The girls are his favourites," Mary whispered.

Sipho was well aware of Mary's words.

"He's not a boy, Mary. He's a grown man."

Mary rolled her eyes and smiled.

Doris made an appearance and told us that dinner was almost ready.

I rubbed my hands in anticipation because Doris is a fantastic cook.

"It's lamb," she said, noticing my sudden excitement. She leaned forward to speak to Ludwig.

"I made some bobotie as well. I know how much you like it, sir."

Ludwig was beaming.

Mary's face, while cheerful, had a strained look about it.

"Mary, you should have said something. We could have postponed dinner," I told her, as she walked beside me.

"Oh no," she said. "He's disappeared in the past, and this is why no one else seems the least bit worried. Not his father, not the girls, none of his friends, except for me. I reported him missing yesterday, and Sipho thought my filing a missing person's claim would not go well, but the police did call me to say that they are looking into the matter."

Sipho joined us again.

"We'll see what they are able to look into; if there is actually something for them to look into," he remarked.

"You're very dismissive about this, even though I told you, and I only have my feeling to go by, that I know something is not quite right. I have a hunch, that is all."

Mary was calm and very composed.

Sipho put his arm around her and he kissed her on her forehead. He squeezed her hand and smiled at us.

Mary looked at her watch and at our drinks, assuring herself, as she often did, that everything was running on time.

"Is everyone ready for dinner?"

"Oh yes," Ludwig called out, raising then withdrawing his hand, as teachers often do.

Kwame raised his hand on the far side of the room.

"Me too," he called out in agreement.

Doris, who had a comfortable relationship with Mary, led us to the dining room, then indicated the dining table where we were to be seated.

Mary often made name cards and we all now looked out for them. Doris had dressed them up a little, adding a small daisy and bow to each. Mary squinted at the display, and then frowned at Doris, who shrugged her shoulders and smiled.

The food smelled wonderful. We were never served in Mary's house, for she insisted on a buffet-style dinner. She did lay quite a beautiful dinner table, with crystal glasses and the finest china.

"I love South African food," Ludwig remarked.

"You've been here a few times," Mary said.

"Oh yes. And I look forward to it each time," he laughed.

Kwame was already chewing the inside of his cheeks.

Mary leaned into the table and looked at me as she spoke jokingly, "Woolworths seen you more than the stove, these days?"

Kwame and Ludwig scrunched their noses at one another, then at me, and nodded. I joined them and there was a short outburst of laughter.

The smell of the lamb, with rosemary, garlic and paprika, was heavenly, and the accompanying sauce, a combination of olive oil, red wine, and soya sauce, drizzled over the lamb as it was cooking, brought a spectacular flavour to the meat. We served ourselves. There was the yellow rice, laced with almonds and raisins that Mary had cooked herself, her own speciality, with the bobotie and the lamb, and roasted vegetables, small boiled corn still on the cob, gem squash cut in half with butter, and small roasted tomatoes. On another, smaller table, Doris had placed green salad, beets, bread, cheese, a baked bean salad and a few sauces. Doris was thoughtful enough to make pap, a mielie meal mixture, or corn cereal, as it is called these days, and I simply loved it.

When all five of us were seated, Sipho, at Mary's suggestion, led us in a small prayer, which was more like an address, a thank you to the supreme God, short and concise and welcoming our presence at their dinner table. Ludwig sat with his hands folded respectfully, as Christian prayers often made him a little uncomfortable. Sipho had asked Ludwig in the past if he objected to the prayers and whether he would feel better if they were not conducted in his presence. Ludwig's response was that being Jewish did not prohibit him from being in the company of those who practised other religions or customs.

We lifted our knives and forks, and hastily tucked in without further encouragement. Sipho had placed himself and Kwame at each head, and Mary sat beside Ludwig, who was placed opposite me. We ate merrily at first with no conversation, as the food was too delicious to spend time talking between forkfuls. We were more than halfway through when Doris stood apologetically at the hallway and asked to be excused. She indicated that she wished to speak to Sipho in the kitchen. Sipho looked at Doris and frowned. He gathered the serviette from his lap and dabbed his lip, before placing it on the table.

"What is it, Doris? Can't it wait?"

"No, sir, I'm sorry, it can't," she replied.

She looked terribly worried.

"And we have to do this in private?"

"Yes, sir."

"Well then!" he exclaimed and excused himself.

Mary called Doris over to her chair, and the woman bent forward as Mary spoke to her in a low voice.

Doris responded by whispering in Mary's ear.

"Thank you, Doris," Mary finally replied.

Doris wrung her hands, and this made all of us ill at ease.

Mary appeared rather cool as Doris left the room. She gathered her serviette and placed it on the table. It was clear that her meal had come to an end. I felt guilty as I ate, unsure what the proper etiquette was. Kwame and Ludwig were completely silent. Finally we all stopped eating.

Mary took a deep breath before she spoke.

"The police are here. Sipho will most likely let them in. I'm not sure why they did not telephone us. Perhaps they have some news about Peter, which required them to come to our home. I don't like policemen arriving here uninvited. These are not the townships and we are not readily at their disposal."

I looked over at Kwame, then at Ludwig.

There was no urgency in Mary's voice. Sipho must have gone to the phone to speak to the gatekeeper, for he returned without the police and raised his brow at Mary, who in turn nodded. Married couples have their own unspoken language.

"Please feel free to finish your dinner. Sipho will take them to the sitting room. I assume it will be more than one, they seem to travel in pairs or packs."

Her face had a blank look on it.

"Mary, we can leave," I suggested in earnest. "We can always come back for a visit another time."

"Oh, nonsense! You'll do no such thing. Whatever it is they've come to tell me, I am prepared to hear. There is no reason for your visit to end just because they are here."

Her hands were neatly folded on the table.

"Kwame, you're a young man. And you're going to Jo'burg next week, aren't you?" she asked.

"Yes, Auntie Mary," he replied, jerking forward to pay attention.

"I am very happy for you. I wish you every success with your audition."

She tilted her head towards the upstairs of the house and went on, "Well, if you need to excuse yourself, and be on your own, then you know where to go. My office is the first one on the right upstairs, and my Internet is all yours for the evening. This will be adult conversation with police here. I shall come and call you myself when they leave. All right?"

"Yes, Auntie Mary," he replied.

I nodded at him, granting him permission to an otherwise forbidden activity in the homes where we were invited for dinner. His computer and television hours were strictly between four and six in the afternoon and he was not allowed to venture off at the homes of others, as many children did, the result of which produced young people who were incapable of social conversation and whose manners left little to be admired.

Ludwig tugged at my arm, asking whether it was really appropriate for us to be at their home.

"It's fine," I replied. "Mary would have said. She's very direct, and does not mince her words. I've known her for more than twenty years."

Ludwig put his arm around me. We took our seats in the sitting room, following Mary's lead.

Sipho was quite a large man. He towered over most people. He walked into the sitting room with one constable in uniform and two policemen in civilian clothes.

The constable was a Xhosa man of medium stature, perhaps in his late forties, and of the two policemen in plain clothes, one was White, the other Xhosa, both young and pleasant, with firm handshakes, and not at all intimidating as policemen often are.

Sipho offered them a drink, leaving the offer open to interpretation, which I thought they'd decline, but they looked at one another and each asked for a whiskey. Ludwig raised an eyebrow at me.

"Mr . . . Mrs, Phokobye," the constable began, "we've sent out a description of your son around the country. Nothing has come in as yet."

Mary frowned, as if to inquire why they had come all the way just to tell her and Sipho that no information had been acquired.

The constable looked towards the young Xhosa policeman and made a small gesture with his head to suggest that it was his time to speak.

"I have to tell you, madam, that often these missing person reports don't amount to much. Sometimes the dates and times and descriptions don't match. Descriptions, like the one you gave of your son, are vague. More than fifty percent of our reports are about Black men, all between the ages of thirty and forty-five."

Mary nodded. Sipho was not on board, not yet.

The young constable then shifted about in his chair.

"Madam, we have several Black men in our morgue, unclaimed by relatives, and not matching any of the descriptions that have been filed. They come in every day, from all over the city. The same can be said about Durban, Jo'burg, and other major cities."

Mary sighed but still looked quite composed.

The constable cleared his throat and continued.

"We have in our possession the bodies of several Black men, killed within the last ten days, which have not been claimed. It is not an easy task, Madam. I suggest, to rule out further investigation, that you and your husband, or one of you, whoever is best at this, come down to our morgue with us and see whether any of these men is your son."

Sipho paced up and down. He was cracking his knuckles, first one hand, then the other.

Mary raised herself from her chair.

"I'll go!" she said.

Sipho looked at her and shut his eyes, then nodded.

"I'll come with you, if you like, Mary," I suddenly heard myself saying.

Ludwig looked at me with big eyes.

"Thank you, Beauty. I'll go and get changed. Excuse me," Mary said and left the room.

I asked Ludwig to check up on Kwame. I went to stand behind Sipho, who was crouched beside a small cabinet, looking at family photos, and put my hand on his shoulder, using my fingers to gently massage it. He placed his on mine, still with his back turned and patted it.

He went over to the constable, in very close proximity, and asked him, earnestly:

"Sir, do you think, from the description my wife gave you that any of these men could be my son?"

"It's hard to tell, Mr Phokobye. Sometimes, due to the circumstances of the death, the bodies are disfigured, facial features are hard to distinguish, clothes are missing, identity cards and bank cards are missing from their pockets. We often have to look at dental records and even at blood tests to match the blood group of the parents with that of the victim, so that the family can have a burial. These days DNA tests make our process of identification a lot easier. Often, after all is said and done, sir, families just want to bury their children."

Sipho nodded.

The constable edged forward in his chair and looked towards the stairs.

"No offence, sir, but are you sure your wife is up to this?"

"She's a lot better at these things than I am, believe me," Sipho replied in a confessional sort of way, holding his hands clasped together.

The young Xhosa policeman sniffed and took the last gulp of his whiskey, then looked about the house at the display of photographs in the cabinet beside which Sipho had been kneeling.

"Sir, your wife gave the constable a photograph of your son. It wasn't a recent one, hey Constable?" he asked, in confirmation.

"No. Perhaps you can give us a recent photograph, sir. We are not so keen for parents or spouses to look at too many corpses. It is our job. If we can narrow it down to two or three, it makes the process easier. We see dead bodies all the time. Seeing a dead body for most people is a traumatic experience, especially if the body has been disfigured. Decay has set in, even if the body is in the morgue. We do not alter the body in any way, and many of the bodies we receive are in very bad condition."

"Shusssh," the young White policeman gestured, using both his hands to orchestrate his request for a more quiet exchange, looking distinctly in my direction. They were clearly aware that Kwame was in the house and reminded the constable.

Sipho excused himself and announced that he would fetch a recent photograph of his son.

I looked up the stairs and heard Ludwig talking to Kwame. I took the opportunity to look at the family photos in the cabinet, some of which looked familiar to me, from the distance. I did not know Peter and had never met him. Mary had mentioned him over the years, and he had been described as the "problem child," the child with whom they struggled; the child to whom they gave everything; the child they sent to private school when it wasn't really done by members of our community; the child who went from job to job, and who was jobless more often than anyone they knew. The girls were all well educated and did very well at university, and obtained good positions at various companies. They saw little of their brother, and did not want to see him at all. He was never present at any of the family events I was invited to, and Mary shrugged her shoulders most of the time when anyone made inquiries about him. They were known as a lovely, well-off family, with three university-educated daughters—who gave them four grandchildren—and an estranged, troubled, son.

Sipho emerged with three photographs, and handed them to the constable.

"Thank you, sir," the man said.

A combination of concern and curiosity pressed on me, and I found myself moving discreetly in the direction of the constable, who attempted to put the photographs in his pocket. The constable looked at me, and took out an envelope from the small satchel he carried.

"Sipho, I've never met your son. May I have a look?" I asked.

The constable handed the photographs back to Sipho who then handed them to me.

A sudden coldness came over me and I don't think I hid it very well.

"Are you all right?" Sipho asked.

I was breathing heavily and trying to contain myself.

"He looks a lot like Mary," I replied, gulping down my suspicions.

"Yes, he does, doesn't he?" was the short reply he offered.

I was trembling and felt cold all over. Sipho came up to me, quite closely, and I nearly fell into his arms.

"Your face has gone quite white," he said.

I was tearful beyond control and held my hands to my mouth, fearing the worst for what might be emitted from it. I was shaking.

"Beauty here lost a brother to AIDS last year," Sipho said, addressing the policemen as he held me close.

"Sorry, Miss. Sorry, Madam . . . ," offered the three policemen.

I moved away from Sipho and dried my face hastily, as I could hear Mary on the stairs.

Ludwig and Kwame were behind her, Ludwig with a puzzled look on his face as his eyes fell upon mine.

"I'm going with Auntie Mary," I said to Kwame.

Before I could address Ludwig, Mary came to my side. She had changed to a pants suit.

"Thank you, Beauty, I appreciate it. I'll take my car and drop you off at home afterwards."

Then she saw my face and said with concern, "You don't *have to* come with me, you know. I'll be fine." She stroked my face.

"I do want to accompany you, Mary. It's no trouble at all."

Ludwig observed me closely.

"Take my car, Ludwig, I'll see you later," I said quietly.

Ludwig did not particularly like driving in Cape Town, since we drove on the left side of the road, the proper side, as I often said to him when he complained.

"You might want to take extra clothes, ladies," the constable remarked. "It will be rather cold inside the morgue."

He excused himself and flipped open his phone in a grand gesture, like a magician, and rang the morgue. He moved to the far corner of the room with his back turned and conducted his telephone call with some privacy while we looked on.

Mary and I remained silent in the car. She played some light music and looked ahead at the road. There was a moment when we came to a robot, quite close to the morgue, when she reached over and patted my knee, as though I needed the comfort more than she did.

We were ushered into the building by the two policemen while the constable went off somewhere, indicating that he would join us shortly.

When we entered the cold part of the building, my spine froze, and I could not move.

Mary looked at me and squeezed my hand.

"I'm so glad you're here," she said, unaware that my hesitation was due to terror, which I could not convey to her.

The constable came towards us, accompanied by an older White man in a white coat with grey hair who looked almost too old to be employed. The two policemen stood in the far corner and Mary called them over. The young Xhosa policeman was on his cellphone and his partner was looking over some paperwork.

The young Xhosa policeman put his hand out to suggest that Mary wait a while before proceeding.

The constable called him over and handed him the photographs that Sipho had provided.

They nodded, and there was some talk among them, which was not audible to either one of us.

"You don't have to look at them, Beauty," she said. "You can be at my side if you wish. I appreciate you being here."

I nodded at Mary without saying a word.

The old man in the white coat came forward and handed us two scented masks. The constable stood with his hands in his pockets, ready to lead the identification process, waiting for us to put on our masks. Both Mary and I were reluctant, but the silent gazes bestowed upon us and the coldness in the room demanded our participation.

"We'll start with showing you three bodies, Madam," the constable announced, as though he had rehearsed the monologue. "You may take a break after viewing each one. If you would like to leave at any time, then please say so. You are not obliged to go through with the identification process if you find it too unsettling."

Mary pushed her mask down to speak.

"Will they have their clothes on?" she asked.

"No, Madam. They won't. We show busts only. We only show the rest of the body, which has a cover from the waist down to the knees, on the request of the parent or spouse . . . if the identification is uncertain. We have a drawer at the bottom of each stretcher, and we will take out the set of clothes, and all other garments or personal items found on the body when we show you each one. If you answer in the affirmative, and wish to claim the body, you have to be absolutely sure. We will then follow up, with a blood test if necessary, depending on the condition of the body, before we release it. As I told you before, many of the bodies are in quite a bad state. We cannot release them, with identifications made under stress, only to find ourselves in a position, hours after you leave, that another family has also identified the same body. So, you see what I mean, Madam? The matter is not that simple."

Mary nodded and pushed her mask back up.

I clutched my handbag and fumbled about in it for my sunglasses. Mary looked at me and waited for me to put them on, which I needed to, since I could not bear to have my eyes exposed. When the first body was shown, I thought I was going to be ill. I understand now why a mask is used in these situations, since it acts as a barrier to gagging. I turned away.

Mary had her hands folded under her chin, and shook her head.

The constable looked at Mary, and she looked back at him, and nodded again, suggesting that she was ready to proceed.

They went on to the second one.

I did not look at the second body and kept my head in the opposite direction.

Mary shook her head again.

There was some silence, and the same waiting and nodding, before proceeding to the third body, the last one, for viewing.

My body was pressed against hers, and I felt her jerking violently, then clutching my arm she let out a loud shriek. I turned my head instantly, without much thought, and came face to face with a man whose deathly face, still with sorrow, greeted mine, demanding an explanation.

I looked at Mary, then back at the body, then again at Mary. She was shocked but there were no tears in her eyes. The man's wounded face looked familiar, but so, I realized, did every face that had undergone similar, violent maltreatment. I shook my head in deliberation, for when the see-through plastic bag containing his clothing was removed from the drawer, I could see no garment in it that was blue. I sighed with relief, and held my hand to my mouth, feeling the gentle tremble of Mary's body against my own.

Mary nodded several times, and looked towards the plastic bag. The constable handed her the bag. He held the photographs in his hand and looked at each of them, then back at the body, pursing his lips, then sympathetically at Mary, as though he accepted her identification. He put the photographs back in the pocket of his jacket, as though the matter had been settled, and put his hands behind his back, in a manner suggesting that he was paying his respects to Mary's son, having met her and having been to her house, first on duty, then as a guest, in the manner he was treated. Mary's face looked hard and cold. She had a tremor to her body, and her gestures were like those of a mime. She folded her arms over her body, standing solemnly still and tight-lipped.

Mary uncrossed her arms and stuck her hand in the bag and took the blood-stained jacket out, shook it, then turned it inside out. She shook it vigorously, and the blue side of it was now visible, with dried blood and all.

I cried out in horror, "No! No! No!" and everyone was staring at me.

I ran out of the room, threw my mask on the floor and stood against the wall outside in the courtyard, banging my hands against it, coughing, spewing unsightly secretions, and crying, all at the same time.

I did not hear the clanking of Mary's heels but soon felt her presence as she extended her hand to my waist.

"Beauty, pull yourself together, my child. Your brother is in a restful place and there is nothing we can do any longer."

I turned around.

"My brother! My brother! Mary, this is not about my brother. This is about your son! I was there! I was there after he was killed. I was in the yard. I closed his eyes. I wrapped him in a black plastic bag . . . a rubbish bag. I was there, after he was shot. I was there!"

Mary came towards me and put her hand over my mouth. My body curled up into a ball and I collapsed. Mary lifted me up, my legs dangling carelessly, incapable of holding me upright. We stood face-to-face. My back was against the wall, her face pressed against mine, trying to hush me and keep my voice down. She was shaking but still calmer than I was.

"Beauty, tell me what happened. Take a deep breath. Pull yourself together. Tell me what happened."

My mouth was open and I was heaving. Mary moved her face away from mine and took the liberty of removing my sunglasses.

I breathed in and out for what seemed like an endless moment. I began by telling her how the four women of the writing circle had been waiting for Isabel at her home and she was late. I told her about the loud bang in Isabel's garage and how Jazz discovered Isabel with a man in the car who had put a gun into her mouth, how it had gone off and killed him.

"I don't want to hear any more," she said.

My mouth was still open and the word I was meant to utter swelled up inside it. It ballooned then burst into the roof of my mouth, seeped into my nostrils, and pressed against my ears, nose, and throat, until the tears ran down my face and my voice broke into a wail. I sobbed like I had never sobbed before. Mary stood some distance away and looked at me, waiting for me to stop.

I wiped the tears off my face. "Mary, I am so sorry. I had no idea. I am so sorry," I uttered.

Mary looked up into the dark sky as though communicating a silent prayer. I waited for her eyes to meet mine before I spoke again. I wiped my face with my hands.

"Mary, I will contact the women from the writing circle. We will come forward. The matter will be settled."

"You will do no such thing," she said hastily.

"But we have to," I pleaded, "It is the only option we have left."

"Really?" she said, with tilted head and a thoughtful gaze.

"We all assisted Isabel in what we believed was the best solution, given her state and the incident, which left her open to all sorts of accusations. We did what we thought was the right thing . . ."

"Ssssh. Of course you did what you thought was the right thing," she replied.

"And the man at the graveyard, the gravedigger, he . . . that bastard! That bastard! He betrayed us . . . he betrayed us!"

"Whether he betrayed you or not . . . I cannot be the judge of that. He acted in Peter's interest and for that I am glad."

"I will go and tell the constable, Mary, it cannot end like this. He is your son. I am sorry. I have not told anyone about this. Only the women in the writing circle know, no one else does . . . and one of the woman's brothers . . . and another woman's brother-in-law." I was suddenly taken away from the moment, cursing Donny, although I had never met him. Mary touched my face, bringing me back into the moment.

"Beauty, my child, if this matter is brought to the level of confession, then to the courts, there will be forensic tests, evidence required on all of your part, and ours, as his parents, and blood tests, which I don't want."

"But Mary, please . . ."

"Listen to me. Listen to me very carefully. Peter does not have my blood type. He does not have Sipho's blood type either."

I had no idea what Mary was alluding to. My mind raced on its own, trying to make meaning of her words. I let out a loud gasp without realizing it. Mary dragged me away from the wall and found a small space further back in the courtyard and looked me straight in the eye.

"Sipho and I met in Cape Town during the early 1960s. He came here from Jo'burg to go to university. Then, in the mid sixties, Sipho and I were engaged and he wanted me to move to Jo'burg with him. The Rivonia trials were behind us, in a haunting sort of way, and the ANC wanted Sipho in Jo'burg, to work with comrades internationally. I could not just leave Cape Town. My mother was not in the best of health and I could not leave her in the careless hands of my sisters and brothers. He left and I did not follow him. I refused. I broke off with him. I am not a woman who takes well to threats. I started seeing someone else."

I gulped hard. And for the most part, I looked at Mary's mouth, surprised at the sequence of events she now relayed to me.

"All those men, all those *amajonis*,* so sure of themselves, so self-absorbed, so happy to have their lovely admirers around them, expected their wives and girlfriends to be committed to them first, and then to the struggle. Sipho was no different. He hid it, unlike most men, but he was no different. After six months in Jo'burg, he came back here and begged and pleaded for me to take him back and eventually I took him back. The next month we were married. I never saw the other guy again; never breathed a word to Sipho, although a friend of his told me that Sipho knew. Men have their pride. The only thing I did, on my part, was never to mention the other man's name. He went into exile somewhere in Europe. When I told Sipho that I was pregnant a few weeks after our honeymoon, he was happy. Sipho never asked, and I never told him. I think, somehow, he knew, but he was not prepared to give me up or walk away from the marriage."

"Mary, I don't know what to say. I am lost for words. I'm sorry that

* revolutionaries

you lost your son. I cannot say anything more."

"Then don't," Mary replied. "I want to meet with the women from your writing circle, and that is all that I ask. I want to hear from them personally. I want to tell them what I did as a mother, and what Sipho did as a father, and that there were wonderful things about my son that they don't know anything about. I am sorry for your friend, for what he did to her, and I will tell her that, but I don't want Peter to be remembered only as a rapist. It is all I ask of you."

"Mary, you don't think Sipho should hear any of this?" I asked after a moment's silence.

"No, he shouldn't. Sipho will never recover from this. And neither will my daughters and my grandchildren. They will never accept Peter's death if this matter goes any further. The courts will do their job and the newspapers will take us apart. Sipho will be undermined, his portfolio of work on new legislation for women who experience violence will be trashed, the country will focus on our son the rapist, and no one will remember any good that Sipho has done. My family will be shamed. And Sipho will only be the father of the rapist. We have so many in the country already, and we have to stop it, in every way we can. God will cast his judgment on Peter. Damn him! Damn him! Damn you, Peter. How could you do this . . . how could you . . . son of mine . . . how could you!"

Mary shouted her curses into the sky, her hands in the air, fists clenched, as though beating her son, then she lowered her arms and kept them at her side.

"Mary! . . . Mary!" I called out.

"Listen to me. Sipho is not a saint. He has affairs. He sees other women. I know. He doesn't say anything and sometimes I think that he knows that I know. He is very attentive when there's someone else. He's up at that hospital quite a lot. I suspect he's seeing someone there. It is perhaps unthinkable for women of your generation, and I agree, it is not what I want for my children, but it is the aftermath of many years of suffering, and for which there are no more excuses—and I would be the last one to make them on his behalf—but it is a situation that many men of his age find themselves in. I love him dearly and I love my children dearly, and I cannot allow this to go any further."

"Mary!...Mary!" I called out again, holding my hands to my mouth.
"Oh please, Beauty. Pull yourself together. I loved my son. I gave him
all that I could, but there is no excuse for what he has done. I would
have taken him to the police myself, if I had found out. Sipho knows
that Peter was not an angel, but this . . . this is monstrous. This goes
against everything that Sipho and I believe in. Sipho knew. He knew. In
fact, the reason I know that Sipho must have known is that he did so
much more for Peter, more than he did for the girls. But there's nothing
in the world worth falling to pieces over. I'm South African. There isn't
an earthquake or a volcano that can sweep me off my feet. *Aikona!** I am
here to stay. This is my life. I protect my family, and do not put them in
harm's way. I face facts. I don't have time for cheap sentimentality. I have
time for love and respect, but not for sentimentality. I will drop you off
at home. You sleep on this and speak to the women tomorrow. I will call
the constable and tell him that I will let my family know tomorrow
evening, when we are all together in my house, and I will give my son a
funeral. I will ask the constable that nothing further be said. I don't want
the newspapers to get word of this. You set up the meeting and I will
come and meet the women from the writing circle and put the matter
behind me. I suggest you do the same."

"Mary, as mothers, as women, we are always talking about our men,
Black men, Coloured men, not taking responsibility . . . "

I hesitated, and looked at her, fearing that I was overstepping a
boundary, but being clear in communicating my concern for her and her
son. Mary frowned. She squinted, uncertain as to what I was getting at,
and I was uncomfortable putting forward words that seemed inadequate.

"Our Black men . . . I mean his father . . . will you let his father know
. . . I mean, the man . . . who . . . ?"

"Who said anything about Peter's biological father being Black or
Coloured? Besides, Sipho is the only father Peter had ever known and
that's the way it's going to stay."

Mary hooked her arm in mine, firmly and tightly, and walked me
to her car.

* no way; absolutely not

Amina

Saturday mornings are usually busy, and by the time my alarm clock went off at seven, I had already been awake for hours, thinking through the events of the previous night at Isabel's house. I dragged myself out of bed, with red, puffy eyes and an aching body. I was happy to see my mother already in the kitchen, making toast and tea for the girls, and coffee for my father and me. I poured my first cup and headed for the shower. Our maid has Saturdays and Sundays off but she had been kind enough to leave the girls' clothes ready and Abdullah's rugby clothes in his backpack together with his casual Saturday clothes, stacked against his cupboard door for him to collect. With the girls going to madressa and Abdullah to drama in the morning, then rugby in the afternoon, my entire day was accounted for. My older brother, after whom Abdullah is named, usually collects the girls after madressa and takes them to his house for lunch. I had two hours to myself late in the morning, before I fetched Abdullah and took him to his rugby game, and those two hours were reserved for my masseuse. At nine o' clock I had dropped off the girls and Abdullah and headed to Cavendish Square in Claremont. I rang my masseuse from the parking lot, since I had not confirmed the night before, as she expected me to, and was relieved that my weekly Saturday appointment was still standing. Beauty rang, from Isabel's bathroom, just as I got off the escalator and informed me that Isabel had agreed to see Helen, a therapist whom Beauty and I thought highly of. The two were to meet at midday. I was relieved, and I felt my shoulders dropping, my body incapable of coping with the release of so many emotions, and my heart pumping more blood than it could contain. I was suddenly tearful, and my nose was runny. I was forced to blow my nose in public and turned my back in a closed area as I continued my conversation with Beauty. I don't have the constitution to deal with the range of emotions Isabel's ordeal had brought forth, and I don't take lightly to being thrown out of someone's house, someone whom I consider a dear friend. I was relieved when Beauty finally hung up, saying she would let me know when she heard from Helen.

The women in the writing circle had great affection for one another, despite the petty squabbling Jazz often initiated. I asked her why she was so mean to Carmen—when I had a chance, briefly in the passageway as she came from the bathroom in Isabel's house and I was about to enter it, before the policemen arrived—and she responded that she wanted Carmen to tell her about Manjit, her brother.

"If she cannot tell me herself, and fears me, how can she really be my friend?"

I hadn't thought about Jazz's needs but of Carmen's fear, because I identified with fear.

"If I fall down the mountain," Jazz said, "I need to know that my friend can save me? What will her first thoughts be? Will she be able to save me or will she be too afraid that she will fall down the mountain with me? The fact that I have to think about it means that I cannot rely on her. So you see, Amina, if I go easy on her, she'll never learn to stand up to me."

I told Jazz quite firmly that I did not approve of putting one's friends through tests, for they were traps, really, and while I got along with her and also fought with her, there was no question in my mind of her affection for me and vice versa, despite my friendship with Harminder.

I held my hand to my head, thinking through the past few days, and was happy finally to arrive at the office of my masseuse, who always had good coffee, bottles of flavoured water, and wonderful sandwiches for her clients. I was happy to kick off my shoes, and proceeded to the cubicle for my session. Griselda started as usual by asking if there were any particular areas that I wanted her to work on, areas in my body that needed attention more than others. I mentioned briefly that I had the usual shoulder and back pain, and sometimes the pain was stabbing. She raised her eyebrows and nodded. She pointed to her selection of massage oils, which were all soya based, and asked if there was any particular one I preferred. I pointed to the lavender and rosemary blend. Since this was a double session, for ninety minutes, I fell into my robe and felt her warmly oiled and scented hands melt over my face. She started with my scalp, with what is known as the Indian head massage, and I felt every part of my head calmed by her hands, which were loving and soothing—the weekly luxury I craved. The head massage brings calmness, wearing away the tensions stored, but her hands, however soothing in the past, this time brought to the surface all of my despair, and before long, as she rocked my head from side to side and held it in her hands, tears dropped from my face and I burst out crying. Her tenderness was endearing, and the softness of her touch elicited emotions that were not accessible to me under the conditions my life allowed. I have known Griselda for some time, and she was quite struck by the sudden onset of tears. She stroked my face and fetched an extra blanket and covered me with it. She bent down close to me and said quietly, "Let me know if you want me to continue." I nodded. The tears ran down my face and into my ears. Griselda stood behind me and asked if I wanted to talk.

I remained silent, and sniffed. She handed me a box of tissues. I pulled one, then another, then several from the partially opened box. I raised myself up from the massage table and turned on my side, facing her. I did not want to be spoken to while I was on my back; it brought back painful memories.

"Your body is very tense. Your muscles, rock hard," Griselda said. "You need to let go. A lot of my clients cry. It's okay. I can continue with the massage, it's no problem for me at all. You need to let go. Let it out. You can talk if you wish, or cry and just let it out. Let it out. It's good for you. Your muscles are holding back, and your back pain is not going to get any better. My time with you is confidential. I don't offer advice, I just listen."

She spoke in that gentle voice of hers. I nodded and asked her to continue with the massage. I realized that I could not leave without it. I needed her touch in order to carry on with my day, and take its bene-fits with me into the week ahead. How could I tell her that her touch, her massage, was my one and only caress? It was not a sexual caress, but a loving, warm, and wonderful caress. I was deprived of physical affection, the only affection I received in the form of hugs and kisses was from the women in the writing circle. My relationship with Ebrahim had not included any form of touching in the past two years. She took away the tissue papers and started to massage my face. I usually close my eyes, but now I kept them open and I spoke to her.

On Monday I went to work, and as I was settling in, I had a visitor whom I had not invited, but who decided to visit me at my work, at teatime, in order to talk to me about his estranged wife. Harminder and I have been friends since high school. His parents were customers, and although they are Sikh, unlike most they are not vegetarian and prefer to purchase halal meats from my father's butcher. When Harminder got married, I did not know Jazz, but got to know her well in the writing circle. I had no choice but to invite him in and excuse myself from my staff and have tea with him in my office.

"Amina, it can't be over," he said.

I told him that it was difficult for me to discuss his relationship with Jazz and that all I could do was listen.

"I know, I know," he replied. "I'm not expecting you to take sides. I need your advice."

"I'm not sure how I can help, other than to listen, Harminder," I reiterated.

"Amina, Jazz does not know how to be intimate. She does not know how to be with a man . . . well not with me, anyway. First it was the colour of the curtains; then the colour of the bedspread . . . too much red in it, she said, then the sheets, then the colour of the furniture was more red than brown and needed to be changed, which I attended to. Then I had to shave my moustache because it reminded her of someone she did not like. She's avoided me for months and arranged all her hours at work in opposition to mine, so that she does not have to see me. She's living with her parents again, as though our marriage never happened."

He looked over in my direction. My left elbow was firmly on the table, holding up my head. My right hand had settled itself on the teacup and it did not move either. My eyes were cast down, since I could not look at him.

"I'm not jealous of the women in the writing circle or her participation in it, I am jealous of the time she devotes to her friends, and
envy those who find themselves in her company. I want to be with her.
I am not a bad man. I love her. She's pushed me away. She blames me
for wanting intimacy. I am not an aggressive man. I am not forceful. All
I want is for her to recognize that she has a problem, and that she has
to get help for it. Instead, she has blamed me. What do I do? What do
I do?"

He paced up and down in my office, wringing his hands, banging
them together. I could not think of anything to say.

He stood opposite me and looked right at me.

"I'm sorry, Harminder, I don't think I can be of any help to you. I
do sympathize, but I suggest you talk to Jazz."

"I've tried, Amina. I've tried," he replied, with a pleading voice.

"You'll just have to try again."

"But you are with her in the writing circle; surely she must have
said something to you, shared something among all of you that you
can tell me? Surely? I want to know. I need to know. I've tried everything."

I shrugged my shoulders. I was relieved when the buzzer rang and
I asked Harminder to be excused. He nodded and said he would leave.
We were friends and I did like him and thought that he was quite a
lovely man, but my commitment was to Jazz, and to the women in the
writing circle.

Griselda was now doing my front, and worked her thumbs and the
rest of her fingers in circular motion around my pelvis. I was relieved
to be talking to her. I let out a loud burst again, and she used both her
hands and pressed down on my pelvis, releasing the trapped tears. As
I drew my hands to my face, she held them in hers and tugged my arms
gently, then placed both beside me, with my palms facing down on the
table. I could cry without drying my tears.

"Can you imagine, the most sensation I feel in my vagina is when I
go for my pap smear each year, Griselda? Can you imagine going to see
my gynecologist and being asked about my health, my sexual life, and
inventing it, for my doctor's benefit, to justify my presence on her

stretcher, as my legs are mounted into those straps? I lie there, listen-ing to her tell me how gentle she'd be, how pap smears are needed and very necessary, especially for women my age, then feel that tingle, the most rewarding tingle I am allowed and in fact pay for. The tingle then leaves a sensation. A sensation my dead husband said I was incapable of having. The examination is not exactly elegant, but proves every year to be an annual highlight. My 'physical' as she calls it, is about the only physical activity in my life, apart from my massages with you, Griselda, which are now weekly instead of monthly," I said, in a soft voice.

Griselda looked at me and nodded gently.

After Harminder left, I had a meeting. I usually have late lunches on Monday afternoons. Most Mondays I eat in my office, alone. I nearly fell off my chair when my assistant walked in with bulging eyes and told me that there was a man claiming to be a family member outside the building, asking to speak to me. I looked over the railing reluctantly and caught the visitor's eye. I hardly recognized him, but his height, his hairstyle and those lips gave him away. It was Donny. What on earth could he want now? I wondered, as I walked down the stairs and opened the small internal gate for him.

"Come upstairs to my office," I said, attempting to get his visit over as soon as possible and avoiding the inspection my staff would doubtlessly undertake whether he was aware of it or not. I was more taken aback by his appearance, since he looked almost handsome, than by the actual visit.

He did not want to sit but announced, without provocation, that he wanted to see whether everything was all right, after the events of the Friday evening. I did not answer immediately and realized that he had made no apologies for his presence.

"Mmmm, everything is fine," I said, with poor articulation.

"It won't kill you to telephone your sister, you know, just to let her know."

I sighed, fearing that he would now demand more than I had asked for.

"Saturday, I took the girls to madressa and then there's also drama and rugby for Abdullah. I was exhausted. On Sunday, we went to a keefeit. One of my parents' friends' daughter died. I haven't had a moment to myself, really," I said, almost apologetically.

"I see," he said, not exactly accepting the account I offered.

"I will call Janup tonight. I'm sorry," I said, as he shook his head in judgment of me.

"Save the apologies, Amina," he said and started towards the door.

My nosy secretary, whose fuzzy outline I detected through the glass door, rang the buzzer on my door and I called for her to enter.

"*Mevrou**, the *meneer*** of the material is here," she announced in the mixture of Afrikaans and English she seems destined to bring into the workplace whether I like it or not. She is very common but rather good at her job, excellent at her office tasks and has little contact with the clients. Her manner towards most of the delivery men, although questionable, seems to work well, since they are all quite fond of her and all seem rather keen to compliment her on her generous bosom and equally generous bottom.

"He can't be here now," I said, annoyed at her suspicious intrusion, for she inspected Donny from head to toe. I was bothered that sales people were not sticking to the timetable I had worked hard at keeping.

"Tell him I'm sorry but he cannot drop material off now. Our delivery boy is not here to carry anything. This is not a time for delivery. Deliveries get done in the morning and it's not my problem that he's late."

"I can give you a hand if you like," Donny said.

My secretary looked at me. "Godfrey is waiting for that fabric, Mevrou!" she exclaimed.

"Argh!" I sighed. I did not want to get into an argument with Godfrey, our high-maintenance designer, who was producing a children's line of haute couture. He is quite tiresome and can be very temperamental. He struts like a peacock and pouts like a pussycat, and when he is annoyed, there is simply nothing I can do but give in to his demands, however unreasonable. I could not afford any more silent wars with him. He had a Picasso temper and felt completely entitled to it.

"Donny, are you sure you don't mind?" I asked, uncertain whether

* Mrs, madam   ** man, sir

I wanted any more favours from him but desperately aware of the aura of discontent Godfrey's pout generated among the machinists who worked under his fierce instructions.

"Not at all," he said.

He removed his jacket and the smell of his aftershave filled the entire office.

All the young women I employ watched him cart one roll of fabric after another with great enthusiasm. It occurred to me, as I observed their smiling faces, that they all thought him attractive. Each to his own, I thought as I shrugged my shoulders, waiting for the little excitement they were enjoying for the day to come to an abrupt end, since I was about to ask him to leave.

I went downstairs and signed the necessary forms. I looked around for Donny and did not see him anywhere. I had no time to thank him and returned to my office, making sure that all the women were now back at their respective positions in the office—which has an open-plan layout—and engaged at their assigned jobs. I walked into my office and shut the door. I had no idea that he was leaning against the door, putting his leather jacket on, and the speed at which I shut the door forced him to fall forward onto me, his hand brushing past my breast, which he awkwardly tried to avoid, and in so doing fell forward right into me. In my shocked state and fearing the fall, I held my hands up, which he caught, and we then stood there in an awkward, accidental embrace, our noses inches away from one another and his breath on my face. My eyes had nowhere else to look, and it happened so fast, I looked into his eyes and he brought me closer, his lips touching mine, then pulled himself away. The moment was shorter than a second, if there is such a thing, and he stood back and looked at me.

"I'm sorry," he said, "I did *not* mean for that to happen."

Nothing happened, I thought, why is he apologizing?

I stood facing him and could not say a word.

He straightened his jacket out and said something about having come into town to do some business somewhere. He waved and left, and I was left with a hardened nipple, which just did not go away.

"Do you know, Griselda, that I've never felt so much sensation in one part of my body all my life, as what I felt after that man left," I said, looking up at her. She nodded at me and started on my feet. I loved it when she worked on my feet, although it was an indication that the massage would soon be over.

"I don't fancy him," I said. "He is my sister's husband. It is odd, though. I feel like a teenage boy with an erection that won't go away. Do you want to see it?" I asked.

She looked uncomfortable.

"Is it sore or tender?"

I shook my head slowly.

"A bit uncomfortable?" she asked, to ascertain, I suppose, why I wanted her to see it.

"No, it is just hard and erect. It's not uncomfortable. I enjoy the sensation. What bothers me is the source," I said, pulling a face.

She smiled. I smiled.

"It is your nipple. It is your sensation. It is your body. Enjoy it," she said.

There were no more tears. I dressed and thanked her. Her assistant knocked on the cubicle door to announce that Shamila, the woman who did my hair, was already in the waiting room. The hair salon was just three shops down and Shamila regularly walked up and down, and in and out of all the shops.

"Oh, Shamila is very prompt. If she says half an hour, then half an hour it is, and you'll be out of there," the receptionist remarked. Half an hour later I was out of the salon. I checked my watch and headed off to collect Abdullah from his drama class.

I left Claremont for town, the city centre, and fortunately Abdullah was on the stairs at the drama school entrance with several of his friends. We chatted briefly in the car. He was not too happy with the fact that I had not brought any food with me. I assured him that my mother and father would be at the field and they would certainly have food with them; they usually do. Zwanswyk was some distance from the city centre but the highway drive proved quite successful and we arrived at our destination in no time. My parents are always happy to see Abdullah. My mother had brought tons of food, which she usually keeps in plastic containers, and was practically feeding him as he popped his head out of the car to greet her.

Neither my parents nor I were happy with the treatment Abdullah received from his teammates. I observed the exchange among them and was furious. When the boys trotted off to the change rooms, I took the opportunity to speak to Abdullah's teacher about the horrific display of masculinity I observed. My son was practically bullied in broad daylight and Mr Adams had not issued one reprimand. Rugby boys have their own code of conduct, but I will not have my son treated as though his gentleness was a problem and would affect the way the opposing team saw them, as they suggested, when they shouted at him during half time, or taunted him when the opposing team had the ball. Their behaviour was appalling. As a flyhalf Abdullah plays an excellent game, and references to his interest in fashion and design should not be used as criteria to kick him off the team or, worse still, ask him to play then place him on the bench for most of the game. Mr Adams was sympathetic, but I had the feeling that deep down inside he thought the treatment Abdullah received would "make him a man"—as he often suggested, according to Abdullah—part of the spiritual uplifting he preached, thus arousing a desire for unnecessary aggression. Abdullah was featured on SABC TV in a series that focused on young talents, girls and boys who were already working towards their chosen careers in a creative way. He is a gentle boy and I have no desire to transform the sensitivity, or remain silent, as I did in the days when Fuad was alive and tormented and ridiculed him, even though he was so young. Abdullah could not defend himself against a father who was ashamed that he had a son who was gentle. My parents offered to accompany me to see some of the parents of the boys on his team when I angrily told them that my talk with Mr Adams did not go well.

Still fuming, but determined to talk to the parents of the boys and settle the matter, I was stuck in the parking lot, on my cellphone, with both lines occupied. On one line, my oldest brother was scolding me, asking angrily, "So we are not told about the girls Moekalaf?" I was meant to notify everyone in my family that my daughters had had their first menstrual period and there was meant to be a celebration of some sort. Because I had failed in my duty I needed to be reprimanded. Without a husband, or even a boyfriend, I was now a child in his eyes.

I let him have it good and solid, even though he is the oldest. He was gulping for air to complete sentences I was not interested in listening to. On the other line, Donny asked me to meet him somewhere as there was a matter to discuss with me, which apparently demanded the utmost confidentiality. I hung up on my brother without warning, then answered the line again. Ebrahim did not take too kindly to my dismissal of him, suggesting that I was snubbing him. I said, rather plainly, that I had something urgent to attend to. I headed to Groote Schuur hospital, where Donny had asked me to meet him. I was completely taken aback when I arrived, for I found him with three other men from his neighbourhood, in the Emergency Unit. Cold shivers ran down my spine. They were quite rough looking men. But they removed their woollen caps when I approached and greeted me. When Donny introduced me as his sister-in-law, they wiped their hands before attempting to shake mine. I feared the worst.

Donny pulled me aside to tell me what had happened.

"Gamat's son has been raped. He brought the boy here. The boy is in Emergency Unit. The boys lost their mother last year. There was a card game last night at his house. He has three sons and the eldest one, Igsaan, did not wake up this morning. He took a handful of pills. Gamat went berserk. He called one of the women neighbours. The woman came and got the child conscious, you know, with her own remedies. Gamat's not himself. The children said that one of the men . . . a guy who was at the card game came into their room. Gamat got it out of the boys . . . the boys are scared, you know . . . but they told their father . . . and he went over to the guy's house and you know . . . the rest is history. The guy is in the Accident Unit. I don't know if he is going to make it. Gamat beat him pretty bad. Igsaan is twelve. The bastard is telling the police that the boy was responsible. That he wanted it. I mean, how sick can this man be? We need your help, Amina. We need your help."

I looked at the men and they were all shaking their heads.

"What is happening to our people, lady . . . terrible, hey!" the older-looking of the men exclaimed.

"How am I going to make this right, Missus? How? My son will need an operation, Missus! The poor boy never asked for this. We

doan have money, Missus. That man who did this, he's a ses en twin-
tag, a twenty-six. He's done time. But his days are over. My boy isn't
going to get over this, Missus. Not *somer** like that. We need help,
Missus," said the man who was introduced to me as Gamat.

I understood only some of the terminology he used due to the
exchanges I was forced to overhear among the machinist staff I
employed, many of whom had husbands, brothers, and male relatives
in prison. The prison system under which men served their sentences
has its own vulgar language, which Gamat had repeated. I understood
that the man who allegedly committed the rape had acquired the
number 26, which was considered prestigious, for such a person—a
leader of a gang—was known to have forced unwanted sexual relations
with men of a lower ranking.

I sighed as I stepped aside and telephoned my friend Brian Kline,
and he immediately told me to bring the child and his family to his
clinic. He would call the doctor in charge and ask that the boy be
discharged to his care. The boy's father was so relieved he kissed my
hands. I had to withdraw them; I could not afford to smell like fried
fish.

"How did you all get here?" I asked, holding my hands behind my
back.

"I'm a taxi driver, Missus. I drove everyone here," the older man
replied.

"Well, once my friend has called the doctor, we can leave. You'll
have to follow me. So it's the four of you and the boy?"

"Yes, Missus," was the joint reply.

"That's a lot of people. Donny, you can ride with me, to leave more
room for the boy," I suggested.

"Thank you, Missus. Thank you, Missus," the father replied.

It was almost one o'clock in the morning when my mother came to my
room.

"Beauty is here for you, Amina . . . Amina, wake up."

"What now? . . . Beauty?" I asked, squinting at my mother.

"Yes, she's here. She looks very upset."

"Oh God, what now," I muttered aloud. I got my slippers on and

* just like

walked to the window. I was not dreaming. Her car was in our drive-way, and my mother was standing in my room with outstretched hands, holding my robe.

I had just fallen asleep after lying in my bed for hours. The day's events had worn me down, and I could not possibly see anyone. I got back into bed without much thought.

"Amina . . . come on," my mother shouted.

I lifted myself from my bed again.

"Did she say anything?" I asked.

"Ai, Amina. She just greeted and said that she was sorry but that it was urgent. Now, please, *kanala tog*,* I need to get back to bed myself."

I went into my bathroom and washed my face and brushed my teeth and applied some light makeup.

My mother indicated that she was going back to bed and we should keep our voices down.

"Yes, yes," I said, a little irritated

"Go into the small lounge and shut the door," my mother asserted, determined to orchestrate every little detail.

"Yesss," I replied.

I almost did not recognize Beauty. She looked haggard and exhausted, in a worse state than I felt.

"Beauty, whatever is the matter?" I asked. She flew into my arms and held onto me as we hugged.

"Oh Amina, I don't know where to start. I . . ." She burst out crying.

"Beauty, sit down. Sit down," I said.

"Has something happened to Kwame?" I asked.

"No. No. No," she said. She held my face in her hands and looked at me. "Donny has betrayed us," she whispered.

"What? What?" I said, frowning.

She bit her lip and started to cry.

"What do you mean?" I asked, as I took a few steps back.

My whole body went cold and I brought my hands to my face.

"Amina, I don't want you to get an asthma attack. That's why I came. I needed to tell you this face-to-face."

"Just tell me, Beauty, just tell me."

"He took the body of that man to the police."

* a plea; often accompanied by the word please

"He did what?"

"Lower your voice, Amina. No, to the morgue, not the police."

"Beauty, are you sure? I was there. Jazz and Manjit put it in the ground . . . I helped."

She burst out crying, and covered her mouth. She looked towards the door, realizing that her outburst had been quite loud.

"He's Mary's son. The man is Mary's son. My godmother, Mary . . . Mary who lives in Bishop's Court! Mary who lives a few avenues away from you, in this neighbourhood! Mary who used to be a professor!" she exclaimed all at once.

"What?" I replied and stepped even further back.

"Yes! The man is Mary's son."

"No!"

"Yes!"

"It can't be," I replied.

"I was at Mary's house. The police came. Mary said that she had reported her son missing. I've always known that she had a son, but I had never met him. I went with Mary to the morgue. Kwame and Ludwig went back home. When we got to the morgue, Mary identified her son . . . it was the same man. The blue windbreaker, with blood on it, was in the plastic bag. I know . . . I know, Amina. I saw him. I closed his eyes. It is the same man. Donny betrayed us . . . he betrayed us," she cried. Her body shook.

"The bastard! The bloody bastard!" I was beside myself with anger. I could feel my chest heaving.

"Did you say anything to Mary?" I asked, between breaths.

"Yes, of course. I owe her at least that. He is her son. She does not hate me. She wants to meet with everyone tomorrow. I have not called Jazz. She's in a state. Oh my God! What is happening to us! I called Manjit before I called you, to ask him how Jazz was. He was at the beachfront, in Seapoint, sitting in his car. He couldn't sleep. Jazz was sleeping in the car. They had not been home. She had quite an ordeal today. She'll tell you about it, I am sure. I told him to come to my flat. He and Jazz are sleeping at my flat. I couldn't sleep. I couldn't . . . even when I was at Mary's house, I was worried about Jazz . . . oh God."

"Let's go."

"Where to?" Beauty asked, surprised.

"To that bastard . . . that bastard!" I was shaking.

"We can't go now," Beauty said and held onto me.

"We can't go tomorrow either. I will never be able to sleep. Not after this. Donny starts work at midnight," I asserted.

"No, I don't want to see him. I don't."

"Well, I do. I am going to give it to him. That bastard just used me." I took my inhaler and used it for a few seconds.

Beauty stared at me.

"I don't want to cause problems to your health, Amina. I don't want to cause any problems between you and your sister, either," she said and came to stand beside me.

"Oh no, you won't. I'm going to put my jeans on. I am not meeting with the man's mother. God . . . how must she feel? She must feel awful."

Beauty did not reply.

"What have we done? And you say she doesn't hate us."

"No, Mary doesn't. She's upset but she doesn't hate us. She's very angry at Peter . . . oh, that was his name. Mary said she would have reported the matter to the police herself, if she knew."

"But the body was in the ground. It was ready to be buried," I said as I headed towards the door.

Beauty stared at me.

"Are you listening to me, Amina?"

"I'll be back now-now."

I returned with my jeans and my handbag.

"Leave your car here. We'll go in my car," I suggested.

"I am not going to a graveyard in a BMW, Amina."

"Are you okay to drive, though?" I asked, looking at Beauty's tear-stained face.

"I got here, didn't I?" she asserted.

"Okay. I'll speak to the man at the gate."

I was overcome with anger and banged my hand on the small table beside the sofa.

"My God, he's used me . . . used me . . . I am going to get him. He's not getting away with this!"

"Amina, you're scaring me. You need to be calm."

"Calm! I'm calm! I'm always calm . . . that is why people take advantage of me. Bastard! Bastard!"

I walked into my parents' room and shook my mother by her shoulders, then gestured, when she opened her eyes, that she should come to the door.

"In the kitchen, Oemie," I said.

"What are you girls up to, now? Do you know what time it is?"

My mother squinted, then realized that I had changed my clothes and was no longer in the bathrobe she had handed me.

"Ja Allah, Amina, where are you going now?"

"We have an emergency, Oemie. I'm going with Beauty. I'm leaving my car here. I won't be long."

"You can't drive around, two women like you, at this time of the night! It's dangerous."

"Oemie, not now. We each have our cellphones and we won't be long. We'll be back within the hour."

I grabbed my bag and bolted for the door.

Hardly a word was said as Beauty drove out of the gated complex.

"Mary lives down that way," Beauty said and indicated where.

I did not bother to look. I stretched my legs on the dashboard.

I had a vague memory of where the graveyard was and gave my recollections to Beauty, noting the few landmarks I had noticed. She said she knew where it was. There were quite a few cars on the highway. By young people's time, it was still early for a Saturday night. The joyful loud screams from their cars as they passed one another did not make our journey easier. As we approached the graveyard, I nodded to Beauty, indicating that it was the correct location. I looked about, and at the far right side of the location was Donny, dressed in exactly the same clothes as the night I was dragged here by Jazz. It was dark, but he looked in our direction as he saw the car and came to the door before Beauty had pulled the handbrake up, uncertain whether in fact she could park at that spot.

"Any more bodies you want buried?" he said, with a smirk on his face, brushing his hands against his faded jeans.

"You bastard!" I said as I slammed the door, pronouncing the word with utmost vehemence.

"Hey hey, hey. I was just joking," he shouted, then suddenly drew a stern face.

"What can I do for you?" he asked with a squint in his eye.

"Who the hell do you think you are? You used me and abused me. You bastard! You came to my work to try and seduce me . . . and then . . ."

"What the hell are you talking about?" he said, sticking the shovel into the earth and leaning on it.

"Don't pretend, Donny. We know," I said, pointing to Beauty and myself.

"Know what?" he said in that low-class tone he had.

"Where's the grave of that man you buried?" I asked. Where is it?"

"Hey, hey . . . Listen, Amina. I did not go to the police, if that's what you think," he said. "After you left . . . I thought about it, you know. I thought, what if that was me or one of my friends lying there."

"Oh, are you trying to tell me you have a conscience . . .you! You!"

"Guh," he nodded in a self-righteous sort of way. "To you I'm just a labourer, hey. To you I'm just someone who digs graves . . . it is not a thinking man's job. I took that man to the morgue because I thought he deserved better than that."

He leaned on the shovel, his face slanted to one side and his head held high. I was amazed at the position of superiority he took, casting himself as the do-gooder on a matter he had been so keen to assist with, on which he previously had held no opinion.

"Oh, that's not what you said this afternoon. It's not what you said about your friend, and the man who raped his son. You were quite happy for the man your friend beat up to die in the Accident Unit. You didn't seem to care then," I said, shaking my head scornfully. I loathed the sudden appearance of dignified resolution he carried.

"Hey, every man deserves to be buried properly, no matter what he's done. That man will get a burial," he said, picking up his shovel. He whistled over in the direction of the labourers who worked under his supervision.

"Just like that, hey," I said, as I realized that he simply did not think he owed me an apology or an explanation.

"Amina, that was just a hole to you. A ditch? Mmm, . . . maybe?" he said, as though he was in a position to decide on the exact nature of my moral judgment on a matter I was placed in and acted on. I was simply flabbergasted.

"Well, aren't you the wise one here," I said, as I dusted my hands.

"He was just a Black man you wanted to get rid of. That was not a grave. Not to people like you. I am sorry for what he did to your friend, but that was not a burial. That was putting a man in a hole."

He was quite out of order.

"How dare you . . . how dare you think that my intentions were simply to get rid of a Black man!"

Beauty was now nudging me at the arm, urging me that we should leave.

"Listen," he said. "I took his body to the morgue. I watched that entrance carefully, and for that brief window, those few seconds when there was no one in the parking lot, I drove up and I left the body there. I parked a few metres away and I saw them take the body in. I knew someone would come and claim him. You have some nerve to come here, in the dead of the night and speak to me as though I owe you something. I don't owe you a damn thing. Not one damn thing."

"But I . . ."

He did not let me offer a response.

"What you did for that little boy today, you did because it's your duty. You did what you are supposed to do. It's all of our duty. I helped my friend because I am supposed to. You didn't do it for me. You did it for that boy. And if you think I *smaak** you, you'd better think again. Go back to your nice house in Bishop's Court."

It was almost three o'clock in the afternoon when I pulled into Beauty's apartment building. My stomach had been in knots the whole morning. I had managed to get only a few hours of sleep. The girls stayed at my brother's house and I drove Abdullah to join them for lunch, remaining in the car as I spoke to my brother and his wife. I was in no mood to eat, or to explain myself to them, and least of all to Ebrahim, who seemed annoyed and bothered that I had not seen him all week. My cellphone rang all morning. Beauty thought that Isabel was not

* desire; fancy

well enough to join us, and Carmen agreed. Carmen and Beauty both thought it would be wise for Isabel to first see Dr Fitz, and on his and the therapist Helen's recommendation set up a meeting with all of us and Mary.

"She's finished with Tom, you know," Beauty said.

I asked whether she had had much conversation with Isabel in the morning and her response was that she had kept the conversation to a minimum, and that it was Isabel who had offered the information.

Jazz had spent the night at Beauty's flat and Manjit had gone to meet Harminder. Jazz was sober, having rested and recovered from her hangover, which I am glad I was not witness to. I still find the incident hard to believe. Her speech was slower than usual, and she intimated that although she missed work and would have preferred to be at the hospital, life had dealt her a strange hand, and she now had to lay it on the table, open.

"Harminder came to see me," I said, "but there was no time to tell you any of this on Friday."

"Yes, I know. He told Manjit. Manjit may have been right all along."

"Oh," I said, surprised to hear her accept any wrongdoing.

"I mean . . . about Harminder and the fact that we need to see a couple's counsellor. A therapist, you know, someone who works with couples."

I remained silent.

"I don't want to go to this meeting with Mary," I said, sighing into the telephone.

"We have to, Amina. We simply have to," she said.

I sat in my car, recollecting my thoughts and thinking through my life. I had to face that moment when I would have to look into the eyes of another woman and tell her that I was involved in burying her son. Fuad's mother had not looked me in the eye. She did not want to see what her son had done to me and that his death, although I never wished it, brought relief. I turned the ignition on and felt a wave of strength sweep over my body. I was not afraid any more. I could face Mary. I could face her and tell her what I had done.